To Ruchama and Mark
for reasons, as they know,
too numerous to recount

I

EVER SINCE he had been a boy, Yoss had known that the day would come when he must leave the village.

This is how it would happen. It would be a summer's morning. Everyone would gather on the green, and behind them, in the shadow of the Jarrow Oak, tables would already be set out for a feast. Then the leader of the village, who was called the Speaker, would come before the crowd, and he would call on Yoss to step forward. He would tell him that he had reached his fourteenth summer, and the time had come for him to go out of the village, and when he came back, he would be as a man. Then the Speaker would give him a single cake of wheat, as if to say that this was all that the village could give him, and for anything else that he desired he must search outside the village to bring it back. And Yoss would take the wheatcake, and turn, and walk through the crowd, and leave.

Yoss had seen it, as he grew up, year after year, when it was other boys who solemnly marched away, and after they had gone the villagers would spend the day feasting on the green.

Yet the boys were always back the next morning. Suddenly they were expected to work and hunt with the men, as if, overnight, they had grown bigger and stronger. But they looked no different than before, and whatever they had learned outside the village, or brought back with them, didn't appear to have changed them. And what could you learn, anyway, if you left one day and came back the next? And how much could you be changed?

There was another boy who had been born in the same year as Yoss. His name was Herman, and when Yoss left the village, Herman would leave with him.

'It's a just a symbol,' said Herman, as the day approached. 'Don't you understand? It's a symbol of becoming a man, as if you go out of the village to prove yourself.'

'What can you prove in one day?' said Yoss.

'Nothing.' Herman shook his head. '*As if* you go out to prove yourself. That's why it's just a symbol.'

Herman and Yoss had grown up together, and this had made them close, yet they were different. Herman was practical and quick-tempered and had no time for daydreams. He was always whittling at sticks and twigs, and spent as much time as he could in the workshop of Matthew, the carpenter. Already he was becoming skilled as a joiner, and once he had gone through the ritual of leaving the village, Matthew was going to make him his apprentice.

'The Speaker will tell us. You'll see,' said Herman, taking out his knife and deftly stripping the bark off a stick.

The Speaker confirmed it. A week before the boys were due to leave, he called them into his house. The ritual of departure was a commemoration, the Speaker explained, a way of remembering and honouring the hardships suffered by those who came into the mountains to found the village.

'In those days,' he continued, 'when their turn came, the young men were sent out. They left the mountains and went beyond the lake. When they came back, they brought something the village needed. Skills or knowledge. Milling, for example, and carving, metalworking, thatching, quarrying, joining . . .' The Speaker paused. 'But now, we have these things. The wheatcake I will give you is just a symbol as well.

Do you really think that's all the village can provide? No, but it should remind you, when it's time for you to become a man, of the ways our ancestors lived and of all they had to endure to make the village prosperous. And therefore you too should leave, if only for a single night.'

But there were people who had never come back. Yoss had heard of them.

'That was a long time ago,' said the Speaker.

Yoss frowned. He didn't know how long ago it was. The villagers sometimes mentioned such people as if they had actually known them.

'How would you do it, Yoss?' said the Speaker. 'Have you seen the lake? Do you know how big it is? You can't even see to the other side.' The Speaker shook his head. 'And then, where would you go? Think about it. To a town? Towns swallow men up, Yoss. They're hungry. A man disappears into a town and is never heard of again.'

The Speaker paused. He gazed at Yoss searchingly. Then he smiled. Beside him, Herman broke into laughter.

~

THE VILLAGE lay in a high valley enfolded by mountains. In the winter it was covered in a blanket of snow. In the summer, crops grew quickly in the intense warmth of the mountain sun. The slopes above the valley were skirted with thick forest, and further up, rocky crags and ice-filled ravines drifted in and out of cloud. Abundant streams flowed out of the mountains and in the spring they turned into torrents of melted snow.

The village lay so deep within the valley that the clouds on the crags might just as well have been an ocean encircling it, keeping all but the most hardy and adventurous travellers away. But to the people of the village, every peak, every crevasse, every ledge in the mountains had a name, and the names, taken together, told a history of the people in this place, of the hardships they had overcome and of the legends they had created. The highest mountain was the Cradle, named for its twin peaks and the saddle between them. It was always snow-covered, even at summer's height. Here, according to the stories that were told to the children of the village, the snows and blizzards were cradled during the summer, sleeping, to be awoken in the autumn. Other crags were the Piper's Hat and the Boar's Snout, named for their shapes, and the Middlesnag, which rose between the two. High on the Middlesnag was Gotfried's Fall, a ravine where a villager called Gotfried had met his death long before. He went out hunting and failed to return. Before anyone could find him, the first storm of winter struck, and then the snow lay on the ground for months. When the ice melted in the spring his body was discovered at the bottom of the ravine. From the village, Gotfried's Fall looked like a thin crack in the side of the mountain, and there was nothing to show the dizzying depth of the chasm that opened up there.

Now it was summer. The day was warm. High in the still, clear air, the snow on the Cradle glistened. The villagers had gathered on the green. Behind them the tables were already set out under the Jarrow Oak.

The Speaker stood before the crowd. Yoss heard him call his name. Herman was called as well. They stepped forward together, blankets and bags slung over their shoulders. Yoss heard the Speaker talk, saying the symbolic words. He received the wheatcake that was also just a symbol. Then he turned, with Herman beside him, and the crowd of villagers parted in front of them. Yoss glanced and saw tears in his mother's eyes. But he looked straight ahead again, and kept walking.

The villagers watched as they left. The figures of the two boys grew smaller. They passed the mill pond. Then they were moving up the slope towards the deer track that led into the forest. For a while longer the boys could be seen. Finally they disappeared amongst the trees.

The villagers turned to the tables, and the feast began.

~

YOSS AND HERMAN sat high on a ledge of rock.

'Look at it . . .' murmured Herman in wonder.

Yoss nodded. It was two days since they had walked away from the village green. They had slept in the open, under their blankets. They had walked through ravines, along the beds of dry streams, with the summit of the Middlesnag towering above them, and then down into valleys that passed through the peaks beyond. Children of the mountains, they scrambled easily over rocks and found their way down stony slopes with the nimbleness of goats. Yoss had refused to turn back, and Herman had continued with him. Now they sat on the edge of an outcrop and gazed in awe at the sight below them. The lake stretched into the distance.

'It's just like the Speaker said,' whispered Herman. 'You can't see the other side.'

The waters of the lake were grey, and a mist hung low over the surface.

Yoss reached into his bag and broke off some bread. He broke some for Herman as well.

'Haven't you ever *wondered*?' said Yoss.

Herman didn't reply. Yoss glanced at him as he passed the

bread. Perhaps he really hadn't ever wondered. Perhaps Herman really didn't think of anything but being Matthew's apprentice and becoming a carpenter.

Yoss turned back to the lake and chewed on his bread. He peered into the distance, trying to see through the mist for a hint of what lay beyond.

'Whatever's there . . . we'll be all right . . .' he murmured.

Herman looked at him in disbelief. Suddenly he shook his head. He reached into his bag and began to pull out bread, cheese and sausage. Yoss saw him piling the food on the rock between them.

'What are you doing?'

'Take it, Yoss. I'm not going with you.' Herman hesitated. 'Take it!' He grabbed Yoss' bag and began to throw the extra food in himself. When he had finished he flung the bag down, breathing heavily.

Yoss frowned. 'Come with me, Herman.'

The other boy dropped his gaze. 'No.'

Yoss looked inside the bag. It was full to the brim.

'What about you?' he said.

'I've got enough to get back,' muttered Herman. 'Take it, Yoss. Who knows when you'll find more?' Herman tried to smile. 'When you come back, you can repay me with something from there.'

Yoss grinned.

Now Herman grinned as well, but only for a moment, and then his face was serious once more. 'Be careful, Yoss. Don't be one of those who never return.'

They climbed down from the outcrop. They stood, not knowing what to do next. Herman adjusted the strap of his bag. He settled his blanket over his shoulder.

'Goodbye, Yoss,' he said at last.

'Goodbye, Herman.'

Herman gazed at him for a moment longer, then he turned abruptly and walked away.

Yoss watched until Herman was out of sight. When had he last been separated from his friend? He could barely remember a time when he couldn't have found the other boy just by calling out his name. But now Herman was gone. Soon he would be far away.

For the first time, Yoss felt alone.

In the distance, above the clouds, rode the twin peaks of the Cradle, like the last reminders of the village he had left. If he kept going, Yoss knew, soon even they would be out of sight.

He took a breath and turned to face the lake. The Cradle shimmered behind him. In front of him, everything was new.

And so, in his fourteenth summer, Yoss left the village in which he had been born.

2

BESIDE A STREAM, a man was riding a thin, miserable horse. The animal moved slowly, frequently attempting to drop its head towards the moss that grew underfoot. The sharp bones of the horse's rump protruded with each step and its back sagged under its rider's weight.

The rider was a large, fat man, with a pug-nosed face and straw-coloured hair. He was hatless, and wore a plain green tunic and brown trousers. His broad hams bounced against the horse's flanks. Alongside him, on foot, was a younger man, dressed entirely in a suit of black velvet. His boots were black as well, and the leather was intricately carved. The boots came up to his knees, and would have been the most striking thing about him, if not for the shape of his head, which was remarkably narrow and tall, as if someone had squashed it between two boards when he was a baby. His hair came down to his shoulders, black and oily. Usually he wore a high, rimless hat, something like a pot turned upside down, made of black velvet to match his suit. But now, in the heat of the day, and as he had already walked a long distance, he had taken the hat off and was carrying it in his hands.

The heat wasn't the only thing that worried him. The fact that he was the one on foot was another source of complaint. He was constantly complaining, grumbling, muttering, cursing and angrily kicking pebbles out of his path with the toe of his elegant boot.

The straw-haired man, for his part, was inclined to laugh.

From his vantage point on the skinny horse, he looked down on the top of his companion's narrow head, listening to his complaints and even goading him on. Laughter was one of the fat man's habits, and a very useful habit it had often proven itself to be, enabling him to discover secrets from other men while revealing little of himself. Not that there was very much to discover about his companion, who easily revealed his secrets even without the prompting of others. Since taking him under his wing, the fat man had discovered that he had his limitations, did young Gaspar, also known as Gaspar de Balboa, Quick Fingers, Cut Purse, Pot Head and various other names that people had invented from time to time.

'What is it, my little one?' said the fat man, as Gaspar hissed something else under his breath.

'What is it?' repeated Gaspar resentfully, aiming a mighty kick at a pebble lying in his path.

The fat man, whose name was Conrad, laughed.

'Don't you think you should give the horse a rest?' demanded Gaspar suddenly, stopping to look at the bowed, exhausted creature.

'And what kind of a rest do you think I should give it? The kind when you sit on its back?'

'Why not?' said Gaspar. 'After carrying you, it would be like a holiday.'

Conrad laughed again. He gave the horse a kick with his heels. The horse jerked and even trotted for a second, before it reverted to its sad, plodding gait. Gaspar trudged alongside.

'I admit, it does seem unfortunate, one horse for two people,' mused Conrad, gazing at Gaspar's peculiar head. Gaspar's head often put him in a thoughtful mood, and made him wonder about the vagaries of fortune, the prizes it gave, the tricks it played, as would the sight of a cross-eyed serving girl or a web-toed infant. 'Ah, fortune, fortune, Gasparillo,' he cried out in mock bemusement. 'Who can explain its ways?'

'I can explain its ways,' muttered Gaspar venomously. 'Three Kings to a pair of Jacks, that's the explanation.'

Conrad nodded. 'True. But who can explain how those three Kings came to be there, nestled and nuzzled in the barber's hand? That's fortune, Gasparto.'

'That's cheating' said Gaspar.

'True,' conceded Conrad. 'But what were your two Jacks, if not the sons and offspring of cheating as well? The cousins of those Kings, if not the brothers! And to show that he was cheating, you would have revealed what you were up to as well. Now *that's* fortune, my little Pot Head.'

'That's bad signalling,' said Gaspar. He blamed Conrad for the loss of his horse and all their money to the barber two nights before, and nothing Conrad said would convince him otherwise. One minute Conrad, who was standing behind the barber's shoulder, had given the signal for him to raise the stakes, and the next . . . the barber slapped three Kings down on the table, easily trouncing the two Jacks that Gaspar had slipped into his own hand.

'Listen,' said Conrad, 'you still don't understand, do you? It was you who lost that horse, not me.'

'But you signalled—'

'I signalled! Yes. But what about all the other times I signalled? When I wanted you to lose a hand or two? Did you do it? No, backed yourself, didn't you?'

'And I won.'

'Of course you won. Didn't lose a hand, did you? Until you lost the lot.'

Gaspar smirked. 'Didn't lose one until *you* told me—'

Conrad reached down from the horse and and tried to swat him on the head. Gaspar sprang away.

'Why didn't we rob him?' demanded Gaspar, warily walking out of Conrad's reach. 'Why didn't we just take everything back?'

'The horse?' said Conrad.

'Yes.'

'The money? Of course!' cried Conrad, slapping his forehead. 'He went out to relieve himself. We could have followed him out and jumped him then!'

'See?'

'Surprised him, murdered him, grabbed the money, rushed to the stable, got the horse and ridden off . . .'

'Let's go back!' cried Gaspar. 'Let's go back now!'

Conrad would have swatted him again, but Gaspar was too far away.

'Gaspar,' began Conrad quietly, 'in that inn, the barber was surrounded by his friends. *We* were the strangers. Now, you know me, Gasparto. You've seen the things I'll do. But if we'd done what you say, do you know where we'd be now? Lying in a ditch. And our heads would be lying in a different ditch.'

'How could our . . . *Oh!*'

'Try to learn something for a change!' Conrad shook his head in exasperation. 'It's worth the price of a horse if you'll just learn the lesson. He *knew* you were cheating.'

They continued in silence. Gaspar trudged along sullenly. Conrad glanced down at him from time to time, wondering what was going through his mind.

'How did he know I was cheating?' asked Gaspar at length.

'Good. The answer's simple,' said Conrad amiably. 'You're

stupid. You cheat too early. You never want to lose. Give a little early to gain a lot later. No, *you* have to win every single time. Fine. When you're playing with honest men, they'll say it's luck. But when you come up against another practised cheat, like the barber, he'll know exactly what you're doing. He'll simply wait until the time is right.'

'You should have known what he was going to do,' muttered Gaspar.

'No. That's where you're wrong, Gaspar. Not even I can see the future. A man like the barber is only going to cheat once. And because he only cheats once, you don't know he's going to do it, and it's too late once he does.' Conrad paused, trying to see whether Gaspar understood. 'It takes lightning fingers, Gaspar, to pull that caper. Think of the risk. Only the quickest fingers can play that game.'

Gaspar stopped in his tracks. '*Was* he quick?' he asked.

Conrad grinned.

'Quicker than me?' Gaspar whispered.

'Almost,' said Conrad. The horse had stopped, and Conrad jerked on the reins. Unwillingly, it began walking again. 'He was quick, Gaspar. Those Kings were out almost too quickly to see where they came from. He had two in his sleeve and another in his belt.'

'But he wasn't quicker than me?' Gaspar said, almost pleading.

'No, I didn't say he was quicker. You're still the quickest I've ever seen.'

Gaspar smiled. He put his hat on his head and folded his arms in satisfaction.

Conrad sighed. Just as well try to teach a stone to turn a somersault! There he was, sauntering along with a grin on his face and his ridiculous hat on his head. Tell him his fingers were quick and he was happy. And yet, Gaspar's fingers really were the quickest Conrad had ever seen. When Conrad had first noticed him, cheating at cards with a couple of fishermen, he had scarcely believed what he was seeing. And that's what Gaspar would still have been doing now, playing for scraps amongst stinking fish heads, if Conrad hadn't discovered him. But if only Gaspar could combine the great speed of his hands with a little common sense − not great subtlety or fearsome planning, which Conrad himself could supply, but just a little *common* sense − what riches he would win for them both when they came to the town!

Gaspar took his hat off again. The sun was high. Eventually Conrad stopped and dismounted. He let the horse drink. Gaspar drank as well. Conrad knelt beside the stream. He cupped his hands and reached forwards.

Suddenly he stopped. He looked around. Gaspar was resting back on his haunches, watching him. Conrad thought for a moment, how easy it would have been for Gaspar to have jumped up, knocked him into the water and ridden off on the horse, leaving him alone.

Conrad raised an eyebrow. Gaspar grinned. No, thought Conrad, he was too simple, too uncalculating, to do that. Besides, he would be too frightened of what Conrad would do if ever he caught him.

The straw-haired man turned back to the stream and raised the water to his lips. He slurped it from his thick fingers, slaking his thirst.

~

THEY ATE beside the stream. Conrad took bread from the

saddlebag, broke it, and threw a piece to Gaspar. He took the rest for himself. Gaspar had pulled off his boots and was sitting with his feet in the water. His hat lay on the ground beside him. The horse grazed on the thin grass nearby. Conrad sat in the shade under a tree, took a bite and began to chew. Dry bread! He rested his head against the tree trunk and tried to work up some moisture in his mouth. He closed his eyes. Duck! Conrad chewed the bread and tried to imagine he was eating a well-roasted duck, basted in its own fat and stuffed with nuts and apricots, like the one he had eaten at the inn before the barber took all their money. He imagined the rich meat of the bird lined with a full finger's breadth of fat, its oil oozing out of the corners of his mouth, dribbling down his cheeks, dripping off his chin, darkening his tunic.

Fortune! Fortune was a fickle thing, one day duck, the next day bread.

Conrad opened his eyes and looked at Gaspar. The younger man had a fondness for fine clothes and other costly objects. The saddle that he had lost with his horse had been a notable one, and its price had taken the winnings from many cheatings. His clothes were well made, of good fabric, as anyone could see. The hat that lay beside him had been especially commissioned from a milliner. His belt had a fine bronze buckle that others might covet. And his boots, of course, were of the highest quality. Whenever he had the chance, he oiled and worked at them. If Gaspar had to make a choice, he would probably oil those boots, thought Conrad, before he would feed himself. Yet it was just as likely that one day he would lose them in a card game or be robbed of them in an inn, and all the care and fondness he had lavished on them would be in vain.

It was a weakness, thought Conrad, this attachment to

objects. Food was the only thing worth coveting. Food and drink: the finest, the best, and the most one could consume. Once eaten, food could never be taken away, nor could the memory of its savour, nor the anticipation of future delights.

'Don't worry, Gasparillo,' he said suddenly, 'you'll soon have a horse again. In this life, you mustn't worry too much about possessions.'

Gaspar was tearing at the bread with his teeth. He muttered something under his breath.

Conrad wagged a finger. 'Where did you get the horse? Can you even remember?'

'From Michele.'

'And why did Michele give it to you?' said Conrad.

Gaspar sighed. 'Because we were going to fetch his sister from the ship and bring her back to him.'

'And did we bring her back?'

'No. Because she was dead, and they had buried her at sea.'

'And did we take the horses back to Michele?'

'No, because he didn't tell us what to do if his sister was dead.'

'Exactly. And we thought, in his grief, why would he want his horses back? After all, when a man has lost his sister, what difference do a couple of horses make?'

'No difference,' said Gaspar.

'Still, they might make a difference,' said Conrad. 'So, Michele gave you the horse, and now you have given it to the barber. Michele mourns the loss of it, and so do you, and one day the barber will as well. All of you make the mistake of being too strongly attached to it. But think of it like this, Gasparuño. The horse is like a small message, it goes from one person to the next.'

Gaspar thought about that, wiggling his white toes in the water. 'What does it say, this message of yours?' he asked eventually.

'That you should not be too attached to possessions. One horse gallops off, and another comes back. Soon you will have another one, and you will probably lose that as well.'

'But you don't lose yours,' pointed out Gaspar,

'True, but that's because I don't care about it. Look at it, thin, hungry, tired. If it galloped off, do you think I would even notice it?'

Yes, you'd notice, thought Gaspar. He pulled his feet out of the water and stretched them on a rock to let them dry in the sun.

They set off again. At first Gaspar wore his hat, but soon his head was too hot, and he took it off, and soon his feet were aching once more, and he began cursing and muttering under his breath again. But this time Conrad let him curse and mutter, because his mind was becoming increasingly occupied with a more pressing concern.

The stream ran through a forest. All around them were trees, and the air was filled with screeching birdcalls that never ceased. They had been in this forest ever since they had turned off the road that led to the town. This was the innkeeper's advice. The road, according to the innkeeper, looped and curled around the forest for a long distance to the north. But if they turned into the trees, and followed one of the streams, they would come out into the plain around the town. The first thing they would see would be the fish ponds, where peasants cultivated fish for the townspeople, and if they continued past those, through the fields of the plain, soon they would see the walls of the town itself. Conrad had never heard of this route, but he had never approached the town from this direction, and the innkeeper swore it was the quickest. As long as you didn't have a cart or a carriage there was no need to stay on the road. And since they didn't have much food, and since Gaspar's last bet with the barber had left them without money to buy any more, the quicker the route to the town, where a meal was only as far away as the first carelessly guarded purse, the better.

Yet the innkeeper hadn't said how wide the forest was, or how long it would take them to cross it. And they had turned off the road on the afternoon of the day before. And still the forest stretched ahead. Conrad was beginning to think that the innkeeper, after the barber had finished with them, had decided to have his own bit of fun.

Gaspar was talking to him.

'What is it?' demanded Conrad impatiently.

'How much longer must we walk through this forest?'

'Until we've arrived.'

'Until we've arrived,' Gaspar muttered in mimicry. 'Don't ask questions, Gaspar,' he admonished himself. 'Don't answer back! Do as I say! Don't make——'

Conrad reached down and swatted his head.

They continued beside the stream. Gradually, it grew wider and shallower. The trees thinned out. Suddenly they found themselves approaching a stony shore, and ahead of them was a vast expanse of water.

'This is the biggest fish pond I've ever seen!' exclaimed Gaspar. 'How much fish they must eat in this town! Conrad, it's as big as a lake.'

'It is a lake,' said Conrad.

Gaspar frowned. 'But we weren't meant to find a lake. Did the innkeeper say anything about a lake?'

'Gaspar, we're lost.'

Gaspar's jaw dropped. Conrad turned back to look across the water.

Mist shrouded the lake. Above the mist, high, snow-covered crags floated in the air, piercing the cloud.

Conrad gazed at the mountains with awe. He shuddered. He loved towns, the cries and stench of many people, food, wine and noise, the hubbub of the market and the shrieks of festivals, the thievery and cheatery and trickery and knifery and pickpocketry and roguery and fakery and riflery and all the other fine sciences that were taught and practised in the university of the streets. The thought of those barren mountains almost overwhelmed him. To be alone up there, he imagined, would be a kind of icy hell.

'Let's go,' he said suddenly.

'Where?'

'Back. Back where we came from. Does it matter? Away from here!'

'But shouldn't we try to find someone? Maybe they'll have some fish from the lake. Or a horse . . .' Gaspar said with a sly grin.

'Here?' cried Conrad. He threw out an arm and gestured wildly along the shore. 'Find someone here? Are you mad, Gaspar? You pot-headed fool. Look at this place. No one has set foot here in a thousand years. You'll find not a soul, not a trace, not a . . .' Conrad's voice trailed away.

'Not a what, Conrad?'

'Look over there, Gaspar.' Conrad's eyes narrowed. 'Tell me . . . do you see someone?'

3

FOR MOST OF THE WAY around the lake, Yoss had found himself walking over long stretches of flat grey stones, which would have been under water when the lake rose in the spring. Occasionally he came across streams that ran out of the mountains, but they weren't deep, and he splashed through them. Sometimes the lake came right up to an outcrop of solid rock, and for a distance he had to pick his way through the trees that grew above it. But he never had to go far before he was able to come down to the water's edge again.

He heard birdcalls coming out of the forest, and he saw birds wheeling above the water. But he saw hardly any other living thing. In the mountains, if you looked carefully enough, from one slope to the next, you almost always caught sight of mountain goats or deer, picked out against the rock like specks of brown fluff. Here, he peered in vain around the shore of the lake. Sometimes he thought he saw something, a person perhaps, or a bear, but when he looked again, it was always gone. Perhaps it was the trees, he thought, that deceived him with their shapes. Or perhaps he had begun to imagine things.

People did imagine things, Yoss knew, when they were alone. Only a few years earlier, one of the young men of the village, Moritz, had survived for six days alone on the Cradle. He had been caught on the mountain when a springtime blizzard struck. Yoss himself was old enough to remember the storm, which raged through the valley and buried the houses in snow up to their eaves. Moritz had burrowed a hollow out of the snow and that was where he survived, as the winds screamed around him, eating the raw flesh of a mountain goat that he had killed and had been bringing down when the blizzard started. Two of his fingers had been bitten by the frost and later fell off, and of his toes, there were no more than three left on each foot. And later he told how, as the days passed in his icy cavern, when there was nothing to see but the snow above and the snow below, nothing to feel but the cold, slowly, steadily nibbling at his fingers and toes, he had begun to see things, glowing coals, and warm beer, and a roasted joint, and of course Brigitte, whom he loved. It was not the flesh of the goat, but the tender words of Brigitte, he said, which had kept him alive. It was Brigitte who had comforted him, given him hope and kept him from despair, and it was Brigitte who had told him when the storm outside had passed, and that it was safe to emerge, because he wouldn't have known by himself, and might have come out too early, when the blizzard was still raging, or come out too late, when his hands and feet were too frostbitten for him to climb down the mountain.

Yet Brigitte, as everyone knew, had stayed safe in her parents' house all through the blizzard. And even Moritz agreed that she had not really been there, but that the solitude and the fear had made her and all the other things appear before his eyes.

Moritz was much admired by the boys of the village, and of all the men, he was the one whom Yoss respected most. He was tall, strong, capable and never thought of his own comfort when there was work to be done. Even with his damaged feet and hands he remained an expert climber and skilful hunter. But the reason Yoss most admired him was because he admitted that he had been afraid during those six days on the Cradle. There was a lot of courage in admitting fear, Yoss thought. And there was a lot of courage in admitting that your mind had started to imagine things, as well, when you were up there on the mountain by yourself.

But how long did it take before you started to imagine things when you were alone? Yoss wandered along beside the water, engrossed in thought, gazing at the stones under his feet. Moritz had been on the mountain for six days. And it was only a day since he had left Herman. Surely it was too soon to start imagining things after just one day! Of course there were trees here, which could deceive you. Moritz didn't have any trees. He just had the white snow, above him and below him and all around.

Yoss felt something hit his head.

Suddenly he was on the ground.

~

HANDS ran quickly over him, rolled him on his back, ran over him again. They left him. Yoss looked up. A man was standing above him, dressed all in black, with a boot planted firmly on each side of his chest.

'What has he got, Gasparto?'

Yoss craned his neck to see where the voice came from.

'Well?'

The man above him grinned. He held up a small wooden comb, pinching it delicately between thumb and forefinger.

'That's mine!' cried Yoss, and he struggled to get up off the stony ground.

The man put a boot on Yoss's chest. He pressed the point of its toe under his chin.

'A comb?' called the other voice. 'Is that all, a comb? No coins, no jewels?'

The man shrugged. He slipped the comb into a pocket.

There was a laugh. 'Let him up,' said the other voice.

The man stepped aside. Yoss got to his feet and looked around. The second man was under the trees, a fat man with straw-coloured hair. He was holding the bridle of a horse. Now he wrapped the reins around a trunk and stepped forward.

'What's in the bag?' he said.

Yoss turned to see the first man rummaging through his bag.

'Give it back!' he cried, throwing himself at the man. The man shrugged him off, sending Yoss sprawling.

'Food,' he said.

'No duck, I suppose?' inquired the fat man.

'No duck. Bread. Cheese. Oh, here's some sausage.'

'Oh, well, sausage is better than nothing,' said the fat man. He had reached them now. 'What do they call you, boy?'

Yoss shielded his eyes from the sunlight and looked up to see the man's pug-nosed face gazing down at him. 'Yoss.'

'Well, get up then, Yoss. Sausage is better than nothing, even if it isn't duck.'

~

THE TWO MEN sat beneath a tree and helped themselves to the food in Yoss' bag. They pulled out knives and were soon slicing it up. There was a lot left in the bag, but they made short work of it. Yoss hungrily watched it disappearing. The two men didn't give him any. It was as if they had forgotten about him altogether.

But they hadn't forgotten about him. At least, the fat one hadn't.

'So, they call you Yoss,' he said eventually. He belched. 'Nothing else? Yoss of the Lake? What about that? That'd suit, I think.'

Yoss shook his head.

'I know what we should call you. Yoss the Solitary. Would you like that? What are you doing here, anyway, all by your-self?'

Yoss didn't reply.

The fat man finished off a piece of sausage. Then he leaned back against a tree and scrutinized the boy.

'Well,' he said after a moment, 'let me do the introductions. This here, is Cut Purse.' He pointed at Gaspar. 'Now, Yoss, can you imagine why they call him that?'

Yoss shook his head. 'Because he cuts the leather for purses?'

Gaspar laughed. 'Cuts the leather—'

'Be quiet, Gaspar! It's a very good answer. Best answer he could have given.' The fat man turned back to Yoss. 'Good answer, boy. Now, I'll tell you my name. They call me Cut Throat, or Stifler . . .'

'Or Heart Stabber or Head Breaker,' added Gaspar.

'Yes, Gaspar, that's enough. Can't you ever be quiet? All right, Yoss, why do you think they call me that?'

'Because you're a slaughterer?'

'Yes,' said Conrad. He grinned. 'You might say so, after a fashion.'

'He's a slaughterer all right,' muttered Gaspar.

Conrad ignored him. He gazed closely at the boy again, appraising him.

Suddenly he slapped his forehead. 'But here we are, filling our bellies, and we haven't given you a thing! Where's our manners, Gasparto? Lost 'em at the card game, eh? Now here you are, Yoss. Here you are,' he repeated to himself, and he looked inside the bag to see what was left, and found some cheese, which he sliced with his knife, and broke off some bread. 'Share and share alike. Got to stick together. There are bandits here, you know. They'll knock you down, take what you've got and cut your throat, Yoss, just like that.' Conrad clicked his fingers. 'Just like *that*!' he repeated suddenly, and as Yoss jumped, he stabbed his knife towards him, with the piece of cheese impaled on its point.

The knife hovered in front of Yoss' chest.

'Take it,' said Conrad.

Yoss reached out and took the cheese off the man's knife. Then the man held out some bread, and Yoss took that as well.

'Where are you going, Yoss?'

Yoss shook his head, filling his mouth with the food and chewing hungrily.

Gaspar watched, arms folded. He glanced at Conrad, but Conrad's eyes were on the boy. Sullenly, Gaspar began to chew on a piece of bread

'Why did you knock me down?' said Yoss, when he was able to speak again.

'That was just to be sure,' said Conrad. 'There are so many bandits, how could we be sure *you* weren't one as well?'

'But I was by myself,' objected Yoss.

'By himself!' Conrad shook his head with amusement. 'And how did we know there wasn't a whole band of your companions just waiting for us? Tell us that, Yoss the Riddler, if you please. That's the trick some of 'em play, and if you don't know it already, then you know it now. One of them comes out and starts talking, and then, when you're least expecting it, the others rush out and grab you from behind.'

'Have you seen it happen?' asked Yoss with curiosity.

'Seen it! Oh, I could tell you some stories, Yoss. Couldn't I, Gaspar? Gaspar!'

Gaspar nodded. Yoss glanced at him. Gaspar was fiddling with his comb.

'Where are you from, Yoss?' asked Conrad.

'Over there.'

'Across the lake?'

Yoss nodded.

The two men turned their heads and looked across the water.

'Do you see that mountain, far, far away?' said Yoss. 'High up. The one with two peaks. Look, you can just see one behind the other.'

'But that . . . those are clouds,' said Gaspar.

Yoss grinned. 'It's snow, Cut Purse.'

'How can it be snow? It's summer. It's too hot, it'd melt—'

'Be quiet, Gaspar! Listen to Yoss. He knows what he's talking about. Anyone can see that. '

'The snow up there never melts,' said Yoss, 'not even on the hottest days. That mountain is called the Cradle, and my village is in the valley below it.'

'And is there snow there as well?' asked Conrad.

'Not now. It's warm in the valley, and the wheat's growing, and the grapes are starting to bud.'

'And you can't get to the town through there, can you?' said Conrad.

Yoss looked at him uncomprehendingly.

'No, I didn't think so. Someone told us the town was up there. An innkeeper. But he may have been playing a trick on us, I think.' Conrad laughed. 'Have you ever met an innkeeper, Yoss? There's a riddle about them. Who never leaves his house, but is still too fast to catch? Eh, Yoss? They're terrible tricksters, every one. Bigger bandits than any bandit you'll meet on the road.'

Yoss shook his head. 'I've never met an innkeeper.'

'Never met an innkeeper,' Conrad murmured under his breath . . . 'Well, I don't suppose you get many visitors up there, do you, Yoss? No need for an inn.'

'I suppose not,' said Yoss.

'You suppose not . . . And here you are, and you've come all this way, all by yourself, with the bandits all around, and you still haven't told us where you're going.'

Yoss didn't reply. He looked at the lake, and then at the peaks of the Cradle shimmering in the air. 'Are you going to the town?' he asked. 'Is that where you're going?'

'Perhaps,' said Conrad. He leaned forward. 'Would you like to come with us, Yoss?'

Yoss found himself gazing into the fat man's eyes.

Suddenly Conrad sat back and slapped his thighs. 'Have you ever been to a town, Yoss? It's a wonderful thing, a town. Duck liver and calf's muzzles, you'll never be hungry when you're in that stench. And there's no end of work for a pair like Cut Purse and me. No end of purses waiting to be cut. No end of throats to be slit.'

Gaspar laughed. Yoss looked at him to find out what he thought was so funny. That only made Gaspar laugh even more.

'And you too, Yoss. We'll find something for you. Oh, yes, plenty to do for a boy like you. A *man* like you, I should say. Come with us. The town's the place!'

Conrad put a finger in his mouth to extract a piece of sausage that was stuck between his teeth. He set it down on the blade of his knife, examined it for a second, and then then put it back in his mouth.

'Well, Yoss, what's your answer?'

Yoss hesitated. He looked up at the Cradle once more. Then he turned back to Conrad. He clenched his jaw, and nodded.

Conrad laughed. 'That's the way!'

'But Con—'

'You'll need your strength, Yoss,' continued Conrad, cutting across Gaspar's voice. 'Look at us, we've been talking so much, you've hardly had a chance to eat.' Conrad passed him his bag. 'Take what you want, Yoss. Share and share alike.'

'*But Conrad!*'

'Share and share *alike*,' Conrad said in a low voice, and he turned to fix Gaspar with his gaze.

Yoss peered into the bag. There wasn't much left. The sausage was finished. He took out some bread.

'You know what I want?' said Yoss suddenly.

'What?' said Conrad.

Yoss pointed at Gaspar. 'My comb!'

Conrad grinned. 'Your comb? Don't tell me he's still got it!'

Gaspar glanced at Conrad. Then he shrugged. He drew the comb out of a pocket, turned to Yoss, ran the comb slowly through the length of his oily hair, and tossed it on the ground at the boy's feet.

4

ALMOST AT ONCE, Yoss began to realize that the two men were of a different type from anyone he had met before.

Conrad was mounted on his horse again, and Yoss and Gaspar walked alongside. Gaspar, of course, soon started to grumble. Conrad on his miserable, plodding horse, laughed and chaffed him. The boy understood only part of what they said, and misinterpreted much more. What he heard was a lot of talk about a barber and three kings. To his inexperienced ears, it sounded as if the barber and the kings were playing some kind of game together. The kings, it seemed, had un-expectedly appeared and joined in. He couldn't understand how this could happen. It must be very unusual, he thought, for three kings to be together in one place, and even more unusual for no one to know they were expected. And it was almost impossible to believe they would bother about a simple barber once they had arrived. And that they should then start playing a game – this was beyond him entirely.

And for good measure – if you could imagine such a thing – Conrad and Gaspar seemed to have been mixed up in the game as well!

But it wasn't specifically the story about the barber and the kings that made the boy realize how different were these two men from the people he knew in the village. After all, he wasn't a fool, and he soon deduced that there must be something he didn't understand about the story, which, if only he had under-stood it, would have made everything clear. No, it was all the other things they said, especially Conrad. The fat man was always ready with a joke, proverb or story to silence his companion, often in the very middle of one of Gaspar's sentences. And in these jokes and stories appeared many people, a whole parade of them, if you added them up, innkeepers, coachmen, serving girls, butchers, haberdashers, fishermen, coroners, guards, barbers, watchmen, money-changers. There were the names of places as well, a whole list of them, ports, towns, hamlets, ships, crossroads. No one in his village, Yoss realized, could have spoken about such a range of people and places. In the village, one's dead ancestors were more real than anyone who was actually alive outside the ring of mountains that surrounded it. But there was no ring of mountains to constrict Conrad's world. It seemed to Yoss that Conrad, and Gaspar with him, were men who inhabited a world without limits.

It was exciting. For Yoss it was an extraordinary realization to find that he was now part of this world. And he was, surely, if he was walking with these men! He didn't speak, but listened, soaking up Conrad's endless litany of names and places. And at the same time, even as he savoured the thrill of this world into which he had been invited, he became aware that there were also things in it that were confusing, if not dangerous. To listen to the two men, it must be a world of constant trickery and cheating. People took from each other and gave to no one. But it was a cheerful world, apparently, because the straw-haired man never ceased from chuckling and grinning as he responded to Gaspar's mutterings.

And quick fingers – whatever that meant – were important. This, above all things, became clear.

So they walked along the stream, through the forest and away from the lake. The boy, keeping silent, thought he was the only one who was watching and learning. But he was mistaken. From his seat on the horse, the fat man's gaze rarely left his face. If the boy wanted to be silent, he would let him be silent. Conrad's eyes, always probing, watched for any sign of the thoughts that were going through his head.

They stopped for the night in the forest. In the morning, when Yoss awoke, his comb had disappeared. Conrad helped him look for it. They searched in the bags and shook out his blanket. They scoured the ground where he had slept.

'You must have dropped it,' said Conrad eventually.

'I didn't,' said Yoss. 'I'm sure.'

'What other explanation is there?' said Conrad.

'*I* can't think of any,' said Gaspar, leaning against a tree with his arms folded, as they searched.

~

BY NOON OF the second day they reached the road from which Conrad and Gaspar had originally turned off, and they stopped to eat. There was only dried bread and a little cured meat, which Conrad produced from his saddlebags. Conrad and Gaspar shared it with Yoss. Yet the thin strip of meat that Yoss was given did not make up for all the sausage and cheese that the two men had consumed out of his bag the previous day.

Then they continued. Now they followed the road towards the north. There was still forest all around them. Conrad rode the horse, and Gaspar and Yoss trudged alongside him, as before.

'Are you still hungry, Yoss?' said Conrad after a while.

'Not really,' said Yoss, thinking that he shouldn't complain.

'Of course you are!' exclaimed Conrad. 'We're all hungry. Are you hungry, Gaspar?'

'Of course I'm hungry,' replied Gaspar, without even bothering to look up.

'See?' said Conrad, grinning at Yoss, as if being hungry was nothing to worry about as long as you admitted it.

'I wouldn't be so hungry if I could sit on your horse,' grumbled Gaspar.

'That's obvious,' said Conrad.

'And I'd have more to eat if we didn't have to feed this little lake creature here.'

'Gasparto! Where's your gratitude? What a fine feast Yoss brought us yesterday. Yoss, pay no attention. Gaspar has a short memory for favours and a long memory for slights. But so do we all. Give a man a shilling and he'll cut your throat for a pound. Sell him a rabbit for a hare and he'll never forgive you. What do you think, eh?'

'I don't know . . .'

'Listen, if you're hungry, it doesn't matter. That's the thing, Yoss. What do they say? Sometimes your belly's as flat as a tray, but you'll fill it to bursting the very next day! That's life, isn't it? Don't be attached to possessions and eat what you can. Now, Gaspar here is much too attached to possessions, aren't you, my little Cut Pursey?'

Gaspar looked up at Conrad and scowled.

Conrad laughed. 'When we get to the town we'll gorge. Just you wait, Yoss. Starve today, gorge tomorrow. What will you have? Joint of beef? Honeyed ham? No, I know the thing for you. Duck! A lovely roast duck, stuffed with apricots and nuts, and the fat all dripping off it. That's the thing. Watch out, Yoss! The fat's dribbling down your chin. I can see it already.' Conrad laughed. He threw his head back and the sound came right out of his belly. 'Eh, Yoss? What do you say?'

Yoss nodded.

'That's it! Smile, Yoss. That's the way. Now, here's some more advice. If you want to get safely to the town, do as I say. This road isn't safe, that's the first thing. Bandits all over the place. You're lucky we found you, or they'd have picked you off already.'

'And taken your comb,' said Gaspar.

'Be quiet, Gaspar. Don't remind a man of his losses. Do I talk about your horse? Pay no attention to him, Yoss. But he's right. They'd take your comb, not to mention what else they'd do. They rarely leave people alive to tell tales, and why should they? Listen to someone who knows, it isn't like the mountains down here. They attack with surprise and there's no time to defend yourself. So listen, Yoss. If I tell you to do something, you must do it, for your own safety. No questions and no delay, all right?'

Conrad stopped the horse. Yoss looked up. The fat man gazed questioningly at him.

'Can we trust you to do that, Yoss? No questions and no delay.'

Yoss nodded.

Conrad grinned and dug his heels into the horse's flanks. 'Good. You're a fine man to have around, Yoss, reliable and trustworthy. Eh, Gaspar? A *fine* man to have around.'

Later the forest began to thin, and when they stopped for the night they were on the edge of a marsh. The next morning they followed the road through wetlands. Yoss had never seen such low, flat country. Birds flew with harsh, honking cries. Rushes grew in pools of water, and the ground between the pools was heavy and waterlogged. Here and there small hillocks were covered in low, tangled bushes. Nothing grew that was tall and upright. A dull heat hung over the marsh, unlike the dry air of the mountains, heavy and moist. There was a ditch along each side of the road, to drain it, and the water at the bottom was hazy with insects.

The marsh was a desolate place, and it made Yoss think about the bandits that Conrad had mentioned. Conrad was right. If you were alone out here in this marsh, and bandits fell upon you, there would be no one to save you.

So when two horsemen appeared in the distance, Yoss had no hesitation in following Conrad's instructions. He dropped into the ditch beside the road, behind Gaspar, and crouched as low as he could, with no questions and no delay, exactly as Conrad told him.

~

THE SOUND of horses approached. Hoofbeats. Harnesses jangling.

Yoss heard it from the bottom of the ditch. His feet were in the water, and insects flew around him in a cloud. Gaspar was crouching ahead of him.

The noise of the horses stopped. There was silence. Yoss felt his heart pounding

'Good day, sir.' It was Conrad's voice.

'Good day,' came the reply

'Are you travelling far, sir?'

'Far enough.'

'The weather is fair for it,' said Conrad.

'It is. Are you alone? I thought I saw a man walking beside you.'

'No, sir. He passed me. Look, you can see him further along.'

'No . . . I can't see him.'

'You will. You'll soon catch him up. Perhaps your servant might take him on his mule.'

'Perhaps. Well, will you move aside?'

'Move aside?' said Conrad.

'To let us pass.'

'I would move aside, but . . .'

'But what?'

'Each must take what he can, sir!'

Gaspar sprang. Yoss saw a dagger glinting in his hand as he leapt out of the ditch.

There were shouts, scuffling, the whinnying of horses. Yoss threw his arms over his head, huddled even lower, face down, breathing the insects that flew above the water. Then there was silence again.

'Yoss!'

Yoss unfolded his arms from around his head and looked up. A mule leapt across the ditch above him. He ducked again.

'*Yoss!*'

Cautiously, Yoss raised his head above the top of the ditch.

Conrad and Gaspar were each holding a man with a dagger at the throat. Two horses, one of them Conrad's scrawny mount, stood on the road.

'Come out, Yoss!' called Conrad.

Yoss climbed out of the ditch. He stopped at the side of the road. The man whom Conrad held was richly dressed. His velvet cap had been knocked off, and lay at his feet, crumpled. His thinning brown hair was disordered and stood in wisps around his head. The second man, whom Gaspar held, was plainly dressed and was bleeding from a cut above the eye. The blood had gushed down his face and stained his white shirt.

All four men were watching him.

'Come here, Yoss. This man has a chain and begs us to take its weight from his neck,' said Conrad, and as he pulled on the man's cloak with one hand, Yoss could see the glint of a gold chain.

Yoss approached uncertainly.

'That's it. Lift it off now,' said Conrad. 'Come on.'

Yoss reached forward with one hand and took hold of the chain. He began to raise it. He avoided the man's eyes.

Conrad lifted the dagger from the man's neck to make way for the chain, and pushed the man's head forward so that Yoss could lift it free.

'That's it. Give it here,' said Conrad, and he snatched the chain from Yoss and stuffed it in a pocket. 'Now the rings,' he said.

There were four rings on the man's fingers, one of plain gold, and three with stones. One by one, Yoss removed them. The man did not resist, but did not help. His hand hung limply, and Yoss had to take hold of each finger and steady it in order to pull the rings off.

'Here,' said Conrad, and he took the rings as well. 'And now the purse. Remember this, Yoss. Every merchant carries a purse. And no matter what they tell you, that's where the money is. Reach under his shirt now, and you'll find it.'

'*Under* his shirt?'

'Quickly, now, he hasn't got all day. Have you, sir?'

The merchant didn't reply. Reluctantly, Yoss reached inside the merchant's cloak, and pulled up his shirt. The skin was cold, clammy.

'Come on, Yoss. Find it, now.'

Yoss ran his hand up the merchant's side until he felt a cord. His fingers followed the cord and found a purse.

'Let's have it, Yoss. Pull.'

Yoss pulled hard on the cord, and the purse came free.

'Do you know what you're doing, boy?'

Yoss' fingers froze. He glanced up. The merchant's eyes were cold, grey-blue.

'You'll hang,' he whispered. 'You'll hang for this. I'll come after you, boy, and when I find you—'

Conrad slapped his hand across the merchant's mouth.

'What's that, eh? Don't you listen to him, Yoss. We're old acquaintances, and he owes me money. Isn't that right, sir? See, he was trying to get out of the town before we arrived. Lucky we found him on the road. Have you got the purse? Good, give it here.'

Conrad took the purse. Now he let go of the merchant and took a step away from him, still holding his dagger ready, and opened the leather pouch.

'Wait, it's more than he owes.' Conrad shook his head. He fished around inside the purse and took a single copper coin out of it. 'Here. Hold out your hand. All we want is what you owe. Don't let anyone say we robbed you.'

Conrad put the coin on the merchant's palm.

'Now,' said Conrad, 'let's see what's in the saddlebags.'

Conrad turned and began to open the saddlebags on the merchant's horse. The coin sat on the merchant's palm. All this time he was watching Yoss, as if he was not even aware of what Conrad was doing, nor of the fact that Gaspar was still holding his servant with a knife. The intensity of his stare, the threat in the grey-blue eyes, transfixed the boy.

Suddenly the merchant turned, charged, and shoved Conrad to the ground. He leapt into the saddle. Gaspar lunged after him but the horse was already galloping. The merchant's servant, finding himself released, dashed after his master.

Gaspar jumped up and raced after the servant. Conrad climbed slowly to his feet. He watched the chase, rubbing his back where the merchant had hit him. The servant was fast. His lead on Gaspar was growing. Eventually Gaspar gave up.

Far down the road, the horse had stopped, and the merchant waited for his servant to arrive.

Conrad put a hand on Yoss' shoulder. They saw the servant reach his master. The merchant hoisted him up. The horse turned and began to move away.

Conrad laughed. 'Well, let them go, eh, Yoss? We'd never catch them on my horse. Did you see what a fine animal the other one was? I had half a mind to keep it as interest on my loan. Yoss, here's a lesson: beware of merchants. They'll promise you riches but rarely pay. Did you see what he was doing? Shameless! Trying to get away before I arrived, just to avoid paying his debt.'

The boy looked up at Conrad. 'But you took his rings . . . and his chain . . .'

'And why shouldn't I?' demanded Conrad. 'If a man owes you gold, does it matter if it's coins or rings? It's all gold, after all.'

'But did he really owe you all of that? So much?'

'Did he really owe me all of that? Look, we'll ask Gaspar. Gaspar,' shouted Conrad, as Gaspar returned from his chase, 'Yoss is asking whether our friend the merchant really owed us so much. So much and more, didn't he?'

Gaspar nodded. He came back and stood with his hand on his hips, looking around the road for his pot-shaped hat, which had fallen off during the struggle. It had rolled across the road and was on the verge of the ditch.

'See, Yoss,' said Conrad. 'Just as I said. I could easily have taken the horse, and still been owed more. Speaking of the horse, I wonder what was in those saddlebags. I was hoping there might have been some food, and we could have had a meal together before they went on their way. I'm sure the merchant would have enjoyed it. But they left us the mule, at least.'

The mule was standing on a hillock. Its saddlebags bulged.

'Yoss, go and get it. With a bit of luck it's carrying a handsome dinner for us. Go on, Yoss. Don't keep us waiting.'

Yoss clambered across the ditch and began to make his way cautiously into the marsh. Even where the ground look solid, his feet sank into the waterlogged soil.

'That was clever, Conrad,' said Gaspar, chortling. 'A debt! I haven't heard that one before. And the little fool believes it!'

'Every merchant owes a debt,' said Conrad coldly. 'Profit doesn't come from nowhere. What he has, he took from someone else, just as surely as if he cut a purse. What he took, I'll take, and give it back by spending it.'

Gaspar frowned. Conrad's ideas, he often found, were difficult to understand. 'Do you think it's safe to go to the town?' he asked after a moment. 'Perhaps he lives there.'

'Safe? Safest place for us. It's when a man's by himself that he stands out, Gaspariño. With others around him, a man's invisible.'

Out in the marsh, the boy was struggling with the mule. It stood stubbornly on its hillock, refusing to budge. Yoss tugged and tugged on its bridle.

'Hit it!' cried Conrad.

Yoss slapped the animal on its rump. It bucked and kicked.

Conrad laughed. 'Go and help him, Gasparto,' he said, nudging Gaspar in the ribs.

5

INSIDE THE TOWN GATE, two soldiers leaned against a wall. Here they stood every day, with little to entertain them but the mishaps of new arrivals and amusements of their own invention. Mostly, peasants came in through the gate, bowed under sacks or wheeling barrows. Sometimes a wagon appeared, or a coach, clattering over the cobblestones. For the attention of newcomers, beggars lay in the gutters displaying their stumps and wounds, their shrivelled limbs or sightless eyes, calling out to advertise their need. Hawkers, selling pastries or slices of sausage, cried their wares. Cats sniffed at the waste that lay on the ground. Occasionally, a hawker would land a kick on one of the cats and send the beast flying into a wall.

A bell tinkled from outside the gate. The soldiers looked to see who was coming through. First appeared an old draught horse, and behind it a wagon, driven by a peasant. One of the soldiers rolled his eyes. The wagon was piled with sacks of corn, and all around the sides hung dead rabbits, tied by their hind feet to the wood. They bobbed and swung as the cart moved and the bell tinkled, dancing a strange, upside-down jig.

'Dancing the rope,' said the soldier, as one might say about a man on the gallows.

The other soldier grinned.

'Rabbits!' cried the peasant. His face was hidden under a broad, slouching peasant's hat.

'Give us one,' cried the first soldier.

'Give you one?' retorted the peasant. 'Trapped them myself.'

'Then give us two,' cried the second soldier.

A young beggar with a withered arm and leg, sitting beside the soldiers in the gutter, watched with interest to see what the peasant would do.

'Rabbits!' cried the peasant.

'*Sausages!*' cried a hawker.

The soldiers swaggered towards the wagon. The peasant pulled up on the reins.

'No one wants your rabbits,' said the first soldier. 'Give us one.'

His companion raised a foot and rested it on one of the wheel spokes.

The peasant hesitated. Then he leaned down and untied a rabbit at the front of the wagon. He tossed it to the soldiers.

'That's better,' said the one who caught it. 'Off you go, rabbit-man.'

The soldiers walked away. The peasant flicked his reins, and the horse began moving towards the street that led to the market. The rabbits danced the rope all around it.

The soldiers laughed once more at the sight. Then the one with the rabbit held it up to look at it. He sniffed it and grimaced. He held it out to his companion, who waved his hand in front of his nose and brushed the animal away.

The soldier looked down at the withered beggar. He tossed the rabbit onto the ground, not straight to him, but some way in front. The beggar hopped up on his good foot, turned a somersault, and landed on it again, inches from the rabbit.

The beggar gathered up the rabbit and hopped away. The soldiers grinned. Through the gate came a fat man on a horse, and beside him a mule, carrying a man and a boy. The soldiers followed the ensemble with their eyes as it crossed the cobble-stones towards an alley.

'That horse will be dead by nightfall,' remarked one of the soldiers. 'I'll bet you a pint of Stampfer's best beer.'

The other soldier shook his head in disgust. Rarely had he seen an animal so badly starved and neglected by its owner.

~

Yoss had caught his first glimpse of the town from far away, on the plain outside. Across fields and fishponds, he saw a low, shadowy outline in the blue distance, with spires poking out of it like thorns. On the plain itself, people were moving, tramping along the road that led to the town or on the tracks that criss-crossed the plain between the fishponds. Others were on horses, and there were wagons as well. Already, the boy felt as if he had come upon a world of infinite activity. In the village, he only had to raise his eyes to the mountains to find emptiness. Here on the plain, there was not a single place he could look without seeing another person.

Yet the town itself was something unimaginable. As soon as he went through the gate, there were people everywhere. They lay in the gutters, stood by the walls, crossed in front of the mule, ran behind it. Yoss didn't discern them as soldiers, or beggars, or traders, or peasants, he merely saw *people*, people, everywhere, moving and turning and shouting. The noise was something else. The clatter of hooves, the creaking of carts, the cries and pleas and calls of the people that crowded all around. And there was a stench. It was solid. As he came through the gate, it hit him in the face.

Yoss had never smelled such an odour. Vile, dank and rotten. What evil things were in it, he could only imagine.

They crossed the open square in front of the gate, and then Conrad led them into dark, twisting alleys. Here there were fewer people, less noise, but the smell grew. The houses were close on each side and rose to two or even three storeys, jutting out and almost roofing the street. Sunlight barely penetrated. The cobblestones were covered in muck and thick, oily water. The stench was very strong, nauseating.

Conrad knew his way through the stinking alleys. Eventually he stopped. They were at a wooden gate set in a high wall. Conrad climbed down from his horse. He motioned to Gaspar and Yoss to dismount as well. Then he knocked at the gate.

A minute or two passed before a man opened the gate and let them in. Conrad sent him off to get his master.

They were in the stableyard of an inn. It was unpaved, and the earth had been churned into puddles of water and mud. The stable, a long, low building along one side of the yard, was roughly constructed of wood and rotting at the bottom. At its far end it leaned against the inn, which was two storeys high and roofed with thatch. The servant had gone inside through a low door under a small wooden porch.

Eventually the door opened again. A different man appeared. He stooped as he came out under the porch, then he straightened up. Only now did he look to see who had arrived. He stared.

Conrad grinned, and opened his arms, as if to embrace the man, even though half the yard still separated them.

'Host Farber!' he cried.

The innkeeper was tall and very gaunt. His clothes hung from him. Yet there was a flush to his thin, hollow cheeks, and his eyes burned with intensity as he gazed at them.

'Conrad?' His voice was hoarse. 'I hadn't expected to see you again, at least not for a long . . . a long . . .' He stopped and began to cough. The coughing escalated. After a moment he was bent double, gripping his ribs with his arms. The coughs racked his entire frame.

Conrad waited until the coughing subsided. 'Still well, I see. The green doctor has cured you.'

The innkeeper stood straight again. He took deep breaths. Then he spat. He wiped the back of his hand across his mouth. His lips were bright. A smudge of blood stained his hand.

'He cured me, certainly. I hope he cures himself just as well!'

Conrad grinned. 'They never cure themselves, Farber. They know better than to even try.'

Farber grunted.

'No morbid thoughts,' said Conrad briskly. 'Here's something to cheer you. Look what I've brought. Two fine animals. A finer mule you'll never see. And this horse . . . well, this horse, it's a horse, that much I will say!'

The innkeeper cast a glance at the animals. Then he approached, studying them with an expert eye.

'This mule, I would say, you have not had long,' he said after a moment, 'knowing how you use them, Conrad, unless you've changed. Never looked after animals, did you? Always rode them until they dropped.' Farber paused, and glanced at Conrad. '*Have* you changed?'

Conrad shrugged. 'Does anyone change, Farber?'

Farber nodded wearily. He turned back to the animals. 'The horse is yours, though, that much anyone could see. Just look at what you've done to it.'

'Both mine, Farber, let's have no doubt. You can rest easy on that.'

Farber snorted, and began to cough again.

'If he waits much longer he'll be dead before he buys them,' whispered Conrad to Gaspar.

Farber turned suddenly, in time to see Gaspar's grin. 'And these? Who are these?' he demanded, waving a hand at Gaspar and Yoss, as if he had just noticed them.

'These,' said Conrad, walking around them as if they were yet two more animals to be sold, 'are my companions, Gaspar de Balboa and Yoss of the Lake.'

'Which lake?' asked Farber sharply.

'The Grey Lake. Near the mountains. You should see it, Farber. The mountain air would do you good.'

The innkeeper gazed suspiciously at Yoss. 'You should be a fish if you come from a lake,' he muttered.

'Yes, a fish! Very good!' said Conrad. 'Then we could roast him, stuff him and eat him with pickles and mint. Oh, yes, lovely idea!' He approached the innkeeper, and continued in a conspiratorial tone. 'Do you remember Antonio Mercuri, Farber? Do you remember his fingers, how fast they were?'

Farber nodded.

'Never thought you'd see anyone faster, did you? Well, you see Gaspar over there? He'd make Antonio Mercuri look like he was wearing mittens.'

'Really?' said the innkeeper sceptically.

'Gasparto, show us your hands.'

Gaspar held out his hands.

Conrad sighed. 'Move them, lad!'

Gaspar wriggled his fingers. They turned into a blur.

Farber glanced at Conrad. The straw-haired man raised an eyebrow suggestively.

'It's one thing to have fast fingers,' muttered the innkeeper, 'another to know what to do with them.'

'True, but when one is ignorant, another instructs.' Conrad grinned. 'You might have some guests who'd like a card game, Host Farber.'

'Perhaps,' said the innkeeper.

'One or two gentlemen with more money than they know how to take care of?'

'It's possible.'

'The usual arrangement with our host, of course,' whispered Conrad.

Farber glanced at him sharply. 'Of course,' he said. He turned back to the animals. He began to cough again, and his shoulders shook with the effort. Finally he wiped his mouth, and he said: 'I'll give you ten silver pieces for the mule.'

'Ten? He's worth thirty.'

Farber scoffed. 'He's worth thirty to you just to get rid of him, Conrad. You ought to be paying me!'

Conrad sighed. 'And the saddle? Look at the workmanship, the care.'

'I'll keep the saddle,' said Gaspar. 'It'd be wasted on an old—'

'Fifteen with the saddle,' said Farber.

'Done!' said Conrad, ignoring Gaspar's protests.

'Now, this horse . . .' said Farber in a tone that didn't hold out much hope.

'Yes, now, this horse,' said Conrad, 'she may not look like much, and she may not feel like much,' he added hurriedly, as Farber ran his hand over the mare's bony rump, 'but she's as steady as . . . as . . . she's steady, that's one thing, and besides—'

'Wouldn't even pay the cost of killing it,' murmured Farber, stepping back and gazing at the animal.

'*Wouldn't pay the cost of killing it?*' demanded Conrad indignantly. 'Now, this horse, you should know, has carried me from . . . well, far enough, let's leave it at that. And it was once a fine animal, a very fine animal, and there's nothing wrong with it that a few days of plentiful hay and your finest oats won't cure.'

'You've ruined it, Conrad,' said Farber bluntly. 'Don't waste your silver tongue on me.'

'Well, ruined it, maybe. But what's ruined for one man is good for another. If the hen won't lay, we'll eat drumsticks today! Look at that horse, Farber. A gluepot, that's what it is. Nothing less, an entire gluepot all in itself. And the flesh? Put it in your stew, a couple of carrots, a turnip . . .'

Farber scowled.

'Don't tell me you never put horse meat in your stews, Farber. I wasn't born yesterday.'

'A week's lodging,' said Farber suddenly.

'Two weeks.'

'For two of you.'

'Three. The boy needs a place as well.'

Farber examined Yoss, as if measuring him for height and weight.

'Ten days,' he said.

'Twelve.'

'Eleven. And the boy sleeps on the floor.'

'But he gets a blanket.'

'He's got his own blanket. Look.'

Conrad turned to look. 'So he does! You don't mind sleeping on the floor, do you, Yoss? Of course you don't. Boy like you, a mattress would be too soft.'

'Not one of my mattresses,' said Farber, and the flushed skin of his face drew tight over his cheekbones, as his bloodstained lips stretched in a grin.

Conrad nodded, threw back his head, and roared with laughter.

47

6

THEY WERE ON FOOT NOW. Each corner led to another alley, each alley to a corner. Conrad moved quickly, and Yoss and Gaspar hurried to keep up. The houses rose on either side of them, refuse lay thick on the ground and rotted in puddles of putrid waste. Shadows scurried along the walls. The darkness of these streets belonged as much to rats as to humans.

Conrad stopped under an overhanging balcony. He knocked at a door. After a moment, he knocked again.

'He's in there,' he said as they waited. 'Don't worry. He's always in there.'

The door opened a fraction. A hand came out, holding a lantern, and a woman's face appeared behind it. She was pale, with thick eyebrows, and her hair was black, shiny and full. When she saw who was there, her eyes went wide, and her fingers clutched at the neck of her blouse.

'You! I never thought I'd see you again.'

'That's what everybody seems to be saying,' replied Conrad. The woman didn't move.

'Well?' said Conrad. 'You're not making me feel welcome.'

'He won't want to see you.'

'That's what you say, Margret. But he'll want to see *these*.'

Conrad drew one of the merchant's rings out of his pocket.

The woman took the ring and peered at it closely, turning it in the light of the lantern.

'Go on. Take it to him, if you like. I trust you. But tell him I've got more.'

The woman turned to take the ring inside. Conrad put a hand against the door before she could close it.

'You're not going to leave us waiting out here.'

The woman stared at him coldly. She stepped back from the door. When they all were inside, she closed it behind them and hung the lantern on a hook.

They were in a tiny, square anteroom with wood-panelled walls on either side. In front of them hung a heavy curtain.

'Perhaps you'll wait *here*, Conrad,' said the woman, and she disappeared behind the curtain without pausing for an answer.

After a moment Conrad pulled back the curtain and peered around its edge. 'Margret's never liked anyone,' he murmured, as he gazed at whatever was happening behind the curtain. 'Only likes gold, even worse than her father . . .'

Suddenly he let the curtain fall.

The woman reappeared. 'Just you, Conrad,' she said. 'These two stay here.'

'Of course,' said Conrad. 'No peeking,' he warned them, and he wagged a finger at Gaspar and Yoss. The woman watched him with distaste.

Yoss and Gaspar waited. They heard a door close. Then there was silence. Gaspar crept forward and pulled the curtain back a fraction, as Conrad had done. Yoss watched him for a moment, then he crept to the other side of the curtain and pulled it back as well.

Beyond the curtain, there was another room, and on the other side of it was a door. The door was closed but the upper part of the wall beside it was made of glass. Through the glass, Yoss could see Conrad and the woman. The woman had her back turned to him, and Conrad was standing side on. They were both looking down at a third person who must have been seated below the level of the glass. Yoss knew there was a person there, because he could see the top of a round brown cap. Later a hand reached up and took the cap off for a second, and Yoss saw the thin grey hair and shiny scalp of an old man.

Conrad's arm extended. He handed something to the old man. Then he was still for a long time, gazing down. Now he raised his arm, and this time, Yoss could see, he was dangling the merchant's gold chain.

The old man's hand reached up and took it.

'That's it,' whispered Gaspar.

Conrad was watching the old man again. Occasionally his lips moved. Then he turned sharply to the woman, and there was a look of anger on his face. Conrad's eyes bulged, the nostrils of his pug nose flared. It was the first time Yoss had seen him like that. He looked like a wild boar, dangerous, ready to lunge and gore. But then, in an instant, his face changed again, softened, and he turned back to the old man.

Perhaps the old man had said something to calm him. Conrad threw back his head and laughed.

The woman walked past Conrad and left the room through another door. Conrad must have been holding some kind of conversation with the old man. At one point he shrugged, and the old man's hand appeared again, waving dismissively, and Conrad grinned. After a few minutes the woman came back carrying a small casket. She put it down in front of the old man. Now Conrad was gazing attentively again. So was the woman. Finally Conrad put out both hands.

The woman turned towards the door.

Gaspar and Yoss dropped the curtain.

The woman came through, and Conrad followed. She pulled the front door open.

'Let's hope we meet again soon, Margret,' said Conrad.

The woman scoffed, and closed the door behind them.

Conrad grinned. 'Not a word of goodbye! Well, at least the old man knows quality when he sees it. He only gave us half of what they were worth, but she would have given half as little again.'

'Half?' said Gaspar. 'Let me see! Now!'

'Not so impatient, Gaspariño. Not here.'

Gaspar eyed him suspiciously.

'Not here, Gaspar!' Conrad hissed, and he stepped away into the alley.

~

THE ROOM at the inn was small and dark, with a window high in the wall that let in little light. There was one bedstead, which was barely large enough for two, and a narrow strip of floor beside it. A candle burned in a holder nailed to a beam. Conrad was sitting on the bed, and Gaspar was beside him. Gaspar had taken his boots off. There was a bowl of lard on his lap, and he held one of the boots across his thighs, working the lard into it with a rag. The black leather glistened in the candlelight.

Conrad counted out the coins. He was making two piles. The coins were of various sizes. Some were silver, and some were copper, and there were even a number of gold coins. Gaspar frowned as he watched, trying to make sure that Conrad's division was even. His hand went round and round as if by itself, rubbing fat into his boot. The mixture of coins, the various sizes and different metals, was confusing him, and Conrad, if he wanted to cheat him, had surely already done it.

'There,' said Conrad, when he had finished. Gaspar put his

boot down. Conrad pushed a pile towards him. But Gaspar, cunningly, pointed at the other pile.

'I'll have that one,' he said.

'Suit yourself,' said Conrad, and he took back the first pile of coins, and pushed the other towards him.

Gaspar's expression clouded. Conrad waited for him to take the pile he had selected. Gaspar had no choice. He reached out and gathered up the coins.

'What about Yoss?' said Conrad.

The boy was standing in the corner of the room, where he had watched the division of the coins take place.

Gaspar glanced over his shoulder at him. 'What about Yoss?'

'*Everyone* has to take a share.'

Conrad took a copper coin from Gaspar's pile and tossed it towards Yoss. It fell on the floor in front of him.

'Pick it up,' said Conrad.

Yoss looked down at the coin.

'Pick it up, Yoss.' Conrad nodded encouragingly. 'It's yours.'

Yoss bent down and picked up the coin.

'Now put it in your pocket. You can do whatever you like with it.'

'That was mine!' cried Gaspar, and he shot Yoss a venomous glance. 'Why does he get one of mine? Why not one of yours?'

'He has to buy himself a comb,' said Conrad, 'unless, perhaps, you can miraculously find the one he lost.'

~

THAT NIGHT, as Conrad had promised, they gorged themselves at the innkeeper's table. Pike, goose, lamb and duck came out on platters, and soon the oil was oozing off their chins, as Conrad had predicted. There was beer as well, and no one's mug was empty for more than a second before the innkeeper's serving girl refilled it.

'Put some meat over there,' Conrad kept calling out to the girl, when he saw some space on the trencher in front of Yoss or Gaspar, poking a greasy finger in their direction. His own appetite was prodigious. He ate with steady, unsatisfiable determination, reaching out for one joint of meat after another, as if he were capable of chomping and chewing and swallowing and gurgling for the entire night. He belched and farted and sweated with the voluptuousness of his pleasure.

Gaspar, on the other hand, soon satisfied his hunger, and became more interested in the serving girl. He reached out for her each time she came to him, and forced his beer mug to her lips, and eventually he had her on his lap, and she was guzzling and giggling as well. Farber saw it and did nothing to prevent her. Gaspar's hands slipped inside her bodice and began fondling her bosom. The girl squirmed and squealed but didn't try to get away. Yoss stared. The beer that he had drunk made him forget to hide his glances. He couldn't take his eyes off Gaspar and the girl, who were nuzzling and fondling ever closer. Gaspar saw him and grinned, and then he whispered something in the girl's ear, and the girl looked at Yoss and laughed, and shook her bosom at him. Yoss looked away sharply. Gaspar and the girl roared. Conrad hardly noticed, working away at a whole half of a duck. Yoss was beginning to feel ill. The beer made his head swim, and he had eaten too much. Gaspar and the girl were squirming. Conrad was engrossed in his eating. Yoss got up and went to the steep, narrow stairs that led to their room.

He was lying on the narrow strip of floor beside the bed, and was woken by the heavy thud of a body falling on the mattress.

It was Conrad. A smell of vomit came into the room with him. Soon Conrad was snoring. Later the door opened and Gaspar came in and fell on the bed, where he landed on Conrad, and they cursed each other and thrashed about in the darkness. Yoss lay rigid, arms poised, waiting for one of them to roll off and fall on him. But eventually they disentangled themselves and settled. Then Yoss heard the straw mattress rustling, and Gaspar grunting, and a moment later Gaspar's boots flew over the edge of the bed, one after the other, and landed on his legs. Yoss pushed them aside. Conrad was already snoring again. Gaspar soon joined him. Sometimes there was a rustling of straw as one of them moved an arm or a leg.

But now Yoss didn't sleep. The sights, the sounds, and the smells of the town flooded back into his mind. How had it happened? A week ago the village had been his entire world, and he knew everyone in it and everything they did. The biggest question was whether young Peter was going to rebuild his barn, or whether Anna would agree to marry the Speaker's grandson, bald Albisch. And now he was lying on the floor of an inn, with two men who smelled of vomit, and a pair of boots that smelled of pig fat, and he didn't even know where he was or what he was doing here or how he had got here or, to tell the truth, what he had even done on the way. What had happened with the merchant? What had *really* happened out there on the marsh? Was it robbery or was it not? He didn't know, and how it was that you couldn't know the answer to a question like that, when you had been there and even taken part in the event yourself, was a mystery to him. Suddenly he felt like a twig, like a little twig such as you might sometimes see in a stream. The stream takes the twig where it wants, and the twig has no say in the matter. And how this could have happened, that he had turned into such a twig, and how it had happened in the course of only a few days, was something else he couldn't work out.

What was it that the Speaker had said? The town swallows men up. Had the town swallowed him? Maybe that was what was happening.

They ran through his mind, the sights, the sounds, the smells of the town. But that wasn't all. As Yoss lay there, as he breathed the stale air and tossed restlessly seeking relief on the hard planks of the floor, as the hours slowly passed before he fell, at last, into a fitful sleep, another image came back into his mind. It was the merchant, the dishevelled hair, the eyes of grey-blue, cold like the waters of the mountain lake, staring at him as he tore the purse from around his body.

And the voice.

'I'll get you, boy. I'll get you.'

Yoss heard the voice, over and over, as Conrad and Gaspar snored.

7

SO DARK AND DISMAL was the alley in which the inn was situated, and so feeble was the light that found its way through the windows, that the main room required candles even at midday. There was a fireplace in this room, and four or five tables with benches, and a low roof with smoke-blackened beams. The candles that burned night and day left a thick, rancid smell of impure tallow.

For the whole afternoon, once he had emerged from his drunken sleep, Conrad sat like a prince at one of the tables, dining on the food that Farber obligingly kept sending in. Gaspar sat with him impatiently, glancing at others who came in to eat, tapping his feet or his fingers. Each time someone opened the door he looked up sharply, hoping it was the serving girl from the previous night. Sometimes he jumped up and went out in search of her, only to return disappointed and sit down again, tapping and fidgeting and shuffling, until he jumped up and went out once more. Once he pulled out his knife and began carving something in the wood at the edge of the table, perhaps just a series of notches for their own sake, and he stopped only when Farber came in and saw him and cuffed him around the ears, knocking his prize velvet hat off his head. Conrad laughed at that. Gaspar stomped out again. Conrad glanced at Yoss and raised his eyebrows, and eventually the boy returned a smile. But most of the time, Conrad simply ignored Gaspar and hardly bothered with Yoss. The only person who seemed to interest Conrad was Farber. Now and then the gaunt innkeeper would come across to whisper something in his ear. Whenever that happened, Conrad listened attentively, and nodded, or turned to whisper something in reply.

It was hard to tell how much time had passed. The light in the room was always the same dim, smoky yellow, and outside it could have been noon or dusk.

Eventually Conrad spoke to Yoss. Gaspar had gone out again. They were the the only ones in the room, and the straw-haired man was devouring a chicken drumstick. Suddenly he waved it in Yoss' direction.

'Are you sick of sitting here, Yoss?' he said.

Yoss nodded, cupping his chin in his hand. It seemed as if he had been sitting there for hours.

'Sometimes you have to wait,' said Conrad. 'There's much waiting in life. But if you wait, Yoss, it'll be worth it in the end.'

Conrad scrutinized the boy, working at the drumstick. He stripped the flesh expertly off the bone with his front teeth, gnawing and turning it at the same time. Then he dropped it on the floor. For a moment, he took his eyes off Yoss, as he raised his beer mug and took a deep mouthful. Then he wiped his lips with the back of his wrist, and put the mug down again.

'Things will start to get interesting soon,' Conrad said. He grinned. 'You should watch Gaspar tonight. Eh, Yoss? Will you watch him? There'll be a game later. You don't need to do anything. Don't say anything. Just sit and watch our friend Gaspar. But concentrate, do you hear? Don't take your eyes off him.'

'Why?'

'Guess.' Conrad chuckled. 'No? Well, let's see if you can tell me at the end of the game.'

Conrad held out the chicken's other leg. Yoss shook his head.

'Go on, Yoss. Do you remember how hungry you were in the forest? If you have food, Yoss, eat. Always eat. Don't be dainty. Do you know the story about the goat who turned his nose up at nettles? Listen, I'll tell it to you.'

By now it must have been evening, because other people started coming in to sit at the tables in the room, and more food appeared, and beer, and before long the room in the inn was full. And after that, the game started.

~

CONRAD LEFT YOSS on a stool, beside the wall, from which he could watch Gaspar. But the boy's attention, naturally, wasn't directed to Gaspar alone. There was too much happening. Over and over, cards were dealt, discarded and replenished. Coins were thrown onto the table, picked up and pocketed. Men groaned as if they had been stabbed, jumped up, sat down again and shouted in anguish for the cards to be dealt again. Why? Yoss couldn't see what occurred to make some men groan and others shout. Yet the game went on and on, continuously renewing itself. Now Yoss looked at the men who stood around the table. Their eyes were transfixed by the cards and the money on display. Their mouths hung open. Some demanded impatiently to have their turn at the table. Conrad moved amongst them. The innkeeper leaned against a wall, his bright, burning eyes following every movement. Sometimes his body was racked with coughs, and he would wipe his hand across his reddened lips or spit bloodily onto the floor, but even as he doubled up he would twist his head so that nothing escaped his gaze.

All the time the serving girl – the same serving girl from the previous night, who had reappeared – was coming in and out with food and drink. Men grabbed at the food, covering the table with crumbs and grease. Gaspar winked and grinned at her, and she giggled back at him, and finally she came over and stood beside him, rubbing her thigh against his shoulder, while he played his hand. Yoss couldn't help watching her. He could see her back, and the shape of her behind through her skirt as it swayed and rubbed against Gaspar. He wondered what it would be like to have her on his lap, as Gaspar had the previous night.

Suddenly Conrad came around the table and grabbed the girl by the elbow. He jerked her away from Gaspar and leaned down to whisper in her ear, and Yoss caught sight of the look of rage on Conrad's pug-shaped face, the same expression he had glimpsed through the glass at the old man's house. And then he let go of the girl, and she scampered hastily away, throwing a frightened glance over her shoulder, and a moment later Conrad was on the other side of the table. After that the serving girl didn't go near Gaspar. And Yoss, who had forgotten all about watching Gaspar by now, watched Conrad instead, wondering if he would catch another sight of that look.

But the straw-haired man had changed once more. Now he was grinning again. He exchanged a word with a neighbour amongst the spectators, nudged him in the ribs, threw his head back with laughter. He nodded when another neighbour made a remark to him. He was always on the move, shifting around the table, raising his eyebrows, scratching his nose, pinching his lips, throwing in a word here, a joke there, striking up a conversation with a spectator who was in deep concentration on the game, rubbing his forehead, and groaning along with everybody else when one of the players lost all his money on a hand he had expected to win.

A man threw a ring down on the table. He lost that and

threw down his dagger. The spectators were beginning to laugh. When he lost the dagger he jumped up and took his belt off and threw that down. Then he bet his purse, which was quite empty by now. Then he bet his hat. Then he bet his boots. Each time he lost, there was a hush in the room, to see what he would offer next, and a roar of laughter when he produced the article. He bet his shirt. Finally he was sitting there in nothing but his trousers, and he would have bet those, as well, but the innkeeper stepped forward and told him to get out. He gazed around helplessly, and had the expression, Yoss thought, of a sheep when faced with the butcher. Wherever he looked there was jeering laughter. Finally he cursed them all, Gaspar and Farber especially, and vowed to get his revenge. This provoked more laughter than anything else. Farber grinned his ghoulish grin and the man hesitated for a moment, barefoot, bare-chested, unarmed, but he wasn't courageous enough to do anything except curse and when he had gone Farber slammed the door after him. The game had already started again, just as if the man had never been there. And Farber was back at his place, never taking his bright, beady eyes off the game and taking note of every coin and article that was wagered.

That man, Yoss realized, would have played until he had nothing, if he could, until he was stark naked. Even then he wouldn't have stopped. He would have wagered the air from his lungs. Why? Yoss had never seen anything like it. The faces at the table were stoked with greed and passion. The players snatched at the cards, anxiously scanned them, cradled them against their chests like babies, tossed their coins onto the table and gazed longingly at the growing pile in the middle, grimaced with despair when someone else dragged it away. The boy had never seen such lust on human faces, nor could he have imagined that such lust, if it existed, would be directed towards insensible objects, cards and metal coins.

It was late when the game ended. A man who had lost early at the game, and had spent the rest of the night drinking Farber's beer, lay slumped at another table, asleep. Farber woke him up and threw him out. Now only Conrad and Gaspar remained with the innkeeper. There were coins spread over half the table in front of them. The belt, shirt, dagger and other things from the man who had undressed himself were there as well. Conrad was dividing the proceeds. But he was annoyed about something, you could hear it in his voice, and see it in the short, jerky movements with which he divided the coins. And he wasn't trying to hide it.

'That girl!' he was saying. 'Keep your eyes on the game, Gaspar, you fool. Every time she walked in you watched her.'

'Conrad, he's young,' said the innkeeper. 'When he sees a girl like that, such a pretty, plump—'

'None of that, Farber. I know what you're up to.'

Gaspar grinned.

Conrad turned on him. 'I've tried to teach you and teach you! Maybe *this* will help to get it into your head.' He picked up the belt from the table and whipped it at Gaspar in rage. Gaspar shielded himself, then stared at Conrad in astonishment and fear.

'Now, listen to me,' said Conrad, breathing heavily. 'You were playing with idiots tonight. Remember the barber? *Do you?* You were so distracted tonight, even an honest man, with a bit of skill, could have beaten you . . .'

Gaspar sneered. Conrad raised the belt again threateningly.

'Listen to him, Gaspar,' said the innkeeper. 'There'll be

others tomorrow. Word gets around . . .'

'These were little chicks today,' said Conrad contemptuously. 'They were just the bait. Tomorrow the cocks will arrive. And don't think they'll be so easy to pluck. Every cheat and rascal will be here. As quick as you, too, don't think they won't be. You have to be *clever.*'

Conrad jabbed a finger hard into Gaspar's temple. Gaspar jerked his head away, flinching.

'Do what you like with the girl *after* the game,' said Conrad. 'Who cares what you do with her then?'

As if to answer Conrad's question, the door opened and the serving girl came in, carrying a platter of meat and bread. She put it down on the table and glanced slyly at Gaspar, who responded with a sullen shrug.

'Get her out, Farber,' said Conrad. 'And tomorrow, keep her out.'

'Keep her out? Who's going to serve if she can't come in?'

'You, or your mother, I don't care. Keep her out.'

Farber looked at the girl and jerked his head towards the door.

'All right? Are you satisfied, Conrad? Don't blame me if the boy can't keep his hands to himself.'

'Ah, our host isn't happy,' said Conrad to Gaspar confidentially. 'He can't get his mother to serve because he doesn't know who she is!'

Gaspar frowned. Conrad nudged him in the ribs, and Gaspar smiled sourly.

'Let's have the money, Conrad,' said the innkeeper, rubbing his fingers.

Conrad pushed a pile of coins towards him. Farber began to count.

'All copper, Farber. There was no silver or gold tonight.'

Farber shrugged. 'Copper today, gold tomorrow. If he's got such quick fingers, Gaspar de Balboa, he can turn one into the other.'

Conrad glanced at Gaspar. He gazed at his pot-shaped head for a moment. Then he started to laugh.

After a moment he reached out for a joint of meat. He bit into it. 'And you, Yoss,' said Conrad as he chewed, 'what did you see? Can you tell me?'

All three men turned to look at the boy, who was still sitting on his stool beside the wall.

'Did you do as I told you? Did you watch Gaspar? Don't tell me you didn't see anything.'

'I saw Gaspar playing,' replied Yoss

'And?'

They all stared at him expectantly, waiting for his answer.

'And what?' said Yoss.

Conrad laughed again, and took another bite of meat. Gaspar got up angrily and went across to the boy.

'And what? *And what?* I'll show you what!'

Gaspar thrust out his arm. Yoss flinched, thinking Gaspar was going to hit him. But Gaspar merely did something with his hand or his wrist right in front of Yoss' face, something fast and blurry with the edge of his sleeve, and sitting in his palm, from nowhere, was a card.

Gaspar flicked the end of Yoss' nose with the card and walked away.

Conrad nodded, grinning. 'Tomorrow, Yoss, watch his hands. Will you do that? Nothing else. Just watch his hands. If you can see what he's doing, he'll start to teach you. Right, Gaspar?'

Gaspar glanced coldly at Yoss. He held out his hands and twirled his fingers so quickly that they disappeared into a blur.

~

THE NEXT EVENING, Yoss did watch Gaspar's hands. He ignored the food that Host Farber brought in, and Conrad's wanderings around the table, and the cursings and mutterings of the other players. But why? He still didn't know what was meant to be so special about these hands. They did what any hands would do. Sometimes one of them held the cards, sometimes they laid the cards down on the table. Sometimes they were folded together. Sometimes one of them picked Gaspar's nose or dug some wax out his ear. Sometimes one of them wandered into Gaspar's pocket, or tugged his sleeve, or reached down to adjust his boot, or reached back to adjust his belt, or reached up to tilt his hat, or reached around to . . .

Yoss frowned. He had seen something. *Had* he seen something? It was so quick, it was over almost before it began. But it looked as if something had come out of Gaspar's collar. It looked like a card.

Yoss glanced up, still frowning and wondering. Suddenly he noticed that Conrad, amidst the crowd around the table, was watching him. Their eyes met. Conrad raised his eyebrows questioningly, and then he nodded, slightly, as if to say that if Yoss thought he had seen something, then he really *had* seen something, and there would be more to see.

Now Yoss really did watch Gaspar's hands. He leaned forward with his chin on his fists and gazed at every movement of those fingers. So closely did he watch, and so fierce was his concentration, that the other players began to notice, and the innkeeper, on a signal from Conrad, had to step across and interrupt him. Farber pulled on his arm and told the boy to come with him. But by then Yoss had seen enough, and he knew that Gaspar de Balboa was pulling cards out of his sleeve and his boot and his belt and his hat and his collar and probably from other places as well that he hadn't even had a chance to see. Gaspar was cheating. And the next thing Yoss realized, remembering the look that Conrad had thrown him and the nod that had accompanied it, was that it was precisely this, Gaspar's cheating, that the straw-haired man had *wanted* him to see.

The innkeeper took him out of the room. He closed the door behind them. They were in a dark corridor. The only light came from the candle that Farber was holding.

Farber started down the corridor, but after a moment he stopped and turned around. He held the candle out so he could see Yoss properly. He peered at the boy just as he had peered at the animals that Conrad had brought him, as if to study and evaluate him.

'You *didn't* know,' he murmured.

Yoss gazed at him uncertainly.

The innkeeper smiled. His bloodstained lips stretched across his teeth. 'You didn't know, did you, Yoss of the Lake?'

Yoss shook his head.

'Nothing? But you helped them rob the merchant!'

'I didn't – How do you know about that?' Yoss frowned. 'What did you say? We robbed him?'

'What did they tell you, boy?'

'They said it was a debt. Conrad told me the merchant owed him a debt, and he was trying to get away from the town, and that's why he had to stop him.'

'A debt?' Farber began to laugh. 'That Conrad! What a tongue. Always had the gift. Truly, a silver tongue . . .' The innkeeper started to cough. Soon he doubled over with the convulsions, the candle trembling in his fist.

The boy watched him fearfully.

Eventually Farber straightened up. He spat on the floor and wiped his mouth, and he leaned against the wall, catching his breath, gazing at the boy in front of him.

Gradually, the expression in the innkeeper's bright, bead-like eyes, set deep in the sockets of his gaunt and skull-like face, began to soften. Anyone who knew him would not have believed that he was capable of such a gaze. But as he stared at the boy, something was stirring in the innkeeper's soul, some deep, long-buried memory of decency and hope.

Farber was a man who had known and practised every deceit, trickery and fraud of the innkeeper's trade, watering his wines, adulterating his food, shortchanging his customers, prostituting his serving girls, taking stolen goods, even practising outright theft when he could manage it with little risk. The unsuspecting traveller who came to his inn was like a sheep wandering into a wolf's lair, and could count himself lucky to escape with the clothes on his back. Yet the innkeeper was ill, and knew that he would soon die of his illness, despite everything the green doctor said to convince him to keep paying for his cure. He did keep paying, but in his heart he no longer believed the green doctor could save him. Every day he spat more blood, and a man has only so much blood, as everyone knew, and when the last drop of it was spat, he would die. And how many liars and cheats had he seen, thieves, cutthroats, swindlers, how many Conrads and Gaspars, all, one way or another, treading the path to the gallows? And how did it start? With another Conrad or Gaspar leading them on, a silver tongue, sweet lies, false promises, until they had turned into liars and cheats themselves. That was the way, always the same. How many times had Farber seen it? How many times had he himself conspired in it? So when he looked at Yoss that night, coughing and spitting the blood that would soon drain the life out of his bones, something rose up in him, some terrible weariness and revulsion, and just for a moment he wondered if it had to be, always, if there was never any other way, and if it was not too late to stop it, just once, if this boy too must tread the path, as had all the other boys whom he had seen, whom he had helped to lead, in the past.

'Where are you from, Yoss?' whispered the innkeeper.

'A village.'

The innkeeper sighed. He gazed at Yoss for an instant longer. Then he nodded. 'I'll take you to the kitchen. You can have some food.'

Farber led the way along the corridors to the kitchen. A steaming cauldron hung over a fire, and above another fire turned a spit with pieces of meat. Dead chickens hung from hooks, their glazed, lifeless eyes staring blindly. Rabbits dangled beside them. Two haunches of meat, red and bloody, lay across a scarred table. The kitchen was filled by an evil smell, which came from a corner that was piled with refuse, thick with flies. Bones, skin, guts lay strewn on the pile.

Then Yoss saw something else, a huge, brown eye. And when he looked closer he could see what it was, the head of Conrad's horse lying in the rubbish in the corner.

Farber saw where he was looking. He winked and pointed at the stew in the cauldron.

Yoss felt sick. He turned green. The serving girl, who was in the kitchen, began to laugh. There were two other men there, whom Yoss hadn't seen before, and they began to laugh as well.

The innkeeper was laughing, his bloody lips stretched tight.

Yoss' head was spinning. He saw a door. He ran towards it. The stable yard. A gate. He didn't think, didn't look back, didn't heed the shouts behind him. He pushed on the gate and it opened in front of him.

8

YOSS WAS LOST. He had been lost from the moment he ran out of the inn. Into the alleys he had tumbled, and they were dark and twisting. One turned into another, and he followed them blindly, racing, not knowing were he was going, because there was nothing that he was going towards, but only something from which he ran.

His mind teemed with rage. He jabbed at himself again and again with a finger of blame and accusation. How *could* he not have known what Conrad and Gaspar were doing? He must have known. It was a robbery, of course he had known. Who but a thief holds a knife to another man's throat? And if he didn't know, it was only because he had chosen to pretend. He had willingly believed Conrad's lie, and surely that was more contemptible than facing up to the truth. Not only was he a robber, but a coward! Not only a coward, but a fool! How they must have laughed at him, the boy who didn't even know when he had just robbed someone. Calling themselves Cut-Throat and Cut-Purse to amuse themselves at his expense. Every word that he remembered made him cringe. They warned him about bandits – *they* were the greatest bandits on the road!

His heart was pounding. He couldn't get enough breath. He stumbled through the alleys. Stray slivers of light came from chinks in the shutters. No moonlight penetrated past the dark walls of the houses looming up on either side. He splashed through unseen puddles and tried not to imagine what was in them. The head of Conrad's horse. Its huge brown eye stared at him. Flies crawled over its muzzle and into its nostrils. The eye was cloudy, cold, heavy, thick. Yoss felt it growing and heaving in the pit of his stomach, as if he had swallowed it.

He stopped. He reached out to lean against a wall. His stomach heaved. Then it came up, everything that it was in him. It spewed out.

When he was finished, Yoss wiped his mouth. He stood back. The alley, like all the other alleys, stank, and now he had added his own part to the stench. He looked around. Light came out through the cracks in a shutter. There were voices inside the house, but they were indistinct. A shadow flitted along the wall. A rat, perhaps.

The town would swallow men up, the Speaker had said. But the Speaker didn't know what it meant! No, the Speaker had never gone beyond the lake. Yoss couldn't have told how he knew this, but he was certain. The Speaker, like Herman, had turned back.

Yoss looked around again. He could still hear voices from behind the shutter, still muffled. He felt calmer now. Some of the rage and foolishness had gone out of him. He wondered what he should do next. He had no idea. He began to walk again.

How did people live like this? The stench of their alleys, the density of their houses, the noise they made when they were out in the streets during the day! To Yoss, the pure air and the silence of the mountains seemed infinitely far away. He shook his head. What kind of people were they? They all seemed to want what they couldn't have. Take Conrad and Gaspar. They wanted other people's money. Yet others wanted their money. And Farber wanted *everyone's* money. How could any one of them ever feel satisfied or secure? If you wanted what others had, Yoss thought, there was always more that you would be trying to grasp. And if you knew that others wanted the same, how could you ever feel safe in what you had? Give a man a shilling and he'll cut your throat for a pound. It was Conrad who had said that, he remembered. And Conrad would cut your throat quicker than anybody else.

Still, he didn't have a pound, or even a shilling that the others might want. He smiled. That was a good thing! Since they cared only about what they could take, they wouldn't care at all about him, who had nothing that was worth stealing.

But Yoss was new to the town through which he now walked, and of the many lessons that it would teach him, he had learned barely the first. Money isn't the only thing men covet. Just because one has no possessions, it doesn't mean he has nothing that others will want to steal.

~

Yoss found himself at a river. The alley had come to an end, and there was an open strip of ground between the water and the houses, and now the boy stood there, in the darkness, transfixed by what he saw.

In reality, it wasn't an especially wide river, but Yoss knew only the narrow mountain streams of his childhood. The water flowed past him, and glinted magically silver where it eddied and sluiced.

The moon stood in the sky above the opposite bank, throwing its pale light over the scene. There were clouds moving in the air, and they came and went across the face of the moon. The other side of the town was a dark jumble of houses, and above them spires rose like black needles against the sky. Pinpricks of light punctuated the shadows. Upriver was a bridge, and there were houses on this as well, built out over the water. Light came from their shutters and painted the water in ripples of gold.

Yoss sat down. The breeze that came across the river carried the stench of the town, but there was also a smell of rain in it. He gazed at the bridge, with its long, black piles disappearing into the water, and the houses that projected from it.

Suddenly, between two sets of piles, the underside of the bridge lit up, as if a door had opened to a golden cave. As Yoss watched, something appeared between the piles. First came the nose, long and flat, gliding smoothly out of its lair. Then came the body, with a lantern dangling above it. And then the tail, a long pole that trailed into the water. A man, standing upright, held the pole. Yoss saw him draw the pole up, raise it, and plunge it down again. The nose glided forward. In the orange light of the lantern, it looked as if the whole thing were moving in a circle of flame.

If there really were fairies and elves, the boy thought, as little children were told, this is how they would travel, in tiny pods that floated on the water, with orange lights swaying above their heads.

The boatman, who was raising the pole again, stopped and peered at the bank.

'*Hallo!*'

Yoss jumped.

'*Hallo!*' called the boatman again. He began to guide his boat towards the rushes that grew by the water's edge.

'Hallo there! Are you deaf? Where do you want to go?'

The boat nuzzled into the rushes. Its nose cut through them and came right up into the mud.

'Well? I haven't got all night.'

'I'm not going anywhere,' Yoss replied.

'Then you're going to sit there forever, are you?' said the boatman. 'Come on, one last fare before I go home.'

Yoss didn't understand.

'I'll take you,' said the boatman in exasperation, 'wherever you want to go.'

Yoss hesitated. He couldn't help wondering what it would be like to sit in the boat. *That* would be something to tell Herman about!

A moment later he scrambled down the bank.

The boatman laughed. 'In a hurry now, aren't we?' Then he held out his hand. 'All right, show us your money.'

Yoss frowned. 'I don't have any money.'

The boatman threw up his hands. 'And when were you going to tell me, my lord? After I'd broken my back rowing you all the way upriver? You're all the same. Go on, off with you. Who's going to feed *me*, I'd like to know? Who's going to feed my little ones? Oh, yes, you're all quick enough when it comes to getting *into* my boat, but when it comes to taking a coin *out*, then, it seems—'

'Actually, I think I do have some money,' said Yoss.

The boatman's anger turned to friendliness in an instant. 'That's the way, sir. No more beating about the bush, eh? Let's see what you've got.'

Yoss reached into his pocket. The coin that Conrad had given him was still there. He pulled it out.

'In you come, sir. That's the way. Let's have a look at it.'

Yoss stepped hesitantly into the boat. The boatman came towards him, heedless of the boat's rocking. He took the coin and peered at it.

'And where would you like to go with this?' he demanded.

'All the way to the Red Pheasant, I suppose? Well, you've got more chance of flying there on that coin than of *me* taking you.'

'I don't want to go to the Red Pheasant,' said Yoss.

The boatman looked at him. 'Where do you want to go?'

Yoss frowned. 'Well . . . across there,' he said suddenly, pointing at the other bank.

'Boy,' said the boatman, and he held out the coin for Yoss to take back, 'this is all the money you've got, isn't it? Now, do you see that bridge there? Why don't you just walk across it? It'll cost you nothing.'

'Can't you take me?'

'I can take you,' said the boatman.

'Good,' said Yoss.

Still the boatman stared at him, holding out the coin. 'Straight across? That's all? Anyone would think you just wanted to do it for pleasure.'

Yoss didn't reply.

The boatman shrugged. He pocketed the coin. Then he returned to the back of his boat and picked up his pole again.

'Sit down,' he said.

'Here?' said Yoss.

'If you like. Suit yourself.'

Yoss sat down at the front of the boat. The boatman set to work and Yoss found himself swinging out towards the middle of the river. He could feel the current bumping against the prow. He shivered with excitement and trepidation. The prow began to rise and dip as the boatman propelled it. Water splashed in over the boy's knees. He gripped the sides of the boat with both hands. Now the boat was really slicing through the water. Yoss grinned with pleasure. Herman would be *green* with envy when he told him about this.

And then, almost as soon as it had begun, it seemed, it was over. They were in the rushes on the other side. Yoss felt the boat crunch onto the riverbank beneath him.

'Here we are.'

Reluctantly, Yoss stood up. 'Are you here every day?' he said.

'Every day,' said the boatman. 'Who else is going to feed my little ones?'

The boatman waited for Yoss to get out.

'Thank you,' Yoss called after him, when the boatman had pushed away from the bank once more. 'I wish I had more money to give you.'

'So do I,' came the reply. The boatman's voice was already growing fainter. He was moving downstream, and the circle of fire thrown by his lantern was drifting away.

Yoss looked up to see what awaited him. Blank walls and dark shutters. He climbed the bank. Then he turned and looked back across the water. He saw a dark jumble of houses, pinpricks of light, just as he had seen from the other side of the river. There was nothing to show what that shadowy scene concealed, Farber's inn, and the room inside it where Gaspar's cheating, even now, probably continued.

The boat was far downstream. Yoss could just see its light. Finally, it rounded a bend and disappeared from view.

~

THE ALLEYS HERE were dark, narrow and vile, just as on the other side of the river. After a while Yoss came into a wider street. Two men were walking ahead of him, and one was carrying a flaming torch that waved and flickered. They stopped and knocked at the door of a house. Yoss waited beside a wall. After they had gone inside he began to walk again.

There was thunder in the air. The wind was rising. Yoss began to walk faster. Someone came running past him from the opposite direction but didn't stop to look at him. Yoss heard more thunder. He was running now as well, although he didn't have anywhere to go. The first drops of rain began to fall.

The street opened into a square. The rain was getting heavier. Clouds now covered the moon and the night had grown very dark. On the other side of the square was a large building with a roof supported by columns. Yoss ran across the square and didn't stop until he reached it. The shadow here was deep, almost black. Yoss sat down against a column to catch his breath. All around him on the ground were dark shapes that looked like long piles of rags.

Yoss let his head rest against the column and closed his eyes. The rain drummed against the roof of the porch.

'*Move!*' hissed a voice.

Yoss opened his eyes. The nearest pile of rags shifted. In the deep shadow, Yoss could just see the glint of two eyes.

'I'm not in your way,' said Yoss.

'How do you know?'

'Because you're lying there, and I'm sitting here.'

'Quiet!' called another pile of rags.

'I'm not in your way, honestly,' whispered Yoss. 'It's raining.'

'So?'

Suddenly Yoss felt very tired. 'Don't make me go away,' he said. 'Please don't make me go.'

There was silence for a moment. 'All right,' said the voice, 'but don't think that's your place, just because you can stay there tonight. Don't think it's yours.'

'No,' said Yoss. 'I won't.'

The rags shifted again, and the glint of eyes disappeared.

Cautiously, Yoss stretched out, careful not to disturb the man.

The stone of the porch was hard and cold.

After a few minutes, Yoss looked around. The eyes were watching again. A hand stretched towards him, holding a ragged length of blanket.

'Here, you must be cold.'

'Thank you,' said Yoss.

The man grunted.

The blanket was thin, but it gave some warmth. Yoss was tired. Eventually he slept. That night, he dreamt about the village. Herman was working as a carpenter. He had built a wonderful cupboard, and Yoss had to open it, but he couldn't. No matter how hard he pulled, the door remained stuck. Then Herman came over, and with the slightest tug on the handle, the door swung open. Herman disappeared inside, but when Yoss went to follow him, the door had closed once more.

9

IN THE MORNING, the sun rose into a clear sky. The rain had somewhat cleansed the streets and alleys of the town, washing their refuse into the river, and taking much of the stench with it. There was almost a freshness in the air.

As soon as it was light, people began to appear on the square. Its stone paving glistened, still wet from rain. The first cart rumbled across it. There was a fountain in one corner of the square and women came out of the alleys towards it, carrying pots. They talked as they waited their turn to draw water. When they had filled their vessels, they walked away, balancing the pots on their heads and steadying them with a hand.

A little boy ran out from the porch under the columns. No older than three or four years, he was completely naked, and was waving a crust of bread. He raced across the square and darted amongst the women at the fountain. No one moved to stop him. Some of the women laughed. Others shook their heads disapprovingly, and threw glances back at the porch, where the piles of rags that Yoss had noticed during the night were sitting up and transforming themselves into people.

Yoss was still asleep. He lay beside the column where he had slumped, partly covered by the scrap of blanket he had been given. At first he had slept fitfully, disturbed by the cold and hardness of his bed and the chorus of snorings and shufflings that surrounded him. Eventually, through sheer exhaustion, he had fallen into a deep sleep, from which he was not now easily awoken. But around him, people were already squatting or standing, stretching, scratching, tying rags into bundles, chewing on crusts of bread, muttering, clearing their throats and spitting away the first sputum of the day.

At last Yoss awoke. He sat up against the column. Under the porch, people stole curious glances at him. But he gazed out at the square, oblivious to them. The colours, the shapes, were brilliant, bright and crisp. Everything out there was so clear, so fresh, in comparison with the dark memories of the night that came back into his mind.

Two women were walking away from the fountain together. Yoss watched them pass. They were talking, and they paid no attention to the heavy pots on their heads. Suddenly they both started laughing. Yoss couldn't take his eyes off them. There was something wonderful in it, the two women laughing like that, and the sun shining in the sky and the square sparkling with the night's rain. One of the women spoke, and they laughed again. Every morning, Yoss thought, they must meet and walk across the square together.

The thought had a strange effect on him. It filled him with a peculiar sense of longing. Even after the two women had disappeared into an alley, the feeling remained.

A cart clattered into the square. A man followed slowly, bowed under a heavy sack. The naked boy, who had dashed all the way across the square, was running back towards the fountain.

Suddenly Yoss became aware that he was being watched.

It was the man who had spoken to him in the night. He was sitting up, cross-legged, with a rag over his head like a hood. Now Yoss saw the eyes that had glinted in the darkness. They were brown, deep-set in a face that was long and lean. The skin was tanned like leather, and a deep crease was incised in each cheek. The man had a thick moustache, and his jaws were covered with a thick stubble, as if he had not shaven for a week.

Yoss was still warming himself with the ragged blanket the man had given him during the night. Now he took it off and held it out.

'Thank you,' he said, 'it kept me warm.'

The man shrugged. He took the rag and dropped it on the ground beside him. He continued to stare at Yoss.

'What's your caper?' he said eventually.

Yoss didn't understand.

'Your caper?' the man insisted. 'What is it?'

Yoss frowned. 'What's a caper?'

The man shook his head. 'You've got to have a caper. If you don't have a caper, you'll starve. Then *that'll* be your caper. But gentlemen and ladies don't like that particular caper, starving to death, and don't give you much for it. Shall I tell you why? Anyone can do it, and they're all frightened they'll be next!'

'True,' said a voice, and Yoss turned to see that someone else was listening. In fact, a dozen or more of the porch people had drawn close, men and women, to hear what the newcomer had to say for himself.

'What's your name?' said the man.

'Yoss.'

The man shook his head, as if there were something unsatisfactory about Yoss' name. 'Me,' he said, 'they call me Legs.'

'Legs?'

'That's right. Because sometimes I've got two legs, and sometimes I've only got one.'

Yoss glanced at the man with bemusement. He *seemed* to have two legs.

'And him, behind you, that's Eye. And next to him is Eyes.'

Yoss looked around. Two men nodded at him.

'Don't worry, you can't confuse them,' said Legs, 'because one of them's only lost one eye, and the other's blind in both.'

'But—'

'And there's Hump, Cripple, Mad Boy, Seven Fingers, Rose the Duck, and Eyes with Babe. She's blind as well, but has the Babe, of course.'

One of the women smiled at Yoss. She was carrying a thin baby with sparse orange hair. With a flick of her wrist, she brushed away a fly that landed on the baby's head.

'Give us a quack, Rose,' said Legs to another woman.

Rose, a small, grey-haired woman with a stoop to her shoulders, gave a sharp, shrieking quack. Yoss jumped. If it was supposed to be a duck, it sounded as if the duck were about to be slaughtered. The others laughed.

'See, that's her caper,' said Legs. 'We called her Mad Rose before, but when she started the quacking, we called her Rose the Duck. Eh, Rosie?'

Rose quacked again, which everyone thought was a great joke.

'You see, you've got to have a caper,' said Legs, and the others murmured their agreement.

They were all looking at Yoss, waiting for him to say something.

'Well . . . I can do somersaults,' said Yoss eventually. 'Will that do?'

Legs looked doubtful. 'Performers . . .' he muttered disapprovingly. 'All right, then, if you must. Give us a look.'

Yoss stood up, steadied himself, and turned a forward somersault, landing shakily on his feet. Even in the village he wasn't regarded as much of an acrobat. Some of the girls could go from one side of the green to the other turning cartwheels and hand-springs like nymphs of the forest. They laughed whenever Yoss tried one of his shaky tumbles.

The people under the porch weren't impressed either. They shook their heads. Cripple, whose left arm and leg were withered, sprang up and turned a series of three faultless somersaults, landing nimbly on his right foot each time. Yoss watched him open-mouthed.

'He's good,' he murmured.

'I know,' said Legs, 'and somersaults aren't even his caper. His withering is.'

Cripple scoffed and hopped away. The others lost interest and moved off as well. Legs pulled out a crust and started to chew on it. Suddenly Yoss felt hungry. He glanced at Legs out of the corner of his eye. Eventually Legs sighed, and shook his head, and pulled another crust out from somewhere in his rags. He tossed it to the boy.

'People here won't feed you, you know,' he said, 'wouldn't be able to even if they wanted.'

Yoss nodded. It was perfectly clear that these people were the poorest of the poor, and even the crust that Legs had given him was an unexpected gift. It was dry and hard, and there were a few small spots of green which Yoss picked off with his fingernail. He chewed it hungrily. 'Thank you,' he said, between mouthfuls.

Legs chewed thoughtfully. 'I'm sure we could think of a caper for you,' he said after a moment. 'A boy like you, the world's full of possibilities. You're too young to have been hurt in the wars, of course, and too old to be a born idiot. We could make you mad, but there's Mad Boy to consider, and he wouldn't be happy. He might easily slice an ear off your head if . . . well, *that's* an idea, we could just take one of your ears off . . .'

'Or toes,' said Seven Fingers, who had come to join them, bringing his own crust of bread. He sat down beside Legs.

'Tricky,' said Legs.

Fingers nodded. He was a stocky man with unusually low-set ears and a thick tongue, which made his words indistinct. He showed the boy a large, spadelike hand. It had only a thumb and forefinger, and the rest of it was covered in a filthy bandage.

'You see,' said Legs, as Seven Fingers unwrapped the bandage, 'no one really pities you if you've just lost a couple of fingers. It's the *wound* that gets to them.'

The bandage came off to reveal an inflamed, oozing wound where the three fingers had been detached. Concentrating, with his thick tongue caught between his teeth, Fingers squeezed a drop of pus out for Yoss to see.

Yoss grimaced.

'Squeamish, are we?' said Legs. 'That pus is like gold. Remember the Ankle, Fingers? He had a wound that poured a cupful of pus each day. That was pure gold, that wound.'

'Pure gold,' repeated Seven Fingers, smearing the pus carefully across the bandage. Everything he did was slow and methodical.

'Killed him in the end, of course,' said Legs. 'That was a real wound. The Ankle got it in the wars. Used to say the bullet was still in there, but he wouldn't let a surgeon near him. Rather die slowly by himself than quickly under the surgeon's knife, the old Ankle. And who can blame him?'

Fingers nodded. He was wrapping his hand up again. The wound and the bandage were so repulsive that Yoss couldn't take his eyes off them.

'But if the Ankle had a *real* wound . . .' said Yoss. Suddenly he looked up at Legs. 'Don't tell me . . . He didn't cut those fingers off himself, did he?'

'Did you cut them off yourself, Fingers?' cried Legs cheerfully.

Seven Fingers shook his head.

'Of course not,' said Legs. 'Someone did it for him.'

Yoss groaned.

'What's this, Yoss?' Legs turned on him seriously. 'Men must make sacrifices for their professions. The lawyer endures the pleas of his clients. He turns them out of their houses, if necessary, to get his payment. Do you think he enjoys it? The surgeon endures the screams of his patients. He inflicts pain, if necessary, to get his fee.' Legs waved his arm sweepingly around the beggars on the porch. 'Here, we do the same. We make our sacrifices to practise our craft. Tell me something, Yoss. Do you think the world can do without beggars? No. Sooner do without your lawyer and doctor, your bricklayer, wagon-driver, serving boy, merchant, notary . . .'

'And prince!' added Seven Fingers thickly.

'Exactly, Fingers. Yoss, I'll tell you why. What does a beggar do?' Legs smiled, and his tone became soft and insinuating. 'Why, he allows people to give. What does it do, when someone gives? Why, it makes him feel he's better off than someone else. Now I can see you're beginning to understand. Of course, people don't want to give much, do they, Fingers?'

Fingers guffawed.

'Not much, but something. Everyone wants to find someone who's worse off than themselves. Just ask yourself, Yoss, what would happen if they couldn't? Have you thought about it? Of course you haven't. Few people do. Well, let me tell you what would happen. There'd be a revolt. Suddenly people would realize how miserable they really are. Meat once a week, if they're lucky, and a new shirt every two years. They'd look at the lawyer and see him eating sausage for breakfast and a roast for supper. But because there are beggars around, they say to themselves, well, I'm not that badly off, look at so-and-so who sits begging in the market every day. I may have meat once a week, but he's lucky to have meat once a year. You see, that's how it works, Yoss. If it wasn't for us, your lawyer and your doctor, your merchant and your prince, they couldn't sleep safe in their beds.'

Seven Fingers was still fiddling with his bandage, adjusting it, and peering at it, and adjusting it again.

'But why do you need a caper?' said Yoss.

'Because they have to believe you're *badly off*!' Legs replied. He shook his head. 'I thought you were sharper than that, Yoss. It's the whole point. People can't bring themselves to give unless they find someone who can't help himself. At least, someone who they *think* can't help himself. They'll give if they see you crawling in the gutter with one leg missing, but they'll give you nothing if you just walk along and hold out your hand. They won't. They can't. I know it makes no sense, but there it is. That's how people are. It's not our job to change them.'

Legs crossed his arms and gazed intently at Yoss. Yoss thought about what he had said. It all made sense, and yet it all seemed wrong. How could it be right that someone like Seven Fingers had chopped his fingers off so that other people would think he deserved their charity?

'Now, my caper – that's my legs,' said Legs. 'I fought in the war and was wounded in the foot. Had my leg chopped off at the knee. Nip of brandy, bite on a rag and they started with the saw. Horrible thing to go through, Yoss. Hope you never have the misfortune. Painful, terrible. As you can see, saved me from the gangrene, but left me crippled.'

'Which leg?' said Yoss.

'That one,' said Legs, pointing at his right foot. 'Sometimes the other, if I feel like it.'

'I see,' said Yoss. 'Did you fight in the wars?'

'Of course not,' said Legs. 'Why should I go off fighting for someone else? Risk my life for some rich prince? Let him risk his own life!'

Suddenly he jumped up. His legs were thin, spindly and flexible. He folded his right leg at the knee, and pulled it back so far, and so tightly, balancing on his left, that it really looked as if it ended there.

'I know what you're thinking, Yoss. You're thinking I'm a cheat. But am I? Compared with what most men do, this is honest work. Do you think it's easy to sit around with your leg tied up like that? The blood doesn't flow. Your foot goes numb, then the leg. Later on, you can't move it even when you untie it. Stay like that for the whole day and you really will lose it. You don't think I make a sacrifice for my profession? Why, if it wasn't such an important job, I'd become a lawyer tomorrow. You would too, wouldn't you, Fingers?'

Seven Fingers nodded

'You see?' said Legs, and he pulled out a piece of rope to tie his leg back.

~

'WHAT ABOUT AN ARM?' said Yoss, as they walked along the street.

'Arms are difficult,' said Legs. 'You can't really tie them back. They fold the wrong way, you see. No, you'd have to cut it off.

Seven Fingers nodded.

'Or course, you could break one,' said Legs, thinking aloud, 'and set it crooked. Still, it wouldn't be easy. You'd need an expert to make it look really bad. And it'd be expensive. As a rule it's cheaper to cut things off than try to deform them. Most of the time you end up having to cut them off anyway, and you've wasted your money. Besides, you don't have any money, do you?'

Yoss shook his head.

Legs was walking with a crutch. His right leg was tied up fast. But he swung along skilfully, and could easily keep pace with Yoss and Seven Fingers.

'What about a broken spine?' said Yoss suddenly. 'There was a man in my village who broke his spine. He was all twisted up.'

'There's an idea!' said Legs with genuine interest. 'Come on, then, let's see what you can do.'

Yoss arched his back, twisted his neck, and dropped his shoulders, trying to imitate the posture of old Victor, who had spent fifteen years in bed after a tree fell on him and broke his spine. Legs and Seven Fingers stopped to look. A few other people on the street stopped to look as well.

'Not bad,' observed Legs. 'Could you do that for the whole morning?'

'It's already starting to hurt,' said Yoss.

'And people will kick you,' said Legs, 'to see if you're pretending. Do you think you could stay like that when people kick you?'

Yoss straightened up. His back was really hurting. 'I don't think it's a good idea.'

'No, it is,' said Legs, 'you just have to practise.'

They walked on. No one came up with any more ideas. Ahead of them was one of the town gates.

'Well, for today you'll just have to do Deaf 'n' Dumb,' said Legs eventually.

'Oh, no!' exclaimed Seven Fingers.

'What's wrong with deaf and dumb?' asked Yoss anxiously.

'It's not that easy,' said Legs.

'I just sit there, don't I?'

'More or less. But people are always suspicious of a beggar who claims to be deaf and dumb. Ideally, Yoss, your donor likes to see crippling, mutilation or insanity. And even insanity raises suspicions. Deaf 'n' Dumb's the most obvious thing to fake. They'll test you. They'll shout at you. They'll try to surprise you. They'll sneak up from behind and clap in your ears. Whatever happens, you can't show you've heard. Not even a flicker of your eyelashes. If they see you react, they won't give you anything except a cuff over the head. Deaf 'n' Dumb isn't easy, believe me. '

'I can do it,' said Yoss with determination.

Seven Fingers rolled his eyes.

By now they had reached the square in front of the gate. The gates were always popular with beggars, according to Legs, because people arriving at the town often gave something to the first beggar they saw, not realizing how many more they were going to meet inside, and people who were departing, having ignored so many inside, often felt a twinge of guilt at the last one they met.

Seven Fingers nodded earnestly at every word.

Legs shouted a greeting to the soldiers who were stationed at the gate, and one of the sentries raised a hand in reply. The second sentry watched them coldly. Other beggars were already there. Eyes with Babe was wandering back and forth beside the window of a coach, pinching the baby so that it would cry. Cripple lolled against a wall, with his withered arm and leg exposed. From somewhere, Yoss heard a quack.

But Legs didn't immediately take up a position. He turned to Yoss. 'There's one more thing,' he said. 'We beggars have a rule. We never ask where someone comes from. Each of us has his own story, his own mother, his own family, his own home that he has left, for one reason or another. It's not for us to pry.'

Legs paused, and glanced at Seven Fingers. Seven Fingers nodded gravely.

'But there's one thing we do have a right to know. You're with us, and if there's trouble because of you, there'll be trouble for us as well. So this is the thing, Yoss: is anyone looking for you?'

Yoss frowned. Conrad and Gaspar? Were they looking for him? What use was he to them? He didn't have anything they wanted.

'Yoss?'

Even if Conrad were looking for him – which was possible – where would he go if he left the beggars? What would he do?

'No,' murmured Yoss. 'No one's looking for me.'

'Really?' said Legs. 'You don't seem very sure.'

The boy returned Legs' gaze. He shook his head. 'No. No one's looking for me. No one.'

10

———

ALONG BOTH SIDES of Threadneedle Street, the tailors' shops
were lined up like chicken coops at a poultry market. In each
doorway stood a tailor, watching the passers-by and calling
invitingly to those whose clothes suggested that they had
money to buy more. It was a paradox of Threadneedle Street
that those least in need of the street's services were its greatest
customers, while those most in need weren't welcome at all. But
tailors, who live by the vanity of mankind, are amongst the
more philosophical of tradesmen, and the more philosophical of
the tailors, as they stood in their doorways, sometimes thought
about this paradox, and gave hearty thanks for it. Where would
they be without the merchant or lawyer who had five suits, for
example, and suddenly decided that he needed a sixth?

The stream of people along Threadneedle Street never
stopped. The street ran between the Council House square and
the pig market, almost as if it had been placed deliberately to
funnel the entire town, the well-off and the poor, the master
and his servant, between its shops. The tailors had an expert
eye. They perused the pedestrians knowingly. They could sum
a person up – at least, as far as his clothing habits were concerned – at a glance. One might have thought they would tire of
watching the crowds. Yet the more they had seen, the more they
knew that no man can ever claim to have encountered all the
oddities and aberrations in human existence. A town throws up
endless variety, and even a tailor could never tell when something surprising was going to appear around the corner.

And now, one after the other, the tailors in their doorways gazed in puzzlement at the strange pair who were coming towards them along the street. The fat, straw-haired man was dressed no better than a peasant, and would probably wear his shirt until it fell apart on his back. Yet his companion strolled alongside him in an elegant black velvet suit, with a peculiar but well-made hat on his head, and a pair of exquisite leather boots. And what, wondered each of the tailors, was one to make of a pairing like that? The more philosophical, perhaps, might have thought of it as an allegory of tailoring, such as could be seen in a painting in their guild hall. But even if it was an allegory, where had it come from, and, more importantly, at whose shop was it planning to stop?

~

GASPAR WANTED a new suit. One velvet suit, it seemed, was insufficient for the indomitable Gaspar de Balboa. The new one, he had decided, should be red, so as not to be confused with the black suit that he was wearing. What else was he going to do with his share of the money that he was accumulating? Besides, Farber's serving girl had told him he should buy one.

'She told you?' demanded Conrad in disbelief. 'And who is this serving girl to—'

'Alice.'

'Who is this *Alice* to tell you anything? Besides, have you got any money left? How much has she had from you, anyway?'

'She has a sick mother, Conrad. She sends her everything she can spare.'

'Of course she does. She'd be the first serving girl I've ever met who didn't.'

Gaspar didn't respond to that. 'I want a new suit,' he said, 'and I don't think I'll be playing cards again until I've ordered it.'

So Conrad took Gaspar to Threadneedle Street, where he pushed through the crowds with a scowl. Tailors on either side, and each one a greater cheat and crook than the next. Gaspar gazed from side to side with his mouth open. The tailors called to him. He wanted to answer each invitation. Conrad dragged him on. Finally he chose a shop. The tailor followed them in. Two others waited inside. When one of them asked how much he wanted to spend, Gaspar told him exactly how much he had. Conrad shook his head disbelievingly and settled back to watch.

One of the tailors disappeared in the back of the shop. The other two were already circling Gaspar, picking at his suit, sighing with admiration. The first one came back with a length of red velvet. Of course, it was the finest material he had.

'The *finest!*' chorused the others.

Luckily for Gaspar, to make a suit out of it would cost exactly the amount Gaspar had mentioned.

'*Exactly!*' chimed the assistants.

Gaspar beamed. It was his lucky day! The tailors draped the velvet across his chest. Out came the measuring tapes. They hovered around him like flies at a piece of mutton. Conrad stared at the grin on Gaspar's pot-headed face and couldn't bear it any longer.

'Take that rubbish away and treat us seriously,' he growled.

The three tailors looked around.

Conrad walked over, took the red velvet off Gaspar's shoulder and tossed it back at them.

'Treat us seriously,' he muttered.

The tailors exchanged glances

'Well, yes,' stuttered the first tailor, 'now that you mention it, I do have something a *little* bit better.'

'A lot better,' growled Conrad.

'Yes, it is. I've only got a bit, you understand, that's why I didn't bring it out before. But it might be enough for the . . . gentleman.'

The tailor disappeared into the depths of his shop once more. The others glanced anxiously at Conrad, fingering their tapes. The first one came back with a length of red brocade, flecked with gold. He displayed it before Gaspar, smiling nervously at Conrad.

'Yes,' said Gaspar, 'oh, yes.'

'With silk lining,' said Conrad.

'Of course,' said the tailor, wincing, and the others winced with him.

'And a cloak, I think. Would you like a cloak, Gaspar?'

'Oh, yes, I would.'

'A cloak?' said the tailor. 'Well, the price . . .'

'What about the price?'

'Oh, well . . . A short cloak. Yes, quite the fashion now. And it will look just right with your stylish hat, if I may say so.'

'Do you think so?' said Gaspar.

'Oh, yes!' said the tailor.

'It *will*!' cried the others, and all at once they were hovering around Gaspar again, as if to block him from Conrad's view, with their tapes and their pins.

'Come, sir, let's take your measure,' said one.

'What a fine figure you have,' cooed another.

'Up with your fine strong arms, sir, that's the way,' added the third.

Conrad waited as the tailors pranced around Gaspar and took

his measurements, paying him false compliments and promising him the most wondrous suit that man had ever worn. Afterwards, as they pushed their way out of Threadneedle Street, Gaspar looked at Conrad with admiration.

'I didn't know you knew so much about tailoring,' said he.

'I don't,' said Conrad.

'But—'

'Listen, Gaspar,' said Conrad, without slackening his pace, pushing his way towards the pig market. 'If a man tells you he's giving you the best, he's lying. *That's* what I know. Doesn't matter if it's clothes, horses, jewels or a pork pie. He's lying the first time he says it and he's lying the second time and he's probably even lying the third time. When he's gone back for the fourth time, maybe then you can believe him.'

'But you only sent him back once!'

'But you're happy, aren't you? What you're getting is better than he offered, isn't it? And you're getting a cloak as well.'

'I suppose so,' muttered Gaspar.

'Then be satisfied,' concluded Conrad impatiently. He stopped and glanced at Gaspar. It was a mystery to Conrad, why someone like Gaspar was endowed with a set of fingers that could rustle and shake faster and more lightly than leaves in a breeze, while someone like him, with the intelligence to know where to rustle and when to shake them, ended up with a set of pudgy, sausagey fingers that were as stiff as tree trunks by comparison. But no matter how much Conrad tried to explain and to teach him, Gaspar remained as simple and uncomprehending as on the day the straw-haired man had first spotted him flipping cards with the fishermen.

Conrad turned and started walking again. They crossed the pig market amidst the squeals of pigs and the bleating of sheep. Soon they were in the alleys again.

'I know why you're angry,' said Gaspar suddenly.

'Why? Why am I angry?' replied Conrad, and he forced himself to grin, as if nothing were worrying him at all.

'Because of the boy,' said Gaspar.

Conrad snorted. 'The boy? No, wrong again, Gaspartito. The boy will be back. What else will he do? Where can he go? Give him a day or two, let him get hungry enough, and he'll come crawling back.'

'Why don't you go and look for him?' said Gaspar.

'Because that's what *you'd* do.'

'And I'd find him.'

'Yes, you'd find him,' said Conrad. 'And what would happen then? He'd run away again. But if he comes back by *himself*, he'll stay.'

'What if he doesn't come back by himself?'

'*Then* I'll look for him,' muttered Conrad.

They came to a corner and Conrad swung into the alley on their left. Gaspar didn't know his way around the town and followed him blindly.

'Well, I don't understand why you want him to come back, anyway,' Gaspar said as he hurried alongside Conrad.

'That doesn't surprise me,' murmured Conrad.

'I mean, what use is he? If you want my opinion, he's never stolen a thing in his life. And cards? He didn't even know I was cheating. I don't think he even knows what it *means* to cheat. Right from the start, Conrad, I didn't know why you wanted him. Why didn't we kill him that day, by the lake? That's what you were planning to do, wasn't it? Instead, we drag him along with us, feed him, look after him . . .'

'And your point is?'

'I just don't see why you want him back, that's all.'

Conrad sighed. 'You simply don't find a boy like that every day.'

'But why not? What's the use—'

'Because he's innocent!' roared Conrad in exasperation. He stopped and glanced quickly up and down the alley, to see if anyone had heard. An old woman was beating a carpet out of an open window. She stopped and looked down at them.

'He's innocent,' Conrad repeated quietly. 'Do you understand? Who knows where he comes from? Some village.'

Gaspar guffawed. 'Some stupid village in the mountains.'

'Why are you laughing? You fool, Gaspar. You *would* have killed him, wouldn't you? You'd have killed him at the lake, and you'd never have known what you'd thrown away.' Conrad shook his head. 'All you had to do was listen to the things he said. Innocence, Gaspar. Innocence is the rarest thing. Rarer than gold. Gold you can buy, you can steal. Not innocence. The more you use it, the less remains.'

Gaspar stared at Conrad uncomprehendingly.

'The boy knows nothing of the world. He doesn't know what's allowed and what isn't allowed, what's normal and what's forbidden.'

'Why doesn't he know?'

'Because he comes from some *village*!' retorted Conrad, trying to control his exasperation again. 'So he needs to be taught. And the first one to teach him can teach him anything he wants. And that's what he'll believe . . . until the noose teaches him otherwise.'

Gaspar grinned. 'The noose . . .'

'Yes,' said Conrad. Finally, there was something Gaspar understood, the noose. Conrad started walking again. 'A boy like that . . .' he murmured, as much to himself as to Gaspar, 'worth his weight in gold, if you get to him first. But you've got to handle him right. Get him started slowly. Feed him well. Make him feel safe, happy. If he runs away and starves for a night or two, so much the better . . .'

Conrad's voice died away. He was thinking about Farber. *There* was a man who'd understand what he was talking about.

Conrad was silent now. Gaspar walked alongside him, glancing at him from time to time. Conrad, it seemed to him, was always thinking. Gaspar had never met a man who thought as much. It puzzled him. Sometimes it frightened him.

They came back to the inn. At once, Conrad called for Farber.

'What did you say to the boy?' he demanded.

'Say?' said Farber

'What did you say to him?'

'Nothing. I told you everything that happened. He ran out by the gate. That idiot Stefan forgot to lock it. I've told him a hundred times, but he doesn't—'

'Forgot to lock it? Just like that?'

'Conrad. I told you.' The innkeeper threw Gaspar a glance to see if he knew why Conrad was questioning him again.

'All right. So he just ran off,' said Conrad, 'by the open gate. Let's say we believe that. All right. Tell me this, Farber. The boy knows no one in this town. He has no money. Why would he do that?'

'Well, he saw my kitchen,' said Farber. 'He wouldn't be the first to run at the sight.'

Conrad smiled coldly. He didn't take his eyes off the innkeeper.

'He just ran, Conrad. He just ran. Believe me, I don't know why.'

Conrad leaned closer to the innkeeper. 'Listen, Farber, do you think I'm going soft? Do you think, if someone took the boy, I'd just let him go?'

'*Took* the boy? What are you talking about, Conrad?'

'Think about the things I've done, Farber. Take a moment to remember them.'

Farber shook his head. He started to cough. Conrad watched him impassively. The innkeeper leaned forward and his thin frame shook until the coughing had stopped. He turned back and spat against the wall.

'It's funny, isn't it, Gaspar?' observed Conrad. 'No matter how close a man is to death, he still wants as much life as he can get. To take even the last week away from a dying man, is as bad as taking all the years that you or I have left.'

The innkeeper turned his wan face to Conrad. His lips shone in the candlelight.

'Have you got him, Farber?' whispered the straw-haired man. 'Is that what you've done? Have you hidden him away?'

The innkeeper shook his head.

'The boy's mine. I found him. So tell me the truth. Did you get someone to snatch him? Are you hiding him somewhere?'

'Conrad, this is ridiculous. Do you think I'd do something like that to you? The boy ran off. No one's hiding him.'

Conrad gazed at Farber. 'All right. I've asked you. If you do have him, and I find out you've lied to me, I don't need to tell you what I'll do.'

The innkeeper nodded.

'Conrad . . .' said Gaspar.

Conrad ignored him, still gazing at the innkeeper.

'Conrad!' cried Gaspar again, and this time he pulled at Conrad's sleeve.

'What is it?'

'He's here.'

'Who?'

'*Him!*'

Conrad turned. There he was, the boy, standing in the doorway.

But he wasn't alone. Behind him jostled half a dozen soldiers. And pushing past them, pointing his finger at Conrad, was the merchant they had robbed on the marsh.

II

YOSS HAD SAT near the gate for hours, legs in the mud, eyes downturned. Every time a carriage went past, it sprayed him with water and filth. People stopped, peered at him, suddenly shouted or clicked their fingers beside his ear, then slapped his head. Each time he saw a pair of feet halt in front of him, he wondered what was going to happen next. And no matter how rigidly he held himself, how tightly he clenched his muscles, he almost always jumped, or twitched, or reacted in some other way to show that he had heard.

The two beggars beside him received little. Someone dropped a wrinkled apple in the mud. Legs lay with his leg tied back, an expression of pain etched into the deep lines of his face. After a while it was probably real pain, as his leg went numb. Seven Fingers cradled his hand with the wound exposed, rocking back and forth and moaning rhythmically, his thick tongue protruding from his lips, as if the ache were too much to bear. But the Deaf 'n' Dumb beggar with them, so clearly a fraud, stifled compassion. Instead, it seemed to Yoss that he managed to arouse every instinct of suspicion and cruelty. No one could resist trying to catch him out, and most added a slap or a cuff when they succeeded.

Yet the slaps and the cuffs weren't the worst of it. Legs and Seven Fingers were going to go hungry. Yoss stared at his feet, sunken in the mud, and all he could think of was this. Couldn't he do anything properly? Deaf 'n' Dumb! How hard was it just to sit still? He was injuring those who had tried to help him.

Was this why he had left the village, to hurt others, and not just anyone else, but the poorest of the poor? What good was he if . . .

Someone clicked. Yoss jumped. Whack! A slap stung him on the ear.

He shook his head to clear it of the sting. He should leave. He should get up and go. Now, right now. Before he did any more harm. While there was still time for Legs and Fingers to get something for their supper.

Now a voice was shouting at him.

Yoss ignored it, pretended not to hear.

'*Boy! Get up, boy!*'

The voice kept shouting. It was right beside his ear. Now he felt a tugging on his arm. But as if he had truly become Deaf 'n' Dumb, as if he were acting the part for one last moment, acting it as he should have acted it all along, he continued staring obstinately at the ground, impervious to everything.

'*Get up, I said. Get up!*'

The person who was shouting dragged him onto his side. Only now, just as his head hit the stone of the gutter, did Yoss look up.

The eyes. That was what he saw first: the grey-blue eyes that he had been unable to get out of his mind.

The merchant leaned down. He had Yoss tightly by the arm now. He jerked him to his feet. His grip was like a vice.

'I told you I'd come for you, boy,' the merchant was chortling. 'I told him,' he said triumphantly, turning to Legs and aiming a tremendous kick at the beggar's ribs, and as the beggar got up and tried to hop away on his crutch, he aimed another kick at his good leg and brought him crashing to the ground.

~

ON THE BRIDGE, people heard the shouts of the sergeant calling on them to make way. Then they heard the tramp, tramp, tramp of the soldiers' boots. Those who failed to get out of the way were brushed aside. There were six soldiers, and in their midst marched two men. In their wake came two other men, and one of them dragged a dishevelled, dirty boy by the arm. People turned to watch as they passed by. They knew where the soldiers were headed. The jail was on the other side of the river, behind the Council House on the main square.

Gaspar was gazing in numb terror at the blur of faces around him. His hat was balanced high on his head. His cheeks were white, his breathing rapid, his hands tingled with fear. He kept pace, but his legs were moving automatically. Conrad glanced at him and could see the terror taking hold. That worried him more than anything else. A fool is dangerous, but a terrified fool is more dangerous still. Yet no concern showed on Conrad's face. Towards the soldiers he turned a cheerful, confident expression. He even joked with them, as they marched, and he could see that they struggled to suppress their smiles. His mind was alert, alive to every possibility and danger. It wasn't the first time he had been marched off to a magistrate. From this point on, it was a game of wits. This wasn't the end, but the beginning.

He turned to catch a glimpse of the boy over his shoulder.

They came to the square. They went briskly past the fountain and into an alley. They turned into another alley. Then they stopped.

The sergeant rapped at a door. A voice answered. A peephole opened and closed. They waited. Eventually the door swung open. The sergeant went in and the soldiers pushed Conrad and Gaspar inside. The merchant and his servant followed with the boy.

The door closed behind them.

They were in an entrance chamber. The walls were of bare stone, the ceiling low. A spiralling staircase led up from one side of the room, and on the other side a staircase led down. Ahead of them was a large, open doorway. Beyond it was a courtyard with a well, and across the courtyard there was a row of doors, and what was behind those doors was impossible to see, because every one was closed.

'Where's the magistrate?' said the merchant.

'He knows you're here,' said the jailer, who had closed the door behind them. He looked meaningfully at the ceiling.

'Go and get him!'

The jailer shook his head. He put his finger to his lips. Then he folded his arms and leaned against the door. He was sallow, small, and his lower jaw protruded beyond the upper.

The merchant glanced at the sergeant, but the sergeant's gaze was blank.

Conrad shrugged. 'Magistrates . . .' he said, and he sighed dramatically, as if they were *always* a problem.

The merchant angrily ignored him. The minutes passed. The merchant went to the foot of the staircase and looked up, then he paced back again. The jailer watched him with a smirk. Conrad glanced from one to the other. Gaspar was still staring in disbelief. The soldiers stood silently, holding on to their halberds, like beasts that move when they're told to move and rest when they're told to rest.

The merchant kept hold of Yoss, dragging him to and fro in his impatience.

Finally they heard footsteps coming down the stairs. The jailer caught the merchant's eye and grinned.

A man appeared. He stopped on the bottom step. He wore black breeches and a white shirt with cuffs and collar of intricate lace. He was balding, and had a small grey beard, in which a breadcrumb was caught.

The magistrate stayed on the bottom step. He studied the scene for a moment. Suddenly he brushed at the breadcrumb.

'So, these are the two you told me about, Merchant Siebert?' he said.

'They are,' said the merchant.

'You say they stole your purse, a chain, and . . . what was it?'

'Rings.'

'Rings. How many rings?'

'Four. And a mule, and the saddle that was on the mule.'

'Where's Thomas?' said the magistrate to the jailer. He shook his head in dissatisfaction. 'What's wrong with you? This must be written down.'

The jailer shrugged insolently. 'Shall I get him?'

'Not now. Stay. Fetch him later and I'll relate it to him.' The magistrate turned back to the merchant. 'They threatened you, you said.'

'Me and my servant. With knives, and he would have killed us, but I escaped. I knocked the fat one down.'

The magistrate smiled. A couple of the soldiers smiled as well. Conrad grinned, and put his hands on his chest, and threw a questioning glance at the magistrate as if to say: 'Me? Does he mean me?'

'And who swears this?' asked the magistrate.

'I,' said the merchant, 'and him, my servant.'

The magistrate queried the servant, who nodded.

'Well,' said the magistrate. He looked at Conrad. 'What do you say?'

Conrad stepped forward a pace. The soldiers made room for him.

'What can I say, sir?'

'Is there nothing you dispute?' asked the magistrate in surprise.

'How can a man dispute a story of which he knows nothing?' said Conrad. 'How can I say this gentleman lies about me, when I have never seen him before? Perhaps this gentleman *was* robbed, and perhaps his servant was with him. But did I rob him? No, sir.' Conrad paused, and turned to examine the merchant as if looking at him for the first time. 'He does not look like a man who would lie, but looks deceive, and since I have never seen him before, I cannot tell you if his looks are false.'

'Liar!' roared the merchant. 'Never seen me before? Never seen me, you cut-throat thief, you—'

'Sir,' said the magistrate, 'let us listen to this fellow, eh? Let him have his say. And the other one. You. What do you say?'

'M-me?'

'You.'

Gaspar looked at Conrad.

'Well?' demanded the magistrate.

'He's a fool,' said Conrad calmly. 'He hardly knows what he says even when he has something to say. I keep him with me to protect him from evil-doers. Gaspar, they call him. Gaspar the Idiot, on account of his idiocy. Now, when was this theft?'

'When was it, you scoundrel? You cut-throat—'

'Well, when *was* it, sir?' demanded the magistrate.

'Four days ago,' muttered the merchant. 'He knows it as well as I.'

'No, no,' said Conrad amiably, 'Gaspar was with me then. If I didn't do it, he couldn't have done it either. Sir, it seems it's two who say we're guilty, and two who say we aren't. I don't say the gentleman lies. I'm sure he was robbed. But a man who is robbed, I think, is likely to see his robber wherever he looks.'

'In front of me now!'

'Well, if I have his rings, or his sword, or whatever he says it is that I have, then let him find them on me. If not, let me go.'

'It's not two, but three who say he did it,' said the merchant, and he jerked on Yoss' arm.

'Him? He's just a boy,' said Conrad, grinning.

'Old enough to be a thief. Took the chain off my neck. Took the rings off my fingers. Took the purse off my very body.'

'One little boy? All by himself?' said Conrad disbelievingly.

'Well, boy?' said the magistrate from the step.

Everyone looked at Yoss. Even the soldiers turned. Yoss glanced at Conrad. Their eyes met. Slightly, almost imperceptibly, the straw-haired man shook his head.

'I . . .'

'What's that?' said the merchant. 'Louder, we can't hear you.'

The merchant pushed Yoss forward. The soldiers let him through. Now he was face to face with the magistrate.

The magistrate came down from the step.

'Well?'

Behind him, Yoss knew, stood Conrad. In his mind, he saw the look of anger of which Conrad was capable, the bulging eyes, flaring nostrils, like a boar on the charge.

'It's true,' he said suddenly. 'It's true. Only . . . I didn't know they were thieves. I thought it was a debt. That's what *he* said.'

'Who said?'

'Him. Conrad.' Yoss didn't dare to look back. 'He said it was a debt and the gold was theirs.'

Conrad roared with laughter. 'A debt? What? Are we surrounded by idiots? First Gaspar and now this one. A robbery masquerading as a debt? If this boy is such a fool as to believe a story like that, only another fool could believe *him*.'

The magistrate frowned, stroking his beard. 'He doesn't look like an idiot,' he murmured.

'Looks deceive! Looks deceive, sir.'

'Lock them up,' said the magistrate, reaching a decision.

'Sir . . .' said Conrad.

'You! You should talk somewhat less.'

'Yes, sir,' said Conrad, bowing his head hastily.

'If what you say is true,' the magistrate continued in a kinder tone, 'and you're innocent, then I'll discover it and you'll be free. And if this is so, Merchant Siebert will pay the price for making a false accusation, as he knows. This is the law and all men are its subjects.'

Conrad nodded, still bowing his head. A day or two in jail, perhaps, but the merchant would realize he couldn't prove his case, and to avoid punishment he would withdraw the charges. It wouldn't be the first time it had happened. All considered, things were going quite well, Conrad thought.

But he had forgotten about Gaspar.

Gaspar, while all this had been going on, had understood hardly anything. He was scared out of his wits, too scared to listen. He was going to hang! That was all he could think of. The magistrate had just ordered the jailer to lock him up. The soldiers were already taking hold of him. They had hold of Conrad. But the boy? What about the boy? Surely *he* wasn't going to escape!

'What about him?' he cried, pointing at Yoss.

The soldiers hesitated.

'Him!' shouted Gaspar again, pointing at Yoss. 'What about him?'

'What about him?' said the magistrate.

'Don't listen to him, sir!' cried Conrad. 'An idiot. Soft. Can't help it. Dropped as a child. Look at his head.'

'Well, let's just hear what he has to say, this idiot,' murmured the magistrate. He took a step closer to Gaspar. 'What about *him?*'

'Why don't you lock him up?' demanded Gaspar. 'He took the chain. He took the rings. Off his fingers. I saw him. He took *the coin*!'

'The coin?'

'Coin! What coin?' demanded Conrad, and suddenly he lunged at Gaspar, but the soldiers held him. Conrad's breathing was heavy. His eyes glared.

'Take him away,' said the magistrate. 'But leave this one.'

'Away? He's a fool. He doesn't know what he says . . .'

Three soldiers bundled Conrad down the stairs. His shouts grew muffled. At length there was silence.

Gaspar glanced around uncertainly.

'You say he took the coin?' said the magistrate.

Gaspar looked back with a start. 'Yes,' he said with a sneer, as if he were outwitting everybody by revealing it.

'What coin?'

'From the merchant's purse! We gave it to him.'

'So he did help you then? When you robbed the merchant?'

Gaspar nodded. He grinned. 'Conrad told him it was a debt. And he believed it!' Gaspar looked contemptuously at Yoss. 'He's from a village in the mountains. He's more innocent than gold. I would have got rid of him by the lake, but Conrad wanted him.'

The magistrate threw a puzzled glance at the merchant, then turned back to Gaspar.

'But the coin? He took it? One of the coins you stole?'

'*He* stole! He took the purse from under the merchant's shirt. *He* did it. Ask the merchant. Look, he probably still has the coin in his pocket.'

'Boy?' said the magistrate.

Yoss put his hand in his pocket. Then he remembered. 'No, I gave it to a man in a boat. He took me across the river.'

'But you did have it?' said the magistrate.

'Yes,' said Yoss.

'Think carefully, boy, before you answer. The coin came from the merchant's purse?'

Yoss nodded.

'See!' cried Gaspar triumphantly. 'Now lock him up and hang him too.'

The magistrate shook his head in disbelief. Thieves! The fat one had almost convinced him of their innocence, but the second one, simply to make sure the boy would suffer no less than himself, confessed it all.

He waved his hand at Gaspar. 'Lock him up.'

'And him? Lock *him* up!' Gaspar cried, as he was taken down the stairs.

~

THE SERGEANT LOITERED. His soldiers were downstairs, with the jailer, locking the two prisoners away.

The merchant, still holding the boy by the collar, glanced at the sergeant impatiently.

The magistrate sighed. 'The coin makes thief,' he said to the merchant, quoting the old saying. 'I'll have to lock him up.'

'But that's why they gave it to him,' said the merchant, 'to make him as guilty as they were.'

The magistrate shrugged. Yoss stared at him fearfully. He could still remember that coin, the touch of it as he picked it up off the floor.

The merchant approached the magistrate, dragging the boy with him. He whispered something in his ear.

'Why?' said the magistrate.

'Just . . . for a moment,' said the merchant. 'A moment of your time? I'm sure you'll find it's worth your while.'

The magistrate rubbed his chin. He turned to the sergeant. 'Go and see to your men.'

'They'll come back when they're finished, sir.'

'Go and see to them! And don't come back until I call for you.'

The sergeant raised an eyebrow. He went to the stairs and disappeared.

The merchant turned to his servant. 'Take the boy into the courtyard. Look to him there.'

The servant gave Yoss a shove. The gash on his forehead, where he had been wounded by Gaspar on the marsh, was still fresh. He went to the well in the middle of the courtyard and leaned against it. Yoss stood nearby. He watched the two men in the entrance chamber. They were deep in conversation. Now and again they turned, and looked at him, and then conferred some more.

The jailer came back up the stairs. 'Right, I'll have the boy now,' he said.

The magistrate glanced at him over his shoulder. 'I understand the jail's full.'

The jailer frowned. 'Full? No, plenty of room. I'll just shove him in with—'

'It's full. Off you go. Get Thomas so I can give him the deposition. Hurry. And after that you can fetch the wood for my kitchen. The maid's complaining you didn't bring any at all yesterday.'

12

THE MERCHANT'S WIFE was sitting as still as she could. A candle had been placed across the room, on a mantelpiece, and she had been instructed to keep her eyes on it. She was young, with clear skin and a small face. Curls of dark hair poked out from beneath her bonnet, which was a handsome cap of blue silk embroidered with a pattern of orange roses. The strings of the bonnet, untied, trailed across her bosom.

All of the woman's clothes were rich. Her dress was of an orange velvet, and the bodice was trimmed with pearls and gold thread. The sleeves, puffed and billowing, were slashed . with blue silk. She wore yellow slippers embroidered in red with a pattern of roses picked out in pearls.

The chair in which she sat was elaborately carved. Its back, which rose above her bonnet, was decorated with scenes of unicorns nuzzling amongst trees. Her arms lay along the arm-rests so that her hands dropped forwards over their scrolled ends, displaying the rings on her slender fingers. Behind her hung a rich yellow curtain that had been arranged to fall in deep folds. In the future, perhaps, people would dispute its significance. The woman had chosen it because its colour represented charity. Her husband had agreed to it because yellow, to him, represented gold.

The shutters of the room were closed. On either side of the woman's chair stood an enormous candelabrum, throwing a soft, even light over the scene. This was the choice of the painter, Master Hans, who said that no harsher lighting would do justice to the lady's beauty. Candlelight would evince the purity of the lady's skin and give the folds of the fabric behind her great depth and body. Still, the lady found it a dismal way to sit, for hour after hour, in such a dark room, with candles flickering around her.

The painter himself was sitting some way back from the candelabra, at a large canvas. This was not going to be a miserly little sketch, but a fully life-size painting that would hang imposingly in the merchant's great hall. The merchant wanted to preserve the image of his wife's youthful lustre for ever. Now and then the painter poked his head around the edge of the canvas to peer closely at the lady's face, then he would disappear behind it once more.

The woman sighed. Master Hans pretended not to hear. He gripped the palette with a big, paint-stained thumb, and used the brush in his other hand to apply tiny strokes of colour. From the corner of her eye, the woman saw him poke his head out and study her for a moment. That was another irritating thing, the way she could never see him properly, because of the angle at which he had set her head. She fidgeted. She looked down at one of the rings on her hand, and turned it a little, to see the glints of the diamonds flashing and sparkling in the candlelight.

'Eyes on the candle, madam.'

The woman looked back at the candle. Master Hans had a habit of saying this every few minutes or so, even when he hadn't appeared from behind his canvas. At first the woman thought he must have bored a little hole in the canvas so he could see what she was doing. After a while she decided he just did it as a routine, without even looking at her. Yet it never failed to make her jump and resume her pose. It was astonishing how often, when she heard those words, she found that her eyes really had wandered. And once her eyes wandered, of course, her face was likely to turn and her shoulders to drop.

'The eyes are everything,' intoned the painter, still hidden behind his canvas. His voice sounded like the tolling of a bell, deep and rhythmic, as if, like a bell, it were merely repeating a note that it had played many times before. And by now, the woman *had* heard it many times before. 'The eyes are the windows on the soul, madam,' the painter continued sonorously. 'If I am to capture your soul, then I must capture your eyes.'

'Who said I wanted you to capture my soul?' said the woman, still trying to look at the candle.

The painter's head appeared. He gazed at the woman for a moment, tilting his head as he studied her.

'Your husband,' he replied, as he disappeared again.

'Well, if it's my soul, and the eyes are the window to it, I should do with my eyes exactly what I choose. There! What do you say to that?'

The painter said nothing to that. Tiny, fastidious strokes came from the brush he was using, with a faint grating sound.

But the woman wasn't ready to give up all prospect of conversation, even a conversation about windows to the soul, if such things existed. Conversation, she often thought, might have lessened the tedium of the sittings considerably.

She decided to press the point.

'What's the use if you tell me where to look? I should look exactly where I choose, and exactly how I choose to do it.'

Now it was the painter's turn to sigh. The woman tried to suppress a little smile of satisfaction.

'Art is not nature, madam,' intoned the painter eventually from behind the canvas. 'Nature chooses, but art must be directed.'

'Nature chooses, but art must be directed,' repeated the lady under her breath, in as mocking a tone as possible. But that wasn't really very clever, she knew, and she couldn't think of a further riposte. She wished she could. Master Hans was exasperating. Nothing hurried or unbalanced him. The painting, she was sure, would be a wonderful thing when it was finished, and very few women were lucky enough to have an artist as skilful as Master Hans to paint them for posterity, particularly when they were still young and beautiful. But Master Hans seemed to work so slowly that sometimes she wondered whether she would still be young and beautiful when he finished! The sittings dragged on so interminably, stretching for hour after hour in this stuffy, darkened room where the closed shutters and burning candelabra made her think of funeral chambers. And if she was thinking of funeral chambers, her soul would be sad, and if the eyes really were the window to the soul, as Master Hans said, then that was what the painter would capture. She didn't want that. There was sadness within her, she knew. It had accumulated over the few short years of her marriage. But she wanted to hide it. She didn't want that part of her to be the part that eventually stared down from the wall in the great hall, as an eternal reproach to her husband, whom she loved, despite everything.

'Eyes on the candle, madam.'

The woman jumped. She looked guiltily back at the candle. 'Make me cheerful, Master Hans.'

'Yes, madam.'

'Can't you tell me any funny stories that would make me cheerful?'

'No, madam. I'm a painter, not a jester.'

'But you're solemn, Master Hans.'

'Thank you, madam.'

There was silence.

'I'm not sad, you know. Not in myself. It's only this room, and the darkness, and all the candles in here when I know the sun is shining outside, and all we have to do is draw back the curtains to let the light and the warmth in . . .'

The painter poked his head around the canvas again, and for a moment the woman thought he had appeared in order to answer her, but he studied her silently, and withdrew.

'Master Hans?'

'Art must be directed, madam.'

'Will you make me cheerful?'

'I will make you cheerful. Shall I make you chattersome?'

'No, sir! What do you mean?'

The painter chuckled to himself. Then there was silence between them again. The lady could hear the strokes of his brush, like a goosefeather tickling a toe, flick flick flick. Sometimes the sound was as unbearable as if he *were* tickling her toes, and she itched to jump up and run away from it. She tried to put it out of her mind by listening for noises from the street outside. She envied those who were out there, who could have no idea of the torture and tedium she suffered locked up in this darkened room with the painter. She often heard a milkmaid who cried her wares beneath her window. What was it like to be a milkmaid? It must be a wonderful, free way to live, the lady imagined, and the streets were your own. How different was her own life! Every morning her husband went off to the Exchange, where the merchants of the town transacted their dealings, and he was never back before the Exchange closed in the evening. Or he would leave the town altogether and ride off on business, sometimes for days at a time, and she never knew when he would return. Now, for instance, he had been gone for ten days, although he had promised to be back in a week. Yet *she* couldn't set foot out of the house without her maid, and even then she had to be ready with a full account of where she was going and where she had been.

Somewhere in the house, a door slammed. Suddenly the woman was alert. She listened. Another door. Footsteps. Now she heard voices as well!

'Madam, keep your eyes on—'

'No, that's enough for today.'

'But I barely have your—'

The woman jumped up.

'Well, give me a slipper,' muttered the painter grudgingly. 'I'll work on the pattern.'

The lady laughed. She stopped and pulled off her slippers, and tossed them playfully into the painter's lap. Then she ran out of the room.

The merchant was just reaching the top of the stairs. Barely had he opened his mouth to greet her when he noticed that his wife was barefoot. He glanced towards the room, wondering what was going on in there.

The woman, for her part, had thrown out her arms, ready to embrace her husband on his return. But she stopped halfway to the stairs, staring in incomprehension. Standing beside her husband was a strange, filthy, dishevelled boy.

~

'SO HE'S A THIEF, is he?' demanded the merchant's wife, for the tenth time. 'He's a thief, and you just thought you'd bring him here. Why not? Why not? A thief one day, murderer the next.'

The merchant didn't reply. The butler, Josephus, was still in the room. Anything that was said would be repeated to every servant in the household. Josephus was the soul of discretion when he was sober and had the loosest of tongues when he was drunk, and since he got drunk almost every evening, a nightly report was invariably provided to any of the servants who chose to listen.

'Leave us, Josephus,' he said.

'But the wine, master?'

'Give it to me.'

Josephus brought the gold jug and set it down beside the merchant. The woman watched the butler leave impatiently.

'A thief! A thief!' she cried when he had gone.

'Hear me, Eleanor. He is *not* a thief. He's a village boy who fell in with thieves and was deceived.'

'Then he's a stupid boy, which is just as bad.'

'He is *not* a stupid boy. Talk to him and you'll see. He's unfortunate. He's innocent and inexperienced. He came from a village. He didn't know what he was doing.'

'How could he not know what he was doing? Do people steal at knifepoint in villages?' The merchant's wife shook her head disbelievingly. 'Are you telling me that someone – anyone – can hold a knife to a man's throat and not know he's threatening him?'

'He didn't hold a knife. The others did that.'

'Good. He didn't hold a knife. Are you saying you can tear the purse from a man's waist and not know you're taking it? It was *he* who took the purse, you won't deny it. You told me so yourself.'

'He knew he was taking it. He knew I was threatened. But he didn't know it was a theft. Eleanor, consider it. He fell in with clever thieves. They told him they were recovering a debt. It's possible. How could he know they lied? The leader is such a rogue, Eleanor, you should hear him talk. A silver tongue. He almost persuaded the magistrate to let him go. If I were the boy, with so little experience, and this man Conrad said it was a debt, I might have believed him myself!'

The woman folded her arms, still shaking her head.

The merchant shrugged. 'Still, I tell you it is so. He's neither stupid nor dishonest.'

The merchant poked his knife at a piece of smoked fish and put it in his mouth. He tore off some bread and chewed it. A moment later he grinned, and shook his head, still thinking about the boy.

'I tell you, Eleanor, it *is* so.'

The woman didn't reply. The merchant pushed the platter of fish towards her, but she ignored it. He took a mouthful of wine. Then he ate some more. He looked at the bread lying on the table. It was fine white bread, wheaten. For a moment he thought: such fine bread, there are men who have never tasted such bread in all their lives. He thought of the beggars at the town gate. He had never expected to see the boy again, and what should happen but that, returning to the town, the very first person he should spy as he came through the gate, sitting in the gutter with two beggars, was the boy himself? Pretending to be deaf and dumb! It was comical. The two frauds with the boy had soon run off, but not before he and his servant had landed a few good kicks in their arses.

The merchant licked his fingers and took more of the wine. Then he sat back and looked at his wife again.

'The boy told me the story and I believe him.'

'Who would believe a story like that?'

'Exactly. Who would make it up?'

The woman shook her head. She leaned back in her seat, and

gazed at her husband, as if appraising him. 'For a man who is so shrewd in his bargains, Simon, this boy has easily duped you. Are you going soft now? Perhaps you've developed some compassion. You should be careful, it will hurt your business.'

The merchant grinned at the jibe. 'That's where you're wrong, my dear. You think I've been duped? Listen to me, this is the shrewdest bargain of them all. The boy is mine. I own him.'

The woman frowned. 'You own him?'

The merchant raised an eyebrow, smirking at his own cleverness.

'What does that mean? You own him? Who could sell him? Not those beggars . . .'

The merchant shook his head. 'No one could sell him, yet I've bought him,' he said, as if it were a riddle.

'I don't understand.'

The merchant laughed. He jumped up and kissed the woman, and he pulled her up and dragged her around in a jig.

'What?' cried the woman, breathless and laughing as well despite herself. Not for a long time had her husband been in such a buoyant mood with her.

The merchant fell into a chair. 'The boy is a thief, yet he's honest. He's a thief by his actions, but not by his will. He was truly deceived.'

'But he took the coin.'

'He took it, didn't deny it. Any man could have denied it. He didn't even have it with him. Where was the proof? And yet he says the coin came from my purse and that he took it. Now, would any man admit that if he knew what it meant? Ask yourself, Eleanor. Would a thief admit it?'

'No,' murmured the merchant's wife.

'No. And yet he does admit it. Now, he should hang, like the others. But the magistrate, who hears the story, is of the same opinion as me. It's clear. The boy is a thief by action but not by intent. So here, Eleanor, we have a very strange animal: an honest thief!'

'But he must hang.'

'Well, must he?' asked the merchant, warming to the story. 'I have an eye for the bargain, Eleanor, you know I do, no man sharper. The magistrate has an eye for it as well, I hope. So I say to him, let's speak a moment. And then, to broach the question, when we're alone, I say, what is the boy's life worth? I say it simply, and in such a way that the magistrate can choose to understand what I am saying, or not. Well, he understands! But he's a fox. So he says, "Master Siebert, am I God, to put a price on a boy's life?" And what do I say, Eleanor? I say, "You're God in this jail."' The merchant roared with laughter, slapping his thigh at the cleverness and audacity of it. 'You're God in this jail!'

'And?' said the woman.

'Ten pieces of gold. Neither of us knew what the price should be. How could we? He asks twenty. I laugh, of course, and he takes ten. I would have given him twenty. More! The boy's young and strong, honest and impressionable. He knows nothing of the world.' The merchant leaned forward, gazing into his wife's eyes. He took her hands. 'Eleanor, he's like wax,' he said earnestly. 'Whoever holds him can mould him . . . like *this*. . .' He rubbed his wife's hands. Then he let go and sat up again. 'He's mine. If he steps outside this house, he's a thief once more, and liable to be hanged. Out there, he has no life. But in here, he's no thief. He's whatever I choose. This is his world now, and I am his master.'

'Then . . . he's your slave,' murmured the woman.

The merchant sat back. 'Yes,' he said after a moment.

The woman reached for the fish and took a piece. She began to eat it thoughtfully. A fragment slipped out of her mouth, and her pink tongue recovered it deftly from the corner of her lips. The merchant watched her. He was still abuzz with the cleverness of his ploy. Suddenly he felt a great desire for his wife, and wanted to take her to their bed.

'Does he know?' asked the woman suddenly.

'What?' said the merchant, who had been lost in his lustful thoughts.

'Does the boy know you bought him? That he's a slave?'

'I told him he's going to work for me.'

'So he doesn't know?'

The merchant thought about it. 'I suppose not,' he said. 'He'll learn.'

13

THE MERCHANT HAD LEFT YOSS with his foreman. After the moment of surprise at the top of the stairs, finding his wife speechless and staring, he had dragged the boy straight back down again, cursing himself for his clumsiness, and handed him over to the foreman before returning to explain.

The foreman, Garner Zeb, was a tall man with a strong, protruding brow. He looked down at Yoss and scrutinized him coldly.

'Come with me,' he said at last.

Yoss followed him towards the stable. After a moment, he heard footsteps, and when he glanced back he saw that three other men had appeared behind him. They came into the stable as well.

The foreman kicked away an old bridle that was lying in the straw. 'Sit here,' he said.

Yoss sat. He looked up at the foreman, who had folded his arms across his chest. The other three folded their arms as well. One of them was small and wiry. He had inquiring, intelligent eyes. The second, tall, dark and stooped, was frowning. And the last, who was the oldest of the three, had hardly any teeth, and a puckered, squashed face, as if it had been compressed from top to bottom. He wrinkled his nose as he gazed at Yoss.

They had already heard about him. The merchant's servant had told them.

While the master had taken the boy upstairs, the servant hadn't been idle. This was the same servant who had been with the merchant when they were robbed on the marsh, and he had the gash on his forehead to prove it. He had been with him when the merchant found the boy with the beggars, when he had gone to capture Conrad and Gaspar, and when he had marched them to the jail. He had managed to give the beggars at the town gate a few kicks that were just as powerful as those of his master.

Of course, he didn't know the whole story. The merchant had questioned the boy in an inn after seizing him from the beggars, and had made the servant wait outside. And he hadn't heard the details of the bargain his master made with the magistrate after the two other thieves had been led to their cell. But he knew enough, at least in his own estimation, and he was quite capable of filling in the details that were missing. And since there are few things more enjoyable than being the one to bring news of a sensation, and since the servant, whose name was Gregor, rarely had the opportunity to play this part, it was hardly likely that he was going to miss the chance. His master was gone with the boy for only a few moments, but that was time enough for Gregor.

The boy was a thief, a cut-throat and a fraud. That was the gist of what Gregor had to say. He had robbed them on the open highway, he and two friends – a number of colourful details developed in the description which Yoss, for one, might not have remembered as actually having taken place – and to hide the wealth that he had stolen, the boy was dressed as a beggar when they had found him. This was a very common trick of young thieves to avoid detection, Gregor added knowingly. Despite his youth, the boy was clearly an experienced scoundrel who would stop at nothing to get his way.

By this time, not only was Garner Zeb listening, but the

other three workmen had left what they were doing and come over to listen as well.

'What's he bringing him here for?' demanded Garner Zeb.

Gregor raised his eyebrows and gazed at the four men with an air of mystery. Then he ran off into the house as he heard the merchant dragging the boy back down the stairs.

So now, when Yoss sat against the wall in the stable, he did so in the guise of a seasoned criminal. All four of the men in front of him were solid, long-serving employees of the merchant. Garner Zeb had known dishonest workers in the past, and always hounded them out when he discovered them, never without a few choice blows to send them on their way. But they didn't compare with a person who would draw a knife, twirl it in the master's face and punch him gratuitously in the belly while searching for his purse – these were merely some of the small embellishments that Gregor had added to the story – even if this terrible scoundrel and cut-throat actually turned out to be a slim, wide-eyed boy who looked hungry, dirty, and tired.

Still, if even half of what Gregor had said were true, thought Garner Zeb, the first thing the boy needed was a thorough thrashing.

'What's your name?' he said as he looked down at him.

'Yoss.'

The foreman grunted. 'Well, *Yoss,* I've got work to do, so that's where you'll sit, and you won't get up unless I tell you.'

Yoss nodded.

The foreman gazed at him for a moment longer, as if he didn't believe him. Then he turned to the others. 'What are you doing here? Go on. Back to work. Do you think the master pays you to stand around and have conversations all day?'

'You were the one having the conversation,' murmured the small, intelligent one, and he winked at his companions.

Garner Zeb scowled. He threw a disapproving glance at Yoss. 'Beetle,' he muttered to one of the workmen, 'bring a pail of water. Let him get the filth off his face.'

~

LATER the merchant came down again and called the foreman into his counting room.

The foreman was the merchant's longest-serving employee. He had been with him from the start, more than fifteen years, from the very first journey the merchant had made to purchase his first consignment of silk with money borrowed from his father-in-law. In those days, when the merchant's first wife was alive, they lived in a small house with only two storerooms and a tiny stable, and they had used any available space – stable, hall, closets, kitchen, bedroom – to store goods as the merchant's business expanded. Each journey was an adventure, and there was no way of telling what bargains they would strike and what profits they would make before they came back again. That was how Garner Zeb, or plain Zeb as he was called then, came to appreciate the merchant's judgement and extraordinary wiles. What Zeb would have bought for three pieces of silver, the merchant, through patience and shrewd negotiation, got for two, and what Zeb would have sold for two the merchant sold for three. He had known the master, at a fair, buy goods from one merchant and pass it on to another on the very same day, and take the profit without ever having seen or touched the consignment. There was no one shrewder than he at gathering information and deploying it well.

But it was now a long time since Zeb had been on a journey

with the merchant. He was needed to supervise his master's many storerooms and the deliveries that arrived and left them. And it had never occurred to Zeb that his master felt just as nostalgically as he about those early, difficult years, despite all the wealth that the merchant had accumulated.

Yet if the truth were known, the foreman was the merchant's closest friend. Each morning, when the merchant came down from the upper storey of his house, the first thing he did was to disappear with Zeb into the counting room. There they talked about the business of the day, and Zeb, who could neither read nor write, would make notches in a stick with his knife, to remind himself of all the things that needed to be done. But after that the merchant would linger, and tell Zeb about the affairs he hoped to execute, and when he came back from the Exchange in the evening, he would disappear with his foreman into the counting room once more, and there, with a tankard of beer for each of them, he would talk about the pieces of business that had been carried out in the town that day, those that harmed him, those that helped him, those that were rumoured, those that were certain, those that he himself had consummated with cleverness or with the aid of simple luck. In whom else could he confide? When he told his wife about his plans, she tried to show interest, but she had little understanding of the subtle, complicated details that could turn an ordinary piece of business into a triumph, and showed little inclination to learn. Other merchants, of course, would savour such things, but to confide in them was out of the question. Only Zeb understood, listening appreciatively to the merchant's stories, nodding his big, brow-heavy head at his master's cunning, grinning as the merchant chuckled with pleasure. And Zeb, of course, could be trusted to keep secret anything the merchant told him. He was as solid as the the bricks of the merchant's storerooms, as unchangeable as the gold in his safe.

The hours that the merchant spent lounging in the counting room with his foreman were the most pleasant in the day. Sometimes he was almost loath to climb the stairs back to his wife. And so, that evening, over two tankards of beer in the counting room, the story of the merchant's purchase of Yoss, like that of any other of his bargains, slipped out.

By the time the merchant had finished telling the tale, Zeb knew how much of Gregor's version was true, how much of it was exaggeration, and how much the servant had simply invented.

Or course, the merchant didn't disclose every detail. There were some facts he kept back. Having more information than others is always an advantage, the merchant knew, not only in business, but in life, not only against one's competitors, but against one's companions, and even against one's most trusted employee. Yet he told him enough. Soon Zeb knew that the boy had come from a village, was inveigled into crime by two ruffians, but at heart was the most honest child that one could ever meet. He knew how the merchant had saved him from the magistrate and the noose. And he knew – perhaps the merchant told him, but even if he didn't, Zeb would quickly have seen it for himself – that the boy had thus become the merchant's slave.

'There's a bargain. Eh, Zeb?' The merchant raised his tankard and drank deeply. He put it down on the table and grinned. 'Sometimes I even wonder at myself!'

The foreman gazed at him.

'Well, Zeb? What's wrong with you? Nothing to say?'

Zeb frowned. 'That magistrate . . .' he mumbled, searching for a response, 'he was a devil, wasn't he?'

'He was! A devil! Greedy swine. I got him down to ten, though. Would have given him his twenty, but he never knew! Oh, Zeb, you should have seen his eyes when I put the question to him. When I saw his eyes, I knew I'd get the boy. I always know, Zeb. I've told you before. I can always tell.'

Zeb nodded quickly. It was true, the merchant could always foretell a man's answer from the look in his eyes, he had often said it. Zeb looked down into his tankard. At the bottom, reflected in the beer, his own eyes gazed back.

14

THAT NIGHT, Conrad came close to murdering Gaspar. As soon as the cell door slammed behind him, Gaspar told Conrad what he had said, relating it almost proudly. It was as much as Conrad could do to keep from punching the teeth out of his jaw even as he spoke. Later, Conrad lay awake on his straw mattress, tormented by Gaspar's stupidity. He was taking them to the noose, he had put it around their necks, as surely as if he had knotted the rope himself. Conrad's blood boiled. He cursed the day he had met Gaspar and been amazed by the speed of his fingers. Fools always hurt you in the end. Fools always do something you can't predict or control.

'Fool,' he said to himself, for not doing something about it before it was too late.

He couldn't sleep. He got up and kneeled over Gaspar. Moonlight came through the barred window high in the wall, showing Gaspar snoring peacefully, as if, now that he had condemned both of them to death, he could sleep at ease. Conrad gazed at Gaspar's ridiculous head, with its tall, tapering forehead. 'Fool!' he said to himself again. 'Fool!' he hissed, and suddenly his hands, trembling in rage, rose and hovered over Gaspar's throat, and he could almost feel the flesh under his fingers, the woody windpipe cracking under his thumbs.

But he restrained himself. He forced himself to go back to his own mattress. He sat with his back against the damp wall, contemplating Gaspar's sleeping form. The game wasn't finished until the noose tightened, he said to himself, and he kept saying it, over and over, over and over, to keep his hands from creeping back to Gaspar's throat. Before the noose tightened, anything could happen. It was too early to tell what benefit he might extract from Gaspar, far too early to decide whether it was wise to get rid of him. Gaspar had already done the damage, but he still might be of some use.

When Gaspar awoke the next morning, he found Conrad sitting up against the wall, watching him benignly.

'Sleep well?' said Conrad.

Gaspar nodded. He looked around the cell, and frowned, remembering where he was, and then he turned to Conrad with a fearful look, recalling how it was they had come to be there.

Perhaps he also began to have second thoughts about what he had done. 'Conrad,' he said, 'you're not angry, are you? You don't care that I said the boy took the coin?'

Conrad shook his head. 'Of course not.'

'They would have found out, wouldn't they? I mean, it didn't really matter that I told them, because they would have found out for themselves.'

Conrad smiled. 'Of course they would, Gaspariño. It was just a matter of time.'

~

THE CELL they occupied was small, damp and cold. There were two straw mattresses on the floor and a slop bucket in the corner. The cell was underground, and the tiny barred window high up on the wall, just below the ceiling, was actually at the level of the gutter. Outside, in an alley, this window was one of a row of openings at the very bottom of the jail wall, just above the cobblestones. It was one of the tricks of the small boys of the town to come and pee into the windows, in order to punish

the evildoers inside. No one stopped them. On their second day
in the cell Gaspar was sitting on his mattress beneath the
window when the contents of a child's bladder streamed
through the bars and hit him on the head. He was wearing his
hat at the time, and after that the stain of the child's urine in the
velvet upset him whenever he looked at it. His hat also made
him think of the wonderful new red suit he had ordered, with
the short cloak that would have gone so well with it, and that
upset him even more. He'd never have the chance to wear it.
There didn't seem to be any words to express how unfair it was,
although Gaspar often tried to find them. There were other
things, thought Conrad, as he sat listening to Gaspar, that were
more unfair than that.

Gaspar babbled endlessly, sometimes in terror at the prospect
of death, sometimes in despair about his red suit, sometimes
with exuberant, irrational hope at the idea that they might be
released and he would still have the opportunity to possess it.
Conrad no longer bothered to respond to him. There was no
reason for them to be released. If the judges got their hands on
them, he knew, they'd be despatched without a moment's hesitation or a single qualm of conscience, and half the town would
turn out to cheer at the scaffold. People enjoyed an execution. It
was free entertainment and involved suffering for someone else,
an irresistible combination. There were moments when Conrad
was tempted to remind Gaspar of this, as the sight and sound
of him grew more and more irritating. Sometimes, as Conrad
watched Gaspar babble, he thought that it might be better, after
all, to strangle him in the night and silence him once and for all.
Who could tell what other things he would reveal, which of
their other crimes he would mention? But no matter how many
times Conrad stared at Gaspar's sleeping face in the moonlight,

he always managed to restrain himself. He always found a way for calm, cold calculation to quell the rage boiling in his blood. He reminded himself of what he had decided on their first night in the cell. It didn't matter what else Gaspar might reveal because the robbery of the merchant, at knifepoint, was sufficient to send them to the scaffold. And a judge can kill a man only once. So Gaspar had already done his worst. How he could be useful, Conrad still didn't know.

The straw-haired man needed information. He needed facts. In order to exploit the opportunities in any situation, it is necessary to know, at the very least, what that situation is. And like any experienced fraudster, Conrad knew that the more information one has, the higher one's chances of success. Yet there was hardly any information at his disposal. He didn't even know when they were going to be tried.

So while Gaspar babbled, fretted and whined, Conrad waited, watched and listened, gathering whatever scraps of knowledge he could. Alert to every sound that penetrated from outside the cell, he pieced together in his mind a picture of the the routine of the jail that proceeded around them. The jailer came to them twice a day. He came down the row of cells from what Conrad calculated to be the north side of the jail. He was always accompanied by two guards, who waited outside the cell, a kitchen servant who brought food, and a slops servant who emptied the buckets. These were facts. For the moment, they were all that Conrad knew. How they might help him, he had no idea, yet he stored them away, and sifted sounds and sights for others. A fact, no matter how trivial or irrelevant it appears at one moment, has the potential to be important at another.

The jailer, Conrad knew, was their only channel to the outside world. If he were to learn more it must come from this source. Yet the jailer was silent and taciturn, watching over his servants and giving them a helping kick in the arse with barely a word. The fact that Gaspar always babbled hysterically whenever he appeared, as if he were hoping that the jailer were coming to free them, didn't help to stimulate conversation.

It was Conrad's stroke of brilliance – or luck – to put an end to Gaspar's outbursts. Whether he did it because he knew it would provoke some response, or out of a final, overwhelming exasperation with Gaspar, he himself couldn't have said. But one night, as he lay awake again, listening to Gaspar moaning in his sleep, he suddenly jumped up and woke Gaspar from his dreams. He leaned over him, ghostly in the moonlight.

'*From now on, if you say one word when the jailer comes in, I'll kill you.*'

Conrad clenched his hands together in front of Gaspar's startled eyes. Then he turned them apart abruptly, as if snapping a branch.

'*Now go back to sleep.*'

The next morning Gaspar was subdued, glancing at Conrad doubtfully, unsure if he had dreamt the previous night's episode. But when the jailer swung back the door, Conrad had only to put his two clenched hands together – not even to snap the imaginary branch – for Gaspar's face to go pale. And for the first time since the day they arrived, when the jailer came in, Gaspar didn't utter a sound.

The kitchen servant threw them their bread. The jailer glanced at Gaspar.

'You're quiet today,' he said. 'Sick, are you?'

Gaspar shook his head. He didn't dare to speak under Conrad's gaze.

'He thinks the trial's tomorrow and the execution's the day after,' said Conrad.

The jailer snorted. 'Not for another month. They've got you down for the session after Kelmuss Week. Now eat up, boys, we don't want you to waste away. Your necks'll be too thin for the noose!'

The jailer kicked his servants out and slammed the door. Conrad leaned back on his mattress and ignored Gaspar, who was staring at him with renewed fear. Another fact: the trial was a month away. But this was far from the most useful thing that Conrad had learned in his short conversation with the jailer. More important was the discovery that the jailer would actually speak, and perhaps even reveal things he ought not to have revealed, if you caught him off his guard. And the crack about the thin necks . . . now, *that* was interesting. Nasty, violent, cruel. No sympathy or compassion in it. Conrad considered it at length, turning the remark around and around in his thoughts, as if it were a fragment of a map that showed the way into the jailer's mind.

The jailer, Conrad guessed, had a taste for harsh, brutal humour. With a man like that, there was no use making complaints or asking for favours. He'd only take pleasure from your suffering. No, if a man has a taste for something, then to cultivate him, you must feed it.

A couple of nights later there was a commotion in a nearby cell, and there were footsteps and shouts for almost an hour. The whole jail must have heard it. Then there was a series of thuds, and finally silence, and a little later the sound of something being dragged over the stones of the corridor.

'Noisy night,' said Conrad with a grin, when the jailer appeared the next morning.

The jailer grunted.

'Prisoner went mad, I suppose. And then he bashed his brains out on the wall all by himself.'

'That's right, my boy, bashed his brains out all by himself,' said the jailer gruffly. But he winked at Conrad as he closed the door. 'Did you hear that, lads?' Conrad heard him saying to the guards as they went to the next cell. 'Bashed his brains out all by himself. That's exactly what he did, isn't it? We had nothing to do with it.'

After that, Conrad never failed to address a sentence or two to the jailer, never complaining, never inquiring, just a quip, the crueller the better, even if it was at his own expense. He didn't talk to him as a prisoner, fearful of his fate, but as a man who had often been a tormentor, harsh and cruel, who sought no sympathy and gave none to others. The jailer began to respond, exchanging at first a word, a warning, or a threatening joke. They shared brief and brutal conversations, outdoing each other for harshness. Gaspar sat silently, pale-faced and pop-eyed, not daring to open his mouth. Soon the jailer began to spend a few extra minutes in the cell. He began to send his servants out and linger by himself. He began to complain. He complained about his pay, his quarters, the magistrate and the extra jobs he had to do in the magistrate's household.

Conrad remembered the glances he had seen the jailer throw at the magistrate on the day they arrived. Insolent, resentful, self-pitying. How many times had he seen those kinds of looks before? Always meant the same thing.

'Treats you like a serving boy, doesn't he?'

The jailer nodded sulkily.

'Always the same, isn't it? 'Lock 'em up! Bring 'em here!'

Easy to give orders. It's them that carry 'em out that should be rewarded.'

'Rewarded!' said the jailer sarcastically.

'Every man has the right to a bit . . .' Conrad paused, raising his eyebrows suggestively '. . . extra.'

'The magistrate thinks he does. Look what he did with the boy!'

'What?' said Conrad impulsively. 'What did he do with the boy?'

The jailer grinned slyly. He looked over his shoulder at the guards lounging outside in the corridor. 'Now, I couldn't tell you that, Conrad. Could I?'

'No,' said Conrad. He laughed as if he didn't care. It was a mistake, showing his eagerness to know the boy's fate, but he quickly put it behind him. 'You listen, Carl. There's other rewards you could have.'

'Like yours? The scaffold!'

Conrad forced himself to grin again. But he gave the jailer a searching glance, and he could see, in the jailer's eyes, that the other man had taken note.

And that was enough to begin with. That was how Conrad planted the seed.

15

IN THE FIRST DAYS that Yoss lived at the merchant's house, the workmen barely spoke to him. He worked alongside them, under the instructions of the big man with the bulging brow, but the foreman spoke to Yoss only to tell him what to do, and the others passed him silently, sending suspicious glances in his direction. At night, he slept in a room beside the stable, where two of the workmen slept as well, the old man, whose name was Paulus, and the tall, stooping fellow called Beetle, who had a way of scuttling on his long, bowed legs. Paulus and the Beetle made him put his mattress as far away from them as possible. The boy often looked up to find Beetle watching him attentively. When Yoss asked him what he was doing, the Beetle would merely shrug and settle down under his blanket, pretending to ignore him.

But the boy didn't despair. He told himself that he still knew very little about the way people lived in the town. He had seen gamblers and cheats in Farber's inn. He had spent one night with beggars. Perhaps this was the way, he thought, that workmen behaved. Besides, the merchant's workmen really were an odd bunch, and even if Gregor hadn't prepared the way with his tale of murder and mayhem on the highway, the boy still might not have known what to make of them. Beetle was taciturn and morose, an uncomplaining, quiet worker who sighed but never quibbled, no matter how heavy the sacks that Garner Zeb told him to unload. Paulus, who shoed horses and repaired barrels, spent the whole day talking to himself in a high singsong voice. The only way anyone could ever tell he was talking to them was when he stopped and waited for an answer. When he was puzzled he stared, and wrinkled his nose, and then shook his head and started singsonging again. And the third workman, Tomas, was sharp, witty and mischievous. When he spoke, it was usually to mutter some biting remark that drew Garner Zeb's disapproving glance.

Tomas and Zeb had families and lived in the town. They arrived each morning, and there was an hour's work before breakfast. The boy soon came to look forward to this meal as the best in the day. There was a feeling of newness and anticipation about the morning, no one was tired yet from the work, and even though the workers ignored him, there was still an atmosphere of comradeship at the table. There was good solid bread made of rye, which was never more than a day old, and cheese with it, and sometimes cold meat or chicken that had been cooked the day before. They each had a pint of beer, too, which gave them strength. The merchant was the best master a man could have, Garner Zeb would often remind them, and he didn't mind if Yoss heard it. No one cared more about their workers. No one gave them better food. To which Tomas would often mutter that every farmer who wants to get the most work out of his ox knows that he has to feed him. And to which Paulus would usually singsong 'Best food, best food for us', while he sucked on a crust of bread with his toothless gums.

After breakfast the real work began. And far more than anything else, this was the main reason that Yoss wasn't discouraged by the coldness of the workmen towards him, or hardly even noticed it. The bell would jingle, and Garner Zeb would unlock the gate and throw it back, and in would come a wagon loaded with sacks of grain, or barrels of wine, or bolts of cloth.

Or it might be casks of resin or chests of tea. Or sacks of barley or bales of fur. You never knew what was going to turn up next. It might be rice, nuts or honey. Or it might be spices from islands far away, rich, pungent, vivid – pepper, nutmeg, cinnamon, saffron and cloves – all to be stored in the spice room to which Garner Zeb had a separate key and which were so valuable – for a worker, even a small sack of nutmegs was a fortune – that no one else was allowed to enter, even to bring out a sack, except when he accompanied them.

In short, to work in the merchant's courtyard was to feel yourself connected with the whole world. For Yoss, there was a sense of wonder in it. Others might have noticed only the hard work, the weight of the sacks and the effort required to roll a barrel. But Yoss had left the village to discover the world, and here, in a way, the world displayed itself before him.

Day after day, the wagons rolled through the merchant's gate. Everything had to be unloaded and stored in its place. Other wagons had to be stacked with sacks and barrels from the storerooms. Beetle and Tomas scurried and heaved. Paulus sang and hammered at the forge in his long leather apron. The wagon-drivers shouted and cursed, telling the men to hurry up. Tomas shouted back at them. Garner Zeb strode up and down, barking out orders, lending a hand when it was needed, heaving a sack, harnessing a horse, making sure that everything happened according to the plan he carried in his head.

And Yoss heaved and lifted. He harnessed and carried. When he saw the way Tomas shouted at the wagon-drivers, he shouted as well. That made them laugh and shout even louder. He cleaned the stables and groomed the horses, waxed the harnesses, carried wood for Paulus' forge and swept the storerooms. There was no job that he shirked and no instruction from Garner Zeb that he failed to fulfil. When he returned to the village he would tell everyone what he had seen, the spices and silks that never appeared from one year to the next in the mountains, the way they arrived in boxes that had been sealed on islands far across the oceans. But they wouldn't believe him. He would have to take a dozen nutmegs or a handful of peppercorns to prove it. Even then, he knew, Herman would pretend to doubt him, or refuse to be impressed. But in reality he would be as jealous as a plover. *That* would make him wish he hadn't turned back at the lake.

So even though he lay down in the straw at the end of each day with aching muscles, Yoss got up each morning with enthusiasm. It was good work, he thought, that the merchant had given him. Hard but fair. And since he had robbed the merchant – even though he hadn't known he was doing it – it was right that he should repay him in this way after the magistrate let him go. His only worry now was that one of the workmen might ask what he had done before he came to the merchant's house. The story lay buried inside him, like a secret burden, and he could always feel its presence, threatening to make itself known.

But the workmen didn't ask, believing that they had already been told. Besides, they became less and less concerned with it. Who could fail to like the boy? He was always cheerful, ready and willing. One had only to work with him for a day to see that there was nothing thievish or calculating about him. One by one, each in his own way, the three workmen discounted the story that the servant had told them. Paulus, who didn't have much of a memory anyway, simply forgot it after a couple of weeks. Soon he was chattering to Yoss in his singsong voice, as he hammered on a horseshoe or tightened the hoop of a

barrel, as if Yoss had been there for years. Yoss hardly understood a word of what he said, but no one else did either, so it
didn't seem to matter. Beetle wondered about it for a while, in
his quiet way, and decided that the merchant wouldn't have
brought a thief into his house, so it must have been a mistake.
And Tomas assumed that, if there were any truth to it, Gregor
had exaggerated, and he was soon muttering to Yoss about servants whose tongues got the better of their brains.

Zeb, of course, knew the truth. He still treated Yoss sternly, in
deference to the master, but he liked him more and more. At
home he had a son of his own, who was only a year younger
than the boy. Sometimes the foreman would glance at Yoss, when
he was hard at work, and he couldn't help asking himself what
he would feel if it were *his* son there, heaving at a sack in a
stranger's house, under the eye of another stranger like himself.

Something disturbed him in what the merchant had done.
Even on that very first day, as the master told him the story in
the counting room, Zeb had felt uneasy. He had smiled, and
nodded, but his expression had not reflected his inmost
thoughts. To make a boy a slave? Even to think such a thing
was troubling. That first night, as he walked home to his family,
to his own son, he was already beginning to wonder whether
the merchant, in striking this bargain with the magistrate over
the boy, had not driven a bargain too far.

For Garner Zeb, this was an upheaval. To see the slave-boy
working in the courtyard was disturbing enough, but to find
himself questioning the master's action was even more unsettling. He had never had such doubts before. In business, no bargain was forbidden. Zeb idolized the merchant, considering him
the finest and wiliest master a man could find. When a man is
forced to question his idol, he's forced to question himself.

And the merchant? He came and went as usual, gave his instructions to Garner Zeb before he left each morning, spent the day transacting business at the Exchange, returned each evening with new ventures under way. When he passed the boy in the courtyard he had barely a word for him. Sometimes, in the counting room, he inquired about the boy in passing, as if the memory of him had only just recurred. To Zeb it seemed that he gave him no more thought than he would have given to a mule.

But the foreman didn't know everything about his master. He rarely glanced towards the windows of the upper floor. He didn't necessarily notice his master, for instance, early in the morning, standing at the window of his room, sometimes for minutes at a time, gazing down at the courtyard. He didn't see him last thing in the evening, gazing down once again, as the boy ran towards the stable. And it seemed that the merchant only ever stood like this, watching, when the boy was visible, working at one of his tasks or scampering across the cobble-stones.

16

THE MERCHANT wasn't the only one who sometimes stood and gazed down into the courtyard. The upper floor of the house surrounded the yard on all four sides, and there were many windows that overlooked it.

The two floors of the merchant's house were like two separate worlds, each with its own life. The only connection between them was the staircase, and the only person who used the staircase to cross between them was the merchant himself. Everyone else in his household belonged to one world or the other.

The ground floor was the merchant's world of commerce. Here, around the courtyard, were the stable, counting room, spice room, forge, coopery, and the many storerooms that were needed for the merchant's goods. It was a world of rich smells, spilled grain, straining horses, jangling harnesses, heaving workmen, sweat, shouts and curses. This was the world in which Yoss lived. His visit to the upper floor on the day he arrived lasted only a moment, and didn't take him beyond the top of the stairs.

The upper floor was the merchant's world of domesticity. Here were wood-panelled rooms, carved furniture, heavy tapestries, warming fires, maids, butler, wine in gold jugs and the sound of a harpsichord tinkling along the corridor. This was the world which his wife inhabited.

If the merchant had had any children, the upper floor would have been their world as well. But he was childless. His first wife had died four years before. One day she had found a swelling in her neck, hard and craggy, like a pitted rock. The swelling grew, and the more her neck swelled, the thinner the rest of her body became. One doctor after another came to examine her and each one prescribed his particular remedy, a poultice or an infusion or a purge or a course of emetics or a series of bleedings, and still the swelling grew and the woman's body shrank. Eventually she died, and when the merchant lifted her body for the last time, she was as light as a feather, and he thought, while her body was still in his arms, of all the profits he had made, and at that moment it occurred to him how heavy was all the gold he had accumulated, and yet it was not enough to save the life of this wife, whose body was so light. She had been his wife for twelve years and had left very little behind her, some dresses, and a few small daily items such as a mirror and a brush. He gave these to her maid.

But he was not yet thirty-five, and after a year he married again.

At the time of his first marriage the merchant had only intelligence and ambition to his name. His wife was the daughter of a baker, and it was from the baker's meagre savings that he had begun his business. But now he was a wealthy man, with growing influence in the town, and this time he married the daughter of another merchant, whose family had been prominent in the town for generations. She was eleven years younger than he. It was a good match for him, and created considerable jealousy amongst the other merchants. His friend, Krantz, who was unmarried, and his other friend at the Exchange, Pressler, who had made a match only a year before, could barely contain their envy. Perhaps a merchant has no friend when it comes to business. His new wife brought a dowry that added to his capital, from which he could increase his profits, and his new father-in-law also contributed to the purchase of his fine new mansion, with its storerooms and stable on the ground floor and room enough on the upper floor for the many grand-children that were expected.

But there were no children. A year passed, and a second, and then a third, and still the merchant's wife showed no signs of pregnancy. People began to talk, the merchant knew. Now they were saying that even with a second wife, he was unable to give a woman a child. Sometimes, at the Exchange, for example, when he saw a man grinning, he fancied the man was laughing at him. This merely made him work all the harder, drive yet shrewder bargains, make ever more profits and accumulate ever more gold, as if he had to prove his worth over and over in the marketplace if he couldn't prove it by the number of children in his home. And yet, he sometimes wondered why he was doing all this if he was to have no children, and to whom he would leave his fortune. When he was in this mood he sometimes thought about his first wife again, light as a feather when she died. But these dark thoughts only came when he was in the world of domesticity on the upper floor of his house. When he descended the stairs to the harsh, uncompromising world of commerce, *he* was the master, and he felt immediately reinvigo-rated, as if the very smell of the goods in his storehouses entered his body and charged it with energy for the challenges ahead. If he did fancy that a man laughed at him at the Exchange, it would only be a matter of minutes before a piece of business drove the doubt out of his mind, and if the piece of business was with that very man, so much the better, and so much more cun-ning and subtle would be the bargain that the merchant drove.

But the merchant's wife did not go with her husband to the Exchange, and did not see him at business with his rivals. She stayed in the big, empty upper floor, where the walls echoed to the sound of footsteps. Much as she tried, during the long hours of the day she couldn't keep her mind from thoughts of the children she didn't have. Then she would blame herself for being sad, and for not being a cheerful companion for her husband. How could she not notice the eagerness with which he slipped down the stairs each morning, or the way his mood fell when he returned at night? Sometimes, she thought, he would rather spend his time talking to that great hulking foreman in the counting room than come back to talk to her. And she would gaze at the foreman from her window above the courtyard, and suddenly find herself wishing that he wasn't there, that he would just disappear, and occasionally she found herself having thoughts that were even worse.

And then, her husband had suddenly come rushing up the stairs one day, home at last after one of his journeys, and he was boiling and bubbling over, just as in the days when they were first married and he used to come home and excitedly tell her the story of his latest business triumph, stories which always seemed to depend on complicated twists or conditional provisions which gave an extra fraction of profit and hardly seemed reason enough to get excited, even when she did understand them. Only this time, he had that boy with him, and according to the story that he told her . . . it seemed that he had *bought* him.

What did he mean? One couldn't buy a boy, not really. Slavery was a thing of ancient times. Surely her husband knew it as well as anyone. And even if her husband had managed to do it – and if any man could, it would be him – in her heart, the merchant's wife knew it wasn't right. Sometimes she even dreaded that there would be a punishment for such an act. At other times she told herself this was foolish and superstitious.

She didn't dare speak about it to her husband. And besides, somehow, he seemed to be happier now.

She wished she had taken the chance to talk with the boy. That day, when the merchant brought him home, she had been too shocked to speak, and her husband had whisked him down the stairs again. But the boy was bedraggled and filthy, just like a beggar from the streets. And once he was downstairs, what was she supposed to do? Was she supposed to go down and find him in the storerooms herself?

If only her husband had told her about the boy first, instead of flinging him at her like that. Now, she often thought about the things the merchant had explained to her afterwards. The boy was honest and intelligent, and had been deceived. He was innocent and easily shaped, like wax. During the day, when the boy was at work, she would sometimes watch him from her window. She saw him helping to unload the wagons, staggering manfully away under a cask that was too heavy for his young arms, and she found herself laughing and crying at the same time. What was his name? Yoss, that was what her husband had told her.

'Yoss,' she murmured to herself, looking down as the boy pulled on a sack, frowning with concentration and effort.

The merchant's wife threw a glance at her maid. The girl was looking down into the courtyard as well.

'He's pretty, isn't he?' said the merchant's wife.

'Yes, madam,' whispered the girl, and she blushed a little.

Suddenly the woman turned to her maid. She almost felt herself blushing as well. 'Shall we call him up?'

~

SYLVIE THE MAID was somewhat afraid of Garner Zeb. He was a tall, hulking man with a big brow, and she was a slight, short, slip of a girl. From the upper floor, she often heard the foreman's booming voice issuing orders to the workmen, and she shuddered to think what it would be like if it boomed at her. This didn't make her inclined to raise her voice above its customary whisper when the mistress sent her downstairs to talk to him.

'Speak up,' said Zeb, who was used to the crude shouts of the men. 'I can't hear you.'

'I said,' whispered Sylvie, 'that the mistress would like to see the boy.'

'The boy?' repeated Zeb, as if he still doubted that he had heard her correctly.

The maid nodded.

'Which boy? The master's boy? Yoss?'

'Yes,' whispered the maid.

Garner Zeb frowned. He was reluctant. He had begun to feel protective towards the boy. How much did the mistress know of his story? The merchant might have told her anything. Why did she suddenly want to see him?

'When does she want him?'

'Now.'

'No,' said the foreman. 'He can't go now. He's busy. He's got work to do. Tell the mistress she should wait until the master comes back and then *he* can send for the boy.'

The girl bit her lip. 'She said . . .' she began, and she hesitated, and then she blurted it out as quickly as she could, because the merchant's wife had told her exactly what to say and had made her learn it by rote and promise to say it all, every last word, no matter how frightened she felt of the big, loud foreman: 'She said she wants to see the boy *now* and you're not to prevent it and if you prevent it she'll tell the master and the master will deal with you and you'll *wish* you'd obeyed her and you're not to say anything to the master either now or later because the mistress will tell him *herself* and if you mention it to him you'll wish you *hadn't*.'

Zeb stared at Sylvie with an open mouth.

'And I'm to take him,' she added in a whisper, staring at her feet. 'I'm to stay until he comes and I'm not to return without him.'

Well! Zeb folded his arms. He almost wanted to laugh at the girl in front of him. But he was too angry to be amused. Who was the merchant's wife to go issuing orders to him? His loyalty belonged to the merchant, and as far as he was concerned it was nothing more than a matter of chance that his master happened to have a wife who lived upstairs. She wasn't like the merchant's first wife. Any order that *she* had issued, Zeb would have obeyed with alacrity. In the early days, in the small house, they had been like one family, and the baker's daughter had treated him as much like a brother as like her husband's worker. Never a day went by but that she came out to talk to him, ask about his wife and children, give him a good large piece of leftover pie or a pair of turnips for the family. She hadn't been as pretty as the merchant's second wife, nor as dainty, but she knew what it was for a man to be a worker and to struggle to feed his family day after day. Not like the second one. *She* never came down the stairs but to rush across the courtyard with her maid, barely looking to left or right, as if the very glance of a workman might contaminate her. It was as much as she could manage to say good morning. She never inquired about his family, not even for sake of sheer courtesy, might not even have been aware that he had a family for all the interest she showed. And now, she was issuing orders – through her maid, no less – and apparently expected him to obey!

'The master hasn't said a thing about it,' muttered Garner Zeb eventually. 'Not a thing. Why can't she wait?'

Sylvie glanced up at him from under her eyelashes. 'I'm not to return without him, honestly, Garner Zeb. Please understand. I *can't* go back without him.'

Zeb didn't know what to think. 'He hasn't told me the mistress can't see the boy,' he muttered to himself, and the girl nodded, and gazed at him appealingly, as if she couldn't imagine that such a big, kind man as Garner Zeb would refuse such a tiny, harmless favour.

The foreman hesitated. It was even possible that the master might be angry if his wife's request was denied. Zeb had no idea. The situation had never arisen before.

The maid was still waiting.

Garner Zeb sighed and threw up his hands.

His booming voice echoed across the courtyard. 'Yoss!'

17

THE GIRL MOVED SWIFTLY across the cobblestones. She just as much skipped as walked, and a swishing sound enveloped her steps. Her crisp yellow skirt came down to her ankles, and Yoss could see the bow of her apron tied neatly behind her back. He already felt awkward and clumsy, just following behind her.

Yoss, of course, was trying to work out why the merchant's wife wanted to see him. She must still be angry, he decided. She had been angry that first day, when the merchant took him up the stairs to see her, so angry that the merchant had taken him straight down again. And he couldn't think of anything that had happened since then to change her mind.

He didn't blame her. Why shouldn't she be angry? He had robbed her husband, after all. It wasn't the kind of thing that would make a wife feel friendly towards you. Maybe she had finally decided to give him a piece of her mind.

He would have to explain how it happened, Yoss realized. He had already explained it twice, to the merchant and the magistrate, and it was obvious that the details didn't make him seem very clever. He still lived in dread that the workmen might ask him what he had done before he came to the house. Just imagine Tomas' laughter if he discovered the truth! The problem with the explanation was that he appeared to be either a criminal or a fool, and in order to convince people that he wasn't the first, he had to make them believe he was the second. In other words, if he didn't want to be taken for a thief, he had to admit he was an idiot. And not just admit it, but prove it!

The maid had reached the foot of the stairs. Yoss looked up. It was a broad staircase of white stone, and it curved gracefully, narrowing towards the middle and then flaring again at the top. On each side there was a balustrade of small white columns. The girl began to skip up the stairs, holding her skirt and bouncing from one to the next. Yoss began to feel even clumsier.

Well, he would just have to try to seem as stupid as possible, he thought, and hope that the merchant's wife was sympathetic. If a person was stupid enough, others often felt sympathy. In the village there was old Matty, for example, who was born an idiot, and Gerson, whose arms twisted uncontrollably and who could barely get the words out of his mouth because of the stiffness of his tongue, and Katherine and Gussie with their goitres. People looked after them. But perhaps there wasn't as much sympathy here in the town. How much mercy would Conrad or Gaspar, or Farber, show to someone like Gerson? In the town you needed a caper to survive. And what about the merchant's wife? She hadn't looked very welcoming on that first day. She looked beautiful, not sympathetic. But maybe she didn't know what an idiot he had been. If he could convince her that he really was stupid, a complete and utter simpleton, she might relent.

He was at the top of the staircase now. In front of him was a wide corridor, laid and panelled with wood, and on each side was a row of doors. Between the doors, chests stood against the walls, and tapestries hung above the chests.

The maid led him along the corridor. Her footsteps clicked on the wood. Yoss felt his stomach tightening with anxiety.

The maid stopped at a door. She turned around and examined him.

'Straighten yourself up.'

Yoss looked at her questioningly.

The girl shook her head. She waved her hand towards his hair and then pointed at his clothes.

'Oh,' said Yoss, and he patted his head with his hand, trying to smooth down his hair, and shook out the bottom of his shirt, which made it sit straighter on his shoulders. Then he looked back at her inquiringly once more.

The girl didn't speak. She peered at him mischievously. Then she reached out a hand out and pushed a wisp of hair back from Yoss' temple. Yoss felt her fingers brush against his skin.

She giggled, turned with a swirl of her skirt, knocked on the door, and opened it.

'Go in,' she whispered, and she stepped aside.

Yoss hesitated. He took a step towards the door.

'Go on,' she whispered again, and she nudged him forwards.

~

THE MERCHANT'S WIFE was sitting at a small table. She was dressed more plainly than on the previous occasion when Yoss had seen her. If anything, this made her seem even more beautiful and distant. The knot in his stomach tightened.

'Will you come and sit down, Yoss?' said the merchant's wife. She pointed to a chair at the table.

Yoss stared at her.

'Well? Come on, Yoss,' said the woman, smiling, as the boy hesitated.

Yoss sat down. Behind him, the maid went to a sideboard, and she picked up a dish of cakes and put them on the table.

'Will you have one, Yoss?'

Yoss looked at the woman. She nodded encouragingly, and

he took a cake. He began to eat. The cake was good, very sweet, with a lot of honey in it.

'Are they giving you enough to eat?' asked the woman.

'Oh, yes,' said Yoss hurriedly, and the crumbs flew out of his mouth.

Sylvie giggled, and the merchant's wife threw her a stern glance.

Yoss held the cake. He shouldn't have started to eat it so quickly, he realized. The woman had only offered the cake to see what he would do.

'I'm sorry I haven't sent for you before, Yoss.'

Yoss nodded gravely. He put the cake down on the table. Now, he knew, it was going to begin. The woman was going to tell him what she thought of people who robbed her husband on the open road.

'Are you working very hard?'

Yoss stared at her.

'Downstairs,' said the woman. 'Are you working very hard there?'

'Oh,' said Yoss, puzzled. 'Not *very* hard.'

'What do you do?'

'I carry things,' said Yoss cautiously. 'I unload things, and stack them away, and clean up, and . . . all kinds of things.'

The woman smiled. 'Do you like that work?'

'Yes,' said Yoss, wondering why the woman was asking about this. He turned to glance at the maid.

'And you come from a village? In the mountains?'

Yoss looked back at the woman.

'Do you have a sweetheart there?'

Yoss heard the maid simpering behind him.

'Sylvie,' said the woman, 'leave us, please.'

'But madam!' cried the maid.

'Leave us, Sylvie.'

Yoss glanced at the maid again. She glared at him, and then walked sulkily out of the room.

'She'll listen, of course,' said the merchant's wife with a smile. 'At this very moment, she has her ear to the door.' The woman raised her voice. 'Am I right, Sylvie?'

There was no answer. The woman laughed.

'Now,' she said, 'will you tell me about your village?'

Yoss shook his head. Surely the lady knew what he had done. And if she didn't know, he had to tell her. He couldn't bear it any more. He just couldn't pretend, not in front of her.

'I robbed your husband!' he blurted out.

'I know,' said the woman.

'Oh . . .' said Yoss, more puzzled than ever. 'I just wanted . . . I thought I should tell you, that's all.'

'The first time I saw you, you were filthy. Do you remember?'

Yoss nodded.

'You'd been with some beggars. Had you been with them very long?'

'Only a day,' said Yoss.

'Don't you want to finish your cake?'

Yoss looked at his part-eaten cake on the table. The woman reached forward and took one for herself.

'Tell me about your village,' she said.

'What do you want to know?'

'Why you left, for a start. Was there a famine? A flood?'

'No,' said Yoss. 'I left because I had to. Everyone has to.'

'Everyone has to?' The woman took a bite of cake, watching Yoss with interest.

'Yes, but not everyone does.' Yoss took a bite of his cake as well, and frowned as he thought about it. It was the first time he had really tried to tell anyone about the village. It was strange, to hear himself talking about it out loud. It was as if the village, which had been resting quietly in his memory, suddenly leapt into life.

'Many years ago,' Yoss said, 'everyone used to leave. But today it's more of a symbol.'

'What do you mean?'

Yoss tried to explain. Soon he forgot his nervousness and the fact that he was speaking to the most beautiful woman he had ever seen. He told her about the Speaker. He told her that the ceremony of leaving symbolized the way in which the people of the village had gained their skills, by going out into the world and returning with things they had never seen before. He told her how he had left the village with Herman, his friend, and that Herman had turned back at the lake.

'He should have gone on with you,' said the woman eventually. 'Herman shouldn't have turned back like that.'

Yoss shook his head. 'He wants to be a carpenter. Anyway, I think he might have been frightened.'

'And weren't you frightened, Yoss? Not even a little bit?'

'Me?' said Yoss, and he was just about to say that he was never frightened at all, not one little bit, when he saw from the way the woman was looking at him that she already knew the real answer, and he remembered Moritz, whom he had always admired for telling the truth about his fear when he was trapped on the mountain. Yoss looked down at the table, and he played with some cake crumbs for a moment, moving them around with his finger. 'Yes. I was,' he murmured. 'Sometimes I still am.'

He looked up. And he found, to his surprise, that the lady's eyes were full of tears, and she turned away quickly from his gaze.

'Well,' the lady said, after Yoss had told her other things about the village, and she had made him eat another cake, 'I have just the thing for you, if you want to see something you've never seen in your village.'

'Oh, I've seen lots of things already,' said Yoss. 'The storerooms are full of them.'

'Like what?'

'Nutmegs.'

'This is better than nutmegs,' said the lady.

'And . . . you,' said Yoss after a moment, looking at the cake crumbs on the table and blushing with embarrassment. 'I've never seen anyone as beautiful as you.'

'Nonsense,' said the lady, smiling with pleasure. 'You're a flatterer, Yoss. Who would have thought it? You do have a sweetheart, don't you? I bet you've got lots. Well, this thing that I'll show you, it's me and it's not me, if you understand.'

'What is it?' said Yoss.

'Can't you tell? It's a riddle,' said the lady playfully. 'Me and not me. See if you can solve it. But you'll have to tell me whether you succeed.'

'When?'

'Tomorrow. I'll send for you.'

~

THE NEXT AFTERNOON, Garner Zeb saw the lady's maid come down the stairs and walk across the courtyard towards him again. He shook his head, muttering to himself, and went to get Yoss from the coopery, where he was helping Paulus repair some barrels that had cracked.

The maid brought Yoss to a different room this time. She glanced at him sniffily, and didn't speak a single word to let him know whether he had smoothed his hair down properly before he went in. He heard the door close behind him.

It was like night. Many candles were burning. Across the room, the merchant's wife was sitting on a huge chair. She wore a glittering dress this time, and her head was cupped in a blue bonnet. Her eyes were open, unblinking. She was still, very still.

Yoss stared. He forgot that he hadn't been able to think of an answer to the lady's riddle, and that he feared he was going to disappoint her. Suddenly he felt a much greater fear, which put ice into his veins. Was the lady dead, sitting so still in that chair?

'Come here, Yoss.'

Yoss jumped. He saw one of her hands move, beckoning him.

The boy took a few steps forward. 'Why are you . . . Are you all right? Can you move?'

'He doesn't let me,' said the woman.

Yoss looked around. For the first time, he noticed that there was another person in the room. A man was sitting on the other side of all the candles, with a large board angled in front of him.

'Have you solved the riddle, Yoss?' said the woman.

Yoss wondered whether the man had something to do with the riddle. Perhaps he was there to judge the answer. Yoss tried to get a better look at the man. He had a large head, Yoss could see that much, with fleshy jowls and arched eyebrows. The boy wondered what a man like that would do when he discovered that there was no answer for him to judge.

'Go and look,' said the woman, smiling.

'Madam . . .' growled the man.

'You said you would paint me cheerful, Master Hans. What harm can a smile do?'

'Art must be directed, madam.'

'Art must be directed,' intoned the lady, as solemnly as she could. Then she broke into laughter. 'That's all Master Hans ever says, Yoss. Art must be directed. What do you think?'

Yoss didn't know what to think. The man didn't seem very happy that Yoss had brought no answer to the riddle.

'Go and look,' said the woman again.

Master Hans glared at him, raising his arched eyebrows even further.

Yoss approached the painter hesitantly. Now, for the first time he could see what was on the canvas behind him. Yoss stopped. He looked incredulously at the canvas, and at the lady, and back at the canvas.

The merchant's wife watched with amusement. 'So, you think it's a good likeness, do you?'

'It's . . . I've never seen anything like it!'

'Anything like it that's as good, or anything like it that's as bad?' muttered the painter.

'Good! Good, sir. Oh, very good.'

'I thank you, sir,' said Master Hans sarcastically, and he turned back to his work, lifting a daub of colour from the palette which he held with a thick, paint-covered thumb.

'Are you surprised to see such a thing?' asked the woman.

'Oh, yes. I . . .' Yoss' voice trailed away. He watched the man in fascination. The painter was concentrating on the embroidery of the lady's bodice, and with delicate tendrils of yellow paint, and tiny dots of white, was re-creating the shimmering lattice of gold thread, festooned with pearls, that encrusted the velvet.

'Is it better than what you have seen in my husband's store-rooms?'

'Much better,' murmured Yoss.

'Better than nutmegs?'

'Oh, yes, it's more . . .'

'Yes? It's more what?'

Yoss turned to the woman. 'What?'

'Nutmegs, Yoss. We were talking about nutmegs.'

'Were we?'

The woman laughed.

She gazed at the boy. He watched the painter, entranced. His hair stood in tufts, like the hair of a young goat, and his mouth was ajar. His face was fresh and innocent, his cheeks white, his lips red. Suddenly the woman felt a great tenderness swell in her bosom, and tears welled in her eyes.

And this time, the painter, when he stopped to peer at his subject around the edge of the canvas, didn't call at her to look back at the candle. Instead, he dropped his brush and quickly reached for another. With sure, delicate dabs, he worked rapidly on the eyes in the painting, stealing glances at the woman as often as he could. A glistening film of moisture appeared under his brush, shimmering and transparent.

Yoss thought he had never seen such beautiful eyes. But when he looked at the lady again, she was standing up, with her back to them, and her head was shaking, very slightly, although not a sound was coming from her.

'Do you like watching Master Hans paint?' said the lady. She turned back to face him. Now she had a small white handker-chief in her hand.

'Yes,' said Yoss.

'Then you may come to see him as often as you choose.'

'But Garner Zeb wouldn't—'

'Leave Garner Zeb to me. Come to see him as often as you want.'

Yoss smiled. 'Thank you,' he said.

'Yes, *thank you*,' muttered the painter, and he shook his head with a sigh, adding another dab of paint to the canvas under the boy's fascinated gaze.

18

CONRAD HAD GROWN THINNER. Dreams of roast duck don't sustain a man for long when his meals are a lump of bread at breakfast and a watery broth of turnip and potato for supper. His face had lost its heaviness and the weight around his belly was melting away. He looked leaner, harder. It was as if a disguise had dropped from him, showing the true outlines of the bones beneath.

Time had passed. Kelmuss Week approached. And on the other side of Kelmuss Week, the trial loomed. Yet Conrad continued to bide his time, restraining himself whenever the jailer threw him an expectant glance. What were the rewards that the straw-haired prisoner intended? Conrad had hinted at them only once, yet now, it was clear, from the jailer's questioning gaze and the knowing hints in his conversation, the jailer could think of little else. As each day passed, Conrad could see, the other man's appetite grew. But still he pretended to misconstrue the jailer's oblique entreaties. Silence is more potent than words. Once he has begun to dream, no riches are as great as those that a man composes in his own imagination. The trial approached, and a moment would come when Conrad would not be able to wait any longer. But that moment wasn't here yet. It was still a game of wits. And with each day that passed, if only he could hold his nerve, the greater would grow the mountain of wealth that the jailer's greed was conjuring in his mind, and the greater the risk he would take in order to obtain it.

It was the jailer whose nerve broke first.

He sent the servants into the corridor. He glanced over his shoulder at the guards outside the cell.

'Tell me now,' he whispered, 'what are the rewards I could have?'

'Rewards?' said Conrad.

'Don't play me for a fool, Conrad.'

'*You're* not the one who's being played for a fool.'

Conrad paused for one last, searching look at the jailer. The jailer had declared himself. But one risk remained, and there was nothing Conrad could do to eradicate it. If he continued now, he would cross a line from which there was no retreat. Until this moment, Gaspar and the boy had admitted the crime. He had not. If the jailer turned out to be an honest man, playing the prisoner at his own game, Conrad was about to walk into a trap that he had set for himself.

But if the jailer were as corrupt, or as corruptible, as Conrad guessed, then it was *he* who was about to walk into Conrad's snare.

Conrad had already gone over it in his mind. Over and over. The judges wouldn't need his own confession to convict him. He knew this. Therefore, unlike the jailer, he had nothing to lose.

'Well?' hissed the jailer, glancing anxiously over his shoulder again.

Conrad nodded. 'It's the magistrate who's the fool,' he said at last. 'The merchant didn't tell the half of what we took, not the quarter. Did he mention the pearls?'

The jailer shook his head.

'No. Nor the rubies, I suppose.'

'Rubies?'

'Three of them. Big as pigeon's eggs. And the rest! Any

mention of them?' Conrad scoffed. 'Four rings and a purse! Was that what he said? The sly devil. That was barely the beginning, barely the end of it.' Conrad paused dramatically, hunched close beside the ear of the small, sallow jailer. 'Why would a man do that? He was up to something fishy, that merchant, and he didn't want anyone to know.'

He drew back from the jailer, fixed him with a stare, and nodded once, portentously.

'Jewels that a man won't talk about,' he continued in a whisper, 'are jewels a man won't look for. Even if he sees you walking down the street with them, there's nothing he can do.'

The jailer gazed at Conrad. After a moment he turned. The slamming of the door echoed behind him.

~

'WHAT WAS THAT about?' demanded Gaspar. 'What rubies? You didn't tell me about rubies. We were meant to share! And pearls? Where did you find pearls? Conrad, if you took pearls without—'

'Shut up, Gaspar,' said Conrad impatiently. He turned his head slowly towards him. 'There was none of that. You had your half, exactly as we agreed. So if you don't understand what I'm doing, just shut up. And if you do understand, shut up as well. When he comes back, don't you dare say a word.'

Gaspar lapsed into sullen silence. He chewed on his lump of breakfast bread, which was soon finished. Then he took off his hat and began to examine it disconsolately, turning it round and round in his hand, cursing under his breath at the stain in the velvet. Now and again he glanced up at Conrad.

But Conrad was deep in his own thoughts. He had said to Gaspar 'when the jailer comes back'. Someone would come back, that was certain, but he couldn't be sure it would be the jailer. If he was mistaken, and the jailer betrayed him, it would be the magistrate who came to the cell.

All was in the balance. There was nothing more he could do. Even for an experienced trickster, those hours when he knows that the entire swindle is in question, when the victim has been brought to the very edge of the precipice but has not yet chosen to throw himself over, are excruciating. And this, if it worked, would be no ordinary swindle. The straw-haired man was playing for his life.

He would know when the door of the cell opened. He would know as soon as he saw who came through the door.

The minutes passed, and turned into hours. Conrad listened for every sound. He began to calculate how many cells there might be in the prison, and how long it would take the jailer to visit each one. That time passed. He tried to imagine what other things the jailer might have to do, or why he might suddenly be called away. The jailer had often said that the magistrate forced him to do extra jobs in his household. But surely it couldn't take this long, and surely, if the jailer were eager, he would find a way to return.

Or was the jailer upstairs, even now, repeating every word in the magistrate's ear?

Conrad was starting to feel cold and sick. He didn't touch his bread. Maybe the long weeks of confinement and hunger had taken their toll. His nerves, normally so strong, were strained to breaking point.

He began to talk to himself. He knew that in these situations it's natural to assume the worst. He knew that to assume the worst is often a mistake. It means you aren't able to think clearly when you need to. It means you misinterpret things and jump to the wrong conclusions. To assume the worst often makes the worst come true.

You don't know, he said to himself. You don't know it hasn't worked. You know nothing. Assume nothing. Assume nothing until you know for sure. Someone will come back, the jailer or the magistrate. Then you'll know. Assume nothing. Assume nothing until . . .

He looked up. Gaspar was watching him.

Conrad turned away. Assume nothing, he repeated silently to himself. Assume nothing until you *know*.

The key turned in the lock. Conrad's stomach tightened. He watched the door swing back.

Behind it stood the familiar figure of the jailer, with his sallow face and protruding jaw.

~

THE JAILER was alone. He closed the door and crouched beside Conrad. Hungrily, he demanded to know what had been stolen from the merchant. Conrad repeated his lies, adding emeralds, turquoises and a diamond to the haul. He watched the jailer's face as he spoke. He could see the thoughts in the other man's mind, as clearly as eels wriggling in a pond. Now there was no uncertainty. Conrad felt completely calm. Never, he felt, had he controlled anyone as utterly as the man who crouched spell-bound before him now. The jailer had walked over the precipice. Conrad, as if he were a spectator at the top of the cliff, was watching him fall.

'And he can't do anything about it?' said the jailer. 'Even if he sees someone walking down the street with his rubies?'

'Why did he fail to mention them?'

'I'll have half,' said the jailer.

Conrad shook his head, revelling cruelly in his mastery of the jailer. 'One-third.'

'Half!'

'One-third,' said Conrad, waving a hand in Gaspar's direction. 'There are two of us.'

'There'll be *neither* of you if I don't help you get away.'

'And you won't have even a third unless you do.'

The jailer frowned. Then he wagged a finger. 'Conrad, you're a cool one. You'd be wasted on the gallows. One-third, then. But how do I know I'll get my share?'

'You have my word.'

'Your word? No, thank you. I'll have something before I let you go.'

'What's that?'

The jailer turned and pointed at Gaspar's boots.

Gaspar stared at Conrad in despair. But Conrad's gaze choked off any words that might have risen in his throat.

'Pretty, aren't they?' said Conrad.

The jailer nodded.

'Is that all? Would you like the hat as well, perhaps?'

The jailer shook his head. He held out a hand, and crooked a finger, to tell Gaspar to hand the boots over.

'No,' said Conrad. 'They're your pledge of faith as much as ours. You'll get them on the night we leave, not before.'

The jailer grinned. 'You take no chances, do you? I bet you twist the knife before you pull it out, eh, Conrad? We'll do it in Kelmuss Week. There'll be people in the town. Make it easier for you to get away.'

'No later,' said Conrad, 'or the judges'll have us instead.' He nudged the jailer in the ribs.

The jailer laughed. By the time he left the cell, the last

details had been decided.

Gaspar stared at Conrad in astonishment after the jailer had gone. 'And how do you think we're going to give him all those things?' he asked. 'If there really weren't any pearls, or rubies, or whatever else you said, just where are we going to get them?'

Conrad shook his head. He couldn't be bothered answering.

'So your boots, Gaspar, they're worth . . . what? One life each?'

Gaspar frowned. Slowly he began to understand. 'And you told me not to worry about possessions!'

'Oh, I was wrong,' said Conrad. 'I was wrong, Gaspar. You're much the cleverer. After we're out, I'll have to listen to you more.'

19

YOSS NOW WENT to the upper floor of the merchant's house every day. The merchant's wife had sent the maid to tell Garner Zeb that he was permitted to go. She, and she alone, would speak to the master about it.

For some reason, Zeb went along with this. The merchant himself made it easy for his foreman. His inquiries about Yoss, when he remembered to make them, continued to be brief and perfunctory, as if the boy were a matter of indifference as long as he worked satisfactorily. The subject of the boy's absences in the upper floor simply never came up. But that was an excuse, not a reason. Zeb needed no invitation to broach such a matter with the master. Only in regard to this boy had he ever kept such a silence. Yet once he had begun to keep it, the silence acquired a power of its own. How could he reverse it? A week went by, and then another, and each day he sat opposite his master in the counting room, and still he did not speak. Why hadn't he told him earlier? That was what the merchant would ask. And what would he reply? There was no answer to that question but the answer that the foreman hardly dared to give to himself.

In keeping secret what went on each day when his master was at the Exchange, Garner Zeb knew that he had begun to betray him.

In this, he was complicit with the mistress. Yet he felt no affection for her, and she had never done anything to acquire his trust. All of the great fund of his loyalty belonged with the master. But the enslavement of the boy had turned everything upside-down.

So the boy continued to work with the men, as before, in the mornings, and by the time the master returned in the evening, the boy was at work again. But in between, in the afternoon, he climbed the staircase to the upper floor. There the lady gave him sweet cakes, or honey, or fruits, and talked to him, or asked him questions, or just watched him eat. After a while, to tell the truth, he didn't find these visits interesting. And the lady always seemed close to tears, which was confusing. Yoss wondered what he was doing to make her cry. But she never kept him long. She knew what Yoss really wanted to see.

~

MASTER HANS was a large man, and he had grown larger at the tables of his patrons. His face was pale and smooth-shaven, his eyebrows perpetually arched, and his gaze imperturbable. The clothes he wore were plain and dark, and when he worked he wore a simple black cap that covered all his hair except at the very nape of his neck.

He had not requested the boy's attendance. If the lady of the house allowed the boy to come and watch him work, it didn't mean he had to speak to him. Small boys, he knew, cherished noise and uproar, and soon grew bored without them. This boy wasn't so small, but silence, with luck, would drive him away. It didn't. It wasn't the painter's conversation that fascinated Yoss, but his work.

Master Hans wasn't working solely on the lady's portrait. In fact, his main purpose was to decorate the ceiling of the huge hall on the upper floor of the merchant's house. This hall ran the length of an entire side of the building, with one row of soaring windows looking out on the courtyard and another on the street, and might have been one of the most splendid ballrooms in the town. It lacked only a fitting decoration on its ceiling. It was the merchant's wife who had persuaded her husband to invite Master Hans to do the job. He charged a high fee, as was only to be expected from an artist of his calibre and for a work of such magnitude, and he must come from another town, so the merchant would have to provide accommodation, and even then the painter had to be convinced that the task was sufficiently important to justify his talents. Yet eventually he agreed. It was only after he arrived that the merchant also asked him to paint a canvas of his wife, imagining that the artist would add it without extra charge, considering the hefty fee he was already earning. So Master Hans told him that he *could* do it without charge, but then the merchant would get the kind of painting that an artist does for nothing, just as the merchant, for example, *could* deliver a barrel of wine to one of his customers without charge, but what kind of wine would he choose to deliver? On the other hand, if the merchant chose to pay, explained Master Hans, he would get the kind of painting that an artist does if he is receiving a fee, just as the customer would receive the kind of wine a man expects when he is paying. Having dealt with merchants before, the painter thought this was the kind of argument his patron would understand. And then he left it to the merchant to choose, which he soon did, agreeing to pay exactly what the painter demanded.

So for most of the time the painter was not sitting in the candle-lit room with the merchant's wife, but working in the hall where light streamed in through many windows. The ceiling was to be painted with a vast mythological scene. Its centrepiece was the Goddess of Plenty triumphing over Famine and Want. The painter had suggested this theme as an appropriate one for a merchant's house, and the merchant and his wife had agreed. She was to appear as the Goddess, surrounded by nymphs and maidens, and he would appear as an armoured warrior at the head of her host, driving Famine and Want away. Here the painter worked for hour after hour, completely alone and in utter silence, craning his neck as he reached up with a brush, or lying flat on a plank with his nose almost touching the plaster and the paint spattering his eyelids, like a giant black spider under the roof.

When the merchant's wife brought the boy to the hall, it was in disorder. Old sheets and blankets were scattered over the floor to protect its parquetry from the paint. Two rough trestle tables were strewn with lumps of colour and brushes and pots and palettes. Pails lay on the ground, some overturned, some upright, and a basket of eggs was nearby. A framework of poles, lashed together with rope, rose to the roof, obscuring much of the work that the painter had already completed. Yet even from his first glance, from the parts of the painting that he was able to see, Yoss knew that he was in the presence of something extraordinary, that above him, even as he watched, a great work was taking shape.

The painter saw the boy from the top of the scaffolding and pretended not to notice. But Yoss wasn't deterred. Once he knew where the hall was, he kept coming back. Even from the ground, and through the web of the poles, if he found the right position in the hall he could follow the progress the painter was making. In the course of one afternoon, for instance, he saw the bodies of three horses appear on the ceiling. He knew that there would be many more details to discover if only he could climb to the top. The ladder was there in front of him, rising into the scaffolding. But somehow Yoss understood that he ought not touch it. To use it was to ascend into the world that the painter was creating under the ceiling. First, the painter must invite him to climb it.

Sometimes Master Hans came down to the tables that he had set up on the floor. He might slice some chunks off the lumps of colour, or pick up a few eggs, or select some brushes, or pour some water out of one of the pails. He put whatever he needed into two pails that were attached to a short, curved yoke, and then he lifted the yoke and climbed the ladder again with the yoke over his neck and the pails hanging down beside him. The painter was a big man, and Yoss could hear him puffing as he went up the ladder. He might do this once or twice in an afternoon, and each time he threw perhaps a single glance in Yoss' direction before he went back up. Yoss grew accustomed to being ignored. But one day, instead of lifting the yoke onto his shoulders and going back up the ladder, the painter turned to examine this boy, who came in every afternoon and seemed content just to sit and watch him from the floor.

The painter's arched eyebrows flattened in scrutiny.

'You,' said the painter.

Yoss gazed at him. There was no one else in the hall.

'You work out there, do you?' said the painter, tilting his head in the direction of the courtyard.

Yoss nodded.

'You carry things, do you?'

'Sometimes.'

'Are you good at carrying things?'

'I think so.'

The painter scrutinized him for a moment longer, as if he were trying to verify it for himself.

'Well,' he said, 'let's see if you can carry this.'

The painter lifted the yoke. Yoss came forward. He bowed his head and felt the weight of the yoke on the back of his neck. When he straightened up and raised it, the pails swung.

'Well?' said the painter.

Yoss grinned.

'Oh, so you think it's funny, do you? Up you go, then. Let's see if you think *that's* a joke.'

Yoss went to the ladder. He began to climb as he had seen the painter do many times, with his back well arched and his arms bent and holding the ladder at the level of his chest. It was even harder than he imagined. The only thing keeping the yoke in place was the curve of his neck and it was impossible to look up. The pails, hanging in mid-air, swung and bounced against his shins.

He felt some water slosh out of a pail as it hit his leg. He looked down and saw Master Hans staring up at him.

'Come on, boy! You're slowing down.'

The painter started up the ladder beneath him.

Yoss climbed painfully. When he reached the top, he stepped onto the scaffolding and let the pails rest and squirmed out from under the yoke. He straightened his back with a long, painful stretch.

'You cracked an egg,' said the painter, looking down into the pails when he got to the top.

'I'm sorry.'

The painter pulled it out. He tapped the egg against a pole and broke it in half. He held one of the halves out to Yoss. The yolk was very bright, almost orange.

'Drink it,' he said.

Yoss looked at him doubtfully.

The painter continued to hold the eggshell out. Eventually Yoss took it. He glanced at the painter again. The painter stared at him implacably.

Yoss raised the eggshell. He threw back his head, closed his eyes, and swallowed the yolk.

The painter raised his half of the egg and drained it. Then he threw the eggshell hard against the scaffolding, smashing it to pieces. He looked at Yoss.

Yoss slammed his eggshell as well. He looked back at Master Hans, grinning.

The painter didn't grin. But he nodded at the boy. Then he turned to the buckets, pulled out a slice of green colour, and began to pare slivers of it into a bowl.

Yoss glanced up. Staring straight back at him from the ceiling was an enormous face, painted for viewing from the floor below, eyes wide, mouth gaping, hair wild, a warrior in the act of throwing his spear.

~

THIS was the way Master Hans taught the boy to do things. He let him watch, and then, at a certain point, he let him try for himself. Yoss never knew how the painter decided when he was ready for one thing or another. At first Yoss merely carried the yoke up and down. Then the painter gave him his first chance to mix a colour, and soon Yoss was creating the initial mixtures from colour and eggs and water, which Master Hans would test with his brush and then adjust to suit his needs. One day the painter let him apply a first coat of colour. He put a brush in Yoss' hands and watched him smear blue paint onto a patch of the ceiling that he had marked out to appear as sky. After two brushstrokes, Master Hans took hold of his wrist and guided him through the movements, adjusting the pressure of the brush on the plaster, until the colour began to flow smoothly and easily. Then he stood back and watched as the boy continued by himself, and took hold of his wrist again, and watched once more, and after a while he turned around and went on with his own painting.

He rarely spoke. He corrected by example rather than word. Under the ceiling of the great hall, their work proceeded in silence. Yoss could hear the shouts of the men from the courtyard, Garner Zeb's booming voice and Tomas' rasping retorts and the cries of the wagon-drivers who waited for them, but within the hall the only sounds were the soft dabbing of brush against plaster, or the squeak of a plank as Master Hans shifted weight. And for some reason, this seemed perfectly natural to Yoss, and he wasn't tempted to interrupt the silence with questions, although there were many that he might have asked. Sometimes he thought about Herman, and he almost laughed, thinking of what Herman would do if he had to work in silence like that. The best thing about working with the carpenter, Herman always said, was that they sang songs all day as they sawed together.

Sometimes the painter spoke to himself. One day Yoss heard him say: 'Ears are peculiar. They rarely want to look beautiful.' Just that, and then he lapsed into silence again, concentrating on the head that he was painting. He didn't expect a response. Another day he said: 'You're not my student, Yoss. Don't imagine that you are.' Yoss had never thought of himself as the painter's student, but by the time he had considered it, Master Hans was deep in concentration again, and he hardly dared to reply. And there were other things the painter said, single sentences, or even just words. 'Grey?' once. 'Mortal, mortal . . .' another time.

But Yoss didn't require anything more. It was enough to be a part of the great work that was taking shape in the hall. When the painter used a piece of charcoal to mark the outline of a cloud, for example, and told him to apply a base of pale yellow which he had just mixed, he was content to do it, while the painter worked silently on the glittering gold of a lion's-head shield, and the voice of Garner Zeb came booming through the windows.

'Do you like painting?' said Master Hans.

Yoss looked around in surprise. There was nothing to show that the painter had just asked him a question. He was lying on a raised plank close to the ceiling, working at the details of the lion's face on the shield.

'My father was a painter,' Master Hans continued, still working with his brush. 'He was very successful. He had a large studio. He was my teacher.'

'So that's how you learned to paint?'

'He was my teacher,' Master Hans repeated.

The painter was silent for while. Yoss thought he had finished talking. He dipped his brush in his bowl of paint and turned back to his cloud.

'He was a very successful painter. I honestly don't think he was *better* than me. But how can you judge?' There was another pause, then the painter continued once again. 'In portraits, for example, I think I excel him, but I've had more practice. In his day, this is the only kind of work people wanted, to have their ceilings and walls painted. No canvases. But if you ask about success, well, he had a large studio, and earned a lot of money, more money than me. I've never been interested in having a studio. When my father was alive, we used to have terrible arguments about it. At first I tried, but my assistants never stopped talking or asking questions. "Why do you use that

silver ground for that blue dress?" "Why do you place the light
from the left instead of the right?" I always ended up chasing
them away. I wanted to paint, not talk.'

Yoss nodded. Sometimes when he was on one of the mountains at home, high on the Middlesnag, for example, he just
wanted to have silence, and if he was with Herman or some of
the other boys, he just wanted them to stop talking. When they
were talking up there, it was impossible to think. Their words
tore the air. When he felt like that, he would think about
Moritz, and the time when he had been all alone in the snow
cave for six days with the dead mountain goat and the visions
that he saw, and the silence all around him.

Master Hans was speaking again.

'Now I travel from one patron to another. If someone will
pay me, and if they want me to do something interesting and
important, I'll come to them and do it. No, I don't earn the
most money this way. If I had a studio, like my father, and
many assistants working for me, I would be a much wealthier
man. But I paint what I like in the way that I choose. My
father was never able to do that. He had a big studio so he
needed every commission, and he always had to agree to do
what he was told. In the end he hardly managed to paint a
stroke himself; it was as much as he could do to keep an eye on
everybody else. But I work alone and take as long as I like.
That portrait of the lady, the merchant's wife, I could have finished it a month ago. But why should I hurry? The merchant
pays me well and in the meantime I live in his house. He
grumbles, but he's happy. One day he'll boast to his friends
how much that portrait cost him. Merchants don't understand
painting. The more they pay, the better it must be. But I will
paint him a truly great picture. A truly great picture, Yoss. I'll

take as much care and time over it as I want. Of course, they won't appreciate it. They'd be happy with something half as good that would take a tenth of the time. But I don't paint it for them, I paint it for me.'

Yoss stopped painting. 'She's very beautiful, the merchant's wife,' he said.

'Yes,' said the painter. 'In her way. Not perfect, but nature is imperfect. That's the point, isn't it? Her face deserves a great picture.'

'But she's sad,' said Yoss.

'How do you know?' asked the painter.

'She cries.'

'But only when she sees you, Yoss.'

'Then I won't see her again! I don't want to make her sad.'

'But if you didn't see her,' replied Master Hans, 'that would make her even sadder.'

'Then I don't understand!' said Yoss.

Master Hans didn't explain. 'She's sad. You're right. I don't know why. Each person has his reasons. She wants me to paint her cheerful, but I can't. She smiles, and laughs, and makes fun of me whenever she can, but in her soul, she's sad. Do you know how I can tell? In her eyes, Yoss. The eyes are the windows on the soul.'

Yoss frowned. He watched Master Hans. The shield that was appearing under his brush glittered and flashed, as if real sunlight fell across it. A shield like that wasn't for defence, it was a weapon, thought Yoss suddenly. It would blind whoever looked at it.

Yoss turned back to his cloud. Of course, this was merely the first layer of colour, a flat sheet of yellow, and it didn't really look like a cloud at all. Master Hans would later embellish it and make it bubble and billow with flaring greys and blues. Yoss painted just as he had been shown, applying the colour evenly across the plaster. Finally he was finished. He set the brush down beside the paint bowl. Master Hans was still concentrating on his detailed work. Yoss sat on the planks of the scaffolding to watch him. Whites and yellows created the gleaming metal of the shield.

Why was the merchant's wife sad? Why did seeing *him* make her cry?

'I come from a village,' said Yoss suddenly.

He paused. Master Hans continued to work.

'It's far away, and there are mountains all around it, and even after that you have to walk around a huge lake and even after that there's a forest and a marsh before you get anywhere near here. I had a friend with me when I left and when he saw the lake he turned back. His name's Herman and he's a carpenter. Well, he wants to be a carpenter one day. Actually . . . by now he's probably a carpenter's apprentice.'

Yoss paused again. He didn't know whether the painter was listening and, if he was listening, whether he was interested. You could never tell with Master Hans. He just kept working, interrupting himself only to turn his head and change his brushes or dip into one of the paint bowls that were on the plank beside him.

'Why did you leave?' said the painter.

Yoss shrugged. 'Because we had to. All the boys leave, and when you go back, you're a man.'

'And Herman?'

'Herman's already a man by now, because he's gone back.'

'But he turned back at the lake.'

'That doesn't matter. When I told the merchant's wife, she

said he should have come with me. But she's wrong. It's only meant to be a symbol. Long ago boys used to go out and they couldn't return until they found something to bring back to the village, but you don't have to do that any more.'

Master Hans rolled himself off his plank. He sat down on the scaffolding beside Yoss, and then he leaned back on his elbows, to look at what he had done from a greater distance. He stared at it for a while, turning his head one way and the other. He grunted. Then he climbed up again, lay on his back, picked up his brush and smudged some of the yellow paint off the plaster with his thumb.

'What will *you* take back, Yoss?' he said after he had started working again.

Yoss was surprised at the question. He thought the painter must have forgotten about what he had been saying.

'I was thinking . . . maybe I would take some nutmegs,' he replied.

'Nutmegs?'

'No one in the village has ever seen nutmegs. I'd never seen them until I came here.'

'You won't be able to grow them, you know. They only grow in very hot places. On islands, a long way away.'

'I know,' said Yoss. 'It doesn't matter if they won't grow. They're still something no one in the village has ever seen.'

'Maybe they haven't seen them, but they won't be much use, will they? What if people enjoy the flavour? They'll never be able to get any more.'

'But at least they'll have tasted it,' said Yoss.

The painter grunted. He wasn't impressed. Yoss wondered whether he was right. Maybe taking nutmegs back wasn't much of an idea.

'What about this?' said the painter.

'What?'

'Painting. Does anyone know how to paint in your village?'

'Not like you, Master Hans. *Nothing* like you.'

Master Hans climbed down from the plank again. He picked up a lump of brown pigment and began to pare flakes of it into a bowl.

'If you knew how to paint, you could take that back, couldn't you?' he said as he worked with the knife. 'But of course, you'd have to learn.'

'You could teach me!'

'Me?' The painter looked up. 'No. I told you, you're not my student. You'd ask too many questions and I'd chase you away.'

'I wouldn't.'

'Why have I chosen that yellow ground for the clouds, the colour you just put on? Clouds aren't yellow.'

'Why *have* you chosen it?' said Yoss.

'See?' said the painter. 'You've already started.'

'That was a trick!'

'So?' The painter shrugged. He picked up a cup and poured a little water into the bowl. He began to mix the paint, watching it carefully to judge its consistency. 'Everyone will trick you in the town, Yoss. How do you know you're not being tricked right now?'

'Now?' Yoss stared at the painter in bewilderment. 'What does that mean?'

Master Hans added another drop of water and continued to mix. 'You'll never get by in the town if you don't try a few tricks of your own. Haven't you worked that out yet, Yoss?' The painter shook his head, peering into the bowl. 'No, I don't suppose they taught you that in the village. Anyway, if you did want to learn to paint, it would take years, four or five years at least. Think about that. Even then you'd just be ready to begin. And do you know what would happen? So many years would have gone by, you wouldn't want to go back to your village at all.'

'Never!' cried Yoss.

'Oh, yes.' The painter looked up at the boy. 'Stay here, and you'll become a creature of the town. If you ever want to go back to your village, Yoss, go now.'

20

IN THE DAYS before Kelmuss Week, the Exchange had a festive air. Ribbons were tied around the fluted wooden pillars that supported its roof, and fake moneybags were hung from the beams. It was the only time of the year when drink was permitted in the Exchange, and boys from the nearby inns arrived with trays of wine and Kelmuss whisky, and did a brisk trade. Of course, real moneybags were still more important than the fake variety, and commerce continued unabated amongst the wooden pillars and at the desks that lined the walls. But voices were louder and laughter more frequent than at other times of the year, and one might have had the impression that business, at least sometimes, could mix with pleasure, although not a single merchant at the Exchange really believed that it should.

But on this particular afternoon the mood was not one of festivity, but of uproar. Merchant Grossfuss had not appeared to take up his position in front of the column where he had stood every day for the past fifty years. Grossfuss was enormously wealthy and his network of relationships with merchants in other towns was the envy of the Exchange. Rumours were flying. He had fallen stone dead with his face in his soup. He had tumbled downstairs and broken his neck. He had had a stroke and wouldn't last until evening. Grossfuss was so old, and had appeared to be so healthy, that people had begun to think Death had forgotten him. Each morning and afternoon he would make his way to the Exchange on his own two legs, and his pace was faster than that of many who were ten or even twenty years younger. But Death must have finally remembered him, because now people were saying that he would never enter the Exchange again, on his own legs or anyone else's.

The merchant, seated at a desk with Krantz on one side of him and Pressler on the other, watched his fellow members of the Exchange as they worked themselves into a frenzy. The drinks that they were taking from the boys, who swung amongst them with their trays, weren't helping to calm the situation. They stood in small, noisy groups, remonstrating and gesticulating with each other. First Krantz, then Pressler, got up to join the others. Soon they were gesticulating as well. The merchant watched them sceptically. Anyone would have thought the day of judgement had arrived, and they were going to be weighed in the scales against their gold. It was only Emil Grossfuss who was dying, after all.

Suddenly there was a hush. Grossfuss' son had arrived. He stood in the middle of the floor. His father, he announced, was gravely ill. The glum expression on his face suggested that the grave illness would soon be replaced by a less temporary condition.

The merchant got up. He walked from one group to another, listening to what was being said. Now that Grossfuss was gone, the Exchange would never be the same again, the merchants were telling each another. There wasn't a single one there who had known the Exchange without him. Grossfuss was like one of the pillars that held up the roof, they all agreed. The merchant smiled to himself. They all knew that Grossfuss was no pillar and his disappearance would cause nothing to collapse – except the wealth of the Grossfuss family itself. There were two sons. One had bought himself a commission in the army, and no longer believed that trade was a fit profession for a gentleman.

The other, who had arrived with the announcement, was a fool. Old Grossfuss had never allowed him to strike a single deal for himself. What the father had accumulated, the son was certain to dissipate. If the business passed into his hands it would be squandered within a year, and each part that was squandered would pass into the hands of someone else. So old Grossfuss' death was a strange paradox, which a philosophical tailor, for example, might have pondered with interest. His demise represented a loss to the Exchange, as a whole, but a gain to its members, as individuals. And as the merchants remonstrated and gesticulated, took a glass and raised it righteously to old Grossfuss' memory, recalled the legendary bargains he had struck and the men he had ruined, speculated about the splendour of the memorial service that the Exchange must hold to honour him, each was secretly calculating in his mind what part of the spoils he could hope to gain. Because, after all, they were still merchants, even if it was one of their own brother merchants who was dying, and the nature of merchants is to seek opportunity in every event, and few events bring opportunity to one person without bringing loss to another, as Emil Grossfuss himself, always quick to push home his advantage, would have been the first to admit.

And in pushing home the advantage, it was each man for himself. Those who stood commiserating with one another longest would gain the least. A number had already slipped away. Pressler, for example, had disappeared. Perhaps some had gone to the Grossfuss mansion to find out the truth of the situation in the guise of offering condolences to the widow. Some, the merchant knew, would already be on the way back to their counting rooms, to write letters to Grossfuss' partners in other towns.

The merchant had not left the Exchange yet, but that was because he was still evaluating the situation. He liked to know where a course of action was likely to lead before he set off on it. His mind approached the problem coldly, without emotion. The shrewdest bargains are struck by those who are able to see the matter through the eyes of the other party. So often had the merchant applied this rule, that he did it now without once having to stop and think about it. In those other towns, Grossfuss' partners were going to get twenty different letters, all asking for the old man's business. If you were one of those merchants, receiving all those letters, how would you choose between them? Whom would you trust, whom would you favour?

The answer was simple. You would favour the one who didn't send you a letter at all . . . but came in person.

The more the merchant thought about it, the more obvious this course of action appeared. It seemed *so* obvious that he actually had to stop and ask himself whether he wasn't missing some equally obvious objection. But he couldn't think of one. The others wouldn't budge, he knew. They would all want to be home to enjoy the Kelmuss festivities. Besides, they were too greedy. They would write to every one of Grossfuss' partners, hoping to succeed with them all. Consequently, they would succeed with none. But he would choose just one, Grossfuss' most important partner. He would visit him, cajole him, win him over and be back before the old man was even laid in his grave. The others could fight over the morsels – he would seize the plum!

It was Rosteck. He was the jewel in Grossfuss' crown. From Rosteck, as everyone knew, came fine furs, resins, amber and consignments of the best pine lumber that had earned Grossfuss a fortune many times over. While the others were sending messengers in every direction, he would concentrate on Rosteck and Rosteck alone. And while Rosteck would receive twenty different letters, only *one* merchant would come to him in person.

Now the merchant took one last look at his rivals, still standing and talking in the Exchange, and slipped away.

~

'GREGOR!' he roared as he strode across the courtyard.

The servant, who had been taking a nap in the master's smoking room, put his head out of a window.

'Get my things,' the merchant called up to him. 'We're off.'

'Off?' whispered the merchant's wife to herself when she heard her husband's voice. 'What's happened?'

'I'm going to visit Rosteck!' he announced, bursting into her room. He had taken the steps two at a time in his impatience and enthusiasm. 'So kiss me and wish me luck.'

She kissed him. 'But why? It's almost Kelmuss Week.'

'Exactly!' exclaimed the merchant. 'That's why none of the others will go, I'm sure of it. Grossfuss is dead, Eleanor!'

The merchant's wife stared. 'Dead?' she whispered.

'Dead in his soup. Well, that's one of the stories. Very sad. Still, he was an old man. How long could he expect to live? Should've died years ago.'

'Oh, Simon, how can you say that?'

'Exactly. Very sad. But he's dead and no one can change it. It's up to the living to live, and I'm going to Rosteck to get his business.'

'But he's barely cold . . .'

'Warm, cold, makes no difference. I'm off. Won't take more than a few days.'

'A few days? Stay for your supper, at least.'

The merchant shook his head. 'I'm going down to talk to Zeb, and I'll come back up to say goodbye before I go. Will you watch what Gregor's doing, Eleanor? Make sure he doesn't forget anything. And see what food he packs. Last time he brought nothing but pigeon pie. Did I tell you? I couldn't stand the sight of it by the end of the second day.'

'I don't think we have any pigeon pie.'

'Just as well!' called the merchant, who was already on his way to the stairs.

The merchant's wife listened to his footsteps in the corridor, thinking how lonely she would be when he was gone. And at Kelmuss Week! What could be lonelier than to be alone at Kelmuss Week? But she was always lonely, and he never seemed to realize it. If it weren't for the boy . . .

The woman's eyes went wide. The boy!

'Zeb!' cried the merchant as he bounded into the courtyard. 'Zeb! Where are you, Zeb?'

The foreman came out of one of the storerooms.

'Zeb! I've got to — Zeb? What's wrong?' The merchant paused. 'You haven't been sleeping, have you?'

'No, master. You're . . . You're early. You're never back before —'

'Always be early, never be late!' exclaimed the merchant ebulliently. 'There's a lesson for you and I give it for free. Beetle! Tomas!' he cried, seeing the workmen rolling a barrel towards a cart in the courtyard. 'Look lively but take care. That's the way, boys. It's fine wine you're rolling there. If you drank a quart you'd be flat on your face with the biggest smile you ever had.'

Tomas grinned. The Beetle frowned at the joke.

'Give them a jug at the end of the day,' the merchant cried to Garner Zeb. 'Drink to Emil Grossfuss, may he quickly rest in peace.'

'What? A jug of that wine for them?'

'Don't be ridiculous,' muttered the merchant. 'A jug of that horrible stuff we can't get rid of.' The merchant elbowed him in the ribs. 'Come on, Zeb, down to business. Let's go into the counting house. I'm off to visit Rosteck. Grossfuss is dead, haven't you heard?' The merchant turned to him with a grin. 'Just imagine, Zeb, what business I can do with Rosteck. We'll need bigger storerooms by this time next year. Where shall we get 'em, eh? I've heard that Muntz might fold. He has that big warehouse by the Mill Bridge. What do you think, Zeb? We could . . . Zeb? What is it, Zeb?'

'Nothing. Muntz's warehouse. I heard you.'

The merchant gave Zeb a puzzled look. 'Something on your mind?'

'Nothing.'

'Something I should know about?'

The foreman shook his head.

'You're not sick, are you, Zeb? Don't be sick now. I'll be away for a week. You can be sick after I come back.'

Garner Zeb forced a smile. 'I'm not sick.'

'Well, you're acting damn peculiar, then, if you don't mind me saying so.' The merchant shook his head. 'Damn peculiar,' he muttered to himself, as he unlocked the door of his counting room.

The merchant sat down at his desk. The foreman took up his usual place, on a stool beside the wall. The merchant shuffled through his papers, studying the contracts and orders in front of him. He began to read out the deliveries that were expected and those that had to be made. Garner Zeb took out his stick and made a notch for each instruction. When he was finished, the merchant pushed the papers aside. He didn't need to give any other orders. The foreman had looked after his affairs so often that he knew exactly what to do if something came up. The merchant unlocked a safe and took out a purse and emptied the coins on the table in front of him. He had no inhibitions before Zeb. He counted the coins and returned them to the purse. Then he reached into the safe and took out some more coins and added them as well.

'Help me,' said the merchant, and he stood up and raised his shirt, and Zeb tied the purse around his body. 'That's it. Nice and tight, Zeb. I like to feel it's there.'

The foreman nodded. He finished tying the purse and stood back.

'Good,' said the merchant, and he gave Zeb one last questioning glance, but the other man didn't meet his eyes. 'All right!' said the merchant heartily, as if he had decided to put all concerns out of his mind.

They left the room. The merchant's spirits were soaring at the prospect of the journey and the advantages he hoped to gain. Tomas and the Beetle were rolling another barrel. The merchant stopped to watch them. Paulus wandered out of the coopery, singsonging to himself. They were all fine men. Well, maybe not Paulus. Why not? Paulus was a fine man as well! Each had his foibles, each his individual character. Tomas was a bit of a troublemaker. Paulus was a bit soft in the head, and the Beetle, well, who could ever tell what the Beetle was thinking? But they were all honest and hard-working, and if they robbed him at all, it was only a little, never more than a cupful of grain or a handful of nuts for their hungry families.

The sight of them filled him with satisfaction. The world was a great fleshy woman and she suckled him abundantly at her magnificent breast. 'Where's the boy?' he said.

'The boy?'

'Over there, is he, in the grain store?' The merchant chuckled. 'Yoss!'

He was already marching to the doorway of the grain store. Tomas and the Beetle stopped pushing the barrel. They stood up and watched.

'Yoss?' The merchant was on his way to the next storeroom, and then he went to the one after that, still calling the boy's name. Garner Zeb followed him, speechless with dismay.

'Where is he?' The merchant grinned, as if it were a game. 'In the stable?'

Garner Zeb shook his head.

'You haven't left him in the spice room by himself. You know, Zeb, no one in there without you!'

The foreman held up the key to the spice room.

'Then where is he?' Now the merchant's high spirits were turning to impatience.

Zeb tried to speak. Still the words wouldn't come out.

'Well?'

Garner Zeb took a deep breath. 'He's with the painter.'

The merchant stared at him uncomprehendingly.

'He's upstairs with the painter. He goes there. The mistress said he could.'

'He goes there?' whispered the merchant. 'Upstairs?'

Zeb nodded. 'You came back early.'

'He *goes* there? The mistress said he could?'

The merchant went white. He began to shake. He turned, and then he looked back at Zeb, and then he turned and set off for the staircase but at the foot of the stairs he stopped and turned again, and he fixed the foreman with a look that was a mixture of anguish and anger and disbelief, like a man in a duel who looks down and discovers that he has been pierced.

For a moment he couldn't speak. Then he raised a finger, and it was trembling.

'You?' he cried hoarsely. 'You knew, and you didn't tell me? *You*, Zeb?'

~

THE MERCHANT came up the stairs at a run. He brushed his wife away and went storming down the corridor. He threw open the doors to the hall and plunged into the forest of scaffolding that stood inside.

And there, high on the scaffold beside the painter, was the boy.

The merchant crooked a finger and beckoned him to the ground.

'Do you know what you are?' said the merchant, when the boy stood in front of him. His voice was strangely quiet, and even, and one could easily have thought that he was perfectly calm.

The boy didn't reply. The merchant stood over him, lips pursed, eyes narrowed. The painter, high in the scaffolding, gazed down at them. The merchant's wife watched from the doorway, where she had stopped.

'Do you know what you are?' repeated the merchant.

The boy silently shook his head.

'Then I'll show you!'

The merchant seized Yoss' arm. He turned and dragged him away. The woman reached out but the merchant shrugged her off. Down the corridor he took the boy, the woman shouting and running behind him, servants appearing out of doorways, the boy slipping and stumbling and being pulled along on his heels. At the top of the stairs, the merchant stopped.

Everyone in the corridor froze.

The merchant looked down at Yoss. His eyes were blazing with anger.

'So, you don't know what you are?' he said. 'I'll tell you. You're a slave. And do you know where slaves belong?'

'Where do they belong?' whispered Yoss.

'Down there!' snarled the merchant, and he shoved him onto the stairs.

There was an instant when the boy teetered, and might yet have saved himself, had only his hands, reaching out, succeeded in grasping the balustrade. But then he was falling. He tumbled, spun and bounced down the wide marble staircase that lead to the courtyard below.

His body slid over the last of the steps, rolled over a couple of times, and finally came to rest, lying on its side, not far from the bottom of the staircase.

Garner Zeb crouched over him.

'Lock him up,' thundered the merchant. 'Keep him locked up until I get back.'

The foreman looked up. 'Where shall I lock him?' he asked huskily.

'Where? Where he can't get out! Put him in the spice room. And if you let him out before I'm back, Zeb, I swear you'll pay for it. Don't think I won't find out because I will.'

21

'I HAVEN'T TIME. I haven't time for this!' declared the merchant.

'Of course you don't. You need to leave,' retorted his wife. 'There's another bargain to be struck, isn't there? More profit to be made, more gold for your safe. Well, take your gold. Keep it!' She tore one of the rings off her finger and flung it at her husband. It flew past his ear and cracked a windowpane.

The merchant flinched, but he didn't turn around. He continued to gaze out of the window. Below, in the courtyard, Garner Zeb had just disappeared into the spice room, carrying the boy.

'It was an accident. I didn't mean to hurt him.'

'Was it an accident that someone threw him down the stairs?'

'He fell!'

The woman scoffed.

'It's your fault,' murmured the merchant. He turned around angrily. 'Who asked you to let him up here? Who gave you permission?'

'Who gave me permission? Who gave *you* permission to bring him here in the first place?'

The merchant stared in indignation. 'I bought him! He's like a horse, madam. I don't ask your permission when I buy a horse. Why should I ask it when I buy a boy?'

The woman shook her head. She sat down.

'Look at yourself, Simon.'

'What should I look at? Tell me, what?'

'Who ever heard of such a thing, to buy a boy? Perhaps you bought me as well. If you can buy a boy, why not a woman? Well, did you buy me, Simon? Is that what you think?'

'You're mad. I married you. The magistrate *sold* this boy to me.'

'And who is the magistrate to sell a boy?'

'As good as any other man to sell a slave!' replied the merchant sharply. 'Perhaps you forget what the alternative was. Or would you prefer that he should hang? Well, then, take him back. The other rogues stand trial next week, there's still time to add him to the list.' The merchant peered jeeringly at his wife. 'Take him back, madam. Why are you waiting? I write off the cost. Tell the magistrate he can keep the money. Yes, go on. Do as your conscience dictates, Eleanor. I, foolish man, thought I might *save* the boy. Some people would call it charity.' The merchant threw up his hands in exasperation. 'I haven't time for this. I haven't. I must leave.' He moved towards the door.

'You can't buy everything,' said his wife suddenly.

The merchant stopped. 'What does that mean?'

The woman smiled sadly. 'You can't buy a child.'

'Is that what you think?' demanded the merchant, hands on his hips. 'Madam, I will give you a child, more than one, just wait and see.'

The woman shook her head. 'No, you won't. You know you won't. If you could, it would already have happened.'

The man didn't reply. He made as if he were about to speak, then slumped silently in a chair.

The woman took his hands. 'Simon. Simon, do you think I'm not happy? I am happy. You make me happy.'

'How can you be?' he demanded in misery.

'I am. If you don't believe me, *then* I can't be. Simon, look at me. Look at me. You cannot buy this child. If we treat him well, with love, then perhaps he'll love us in return. But you can't *buy* him.' The woman shook her head. She let go of her husband's hands and stood up. 'Sometimes I think you don't know how to treat anything but as a piece of business, something to buy or sell, something from which there'll be profit or loss. He's a boy, not a horse. He's a child and you make him work like a man.'

The merchant looked up at her. Their eyes met.

'I bought him,' the man said quietly. 'He's mine. He'll do whatever he's told.'

'He won't.'

'He will.' The merchant rose. 'He will, I tell you!'

'Simon, what's happened to you? When did—'

The woman stopped. The man had gone. His footsteps echoed on the floor of the corridor outside, growing fainter. She heard him shouting. 'Gregor! Gregor!'

The woman went to the window. She bent down and recovered the ring she had thrown, and she gazed at it wistfully, turning it from side to side in her hand. Then she heard horses in the courtyard. She looked down through the cracked windowpane and saw her husband leaving with his servant. The tall figure of Garner Zeb closed the gate behind them.

'Simon,' she murmured, pinching the ring between her fingers, 'when did you become so hard?'

22

IN A ROOM above the jail, the magistrate and his family were at table. The magistrate's wife was a large, plump woman, and there were three children, a son of eight, and two younger daughters, twins. There was bread in front of them, and a pie, of which the crust was burnt. But they were eating it anyway. The girl who helped the magistrate's wife was young and very inexpert, and the woman thought she was probably somewhat soft in her head as well. She came from one of the villages on the plain outside the town, and everyone knew that in such villages uncles married nieces and brothers raped their sisters and all kinds of idiots, cripples and monsters resulted from the unnatural unions. It seemed that pie-baking wasn't something the girl was capable of learning, nor stew-making, for that matter, nor anything else that involved cookery or care.

One of the little girls screwed up her face at a piece of the burnt crust. The other little girl giggled. The boy watched. He itched to throw some crust at them. He stole a glance at his father to see if he was looking.

One of his sisters took a nibble of her pie and pretended to choke. She clutched her neck. The other one almost collapsed in laughter.

'That's enough!' said the woman. 'If this isn't good enough, then maybe you'd be happier with nothing at all.'

The little girls became serious. They stared at their plates, their lips pursed, their eyes downcast, like two angelic little peas from the same pod. All they had to do was put on their serious faces, and they could get away with anything. Their brother swung his leg under the table, trying to kick one of them, but he couldn't reach.

All three of the children knew what was coming next.

'Just think of all the people who'd kill for a piece of pie like that. Just think of all the people *downstairs*. Right, Walther?'

The magistrate nodded. The children looked at him. He raised one eyebrow, just a fraction. They tried to stifle their giggles.

Downstairs. Their mother was always threatening the children with *Downstairs*, but they weren't frightened of it at all. They had never been to the cells. Their only knowledge of what existed in the jail beneath them came from their father, and he was always telling them funny stories about the rogues and beggars who ended up there, and the curious things they did and how he always let them go in the end. In their minds, the place was a kind of community of naughty clowns and repentant robbers. And even though they saw, from their windows, the processions that regularly left the jail on their way to the gallows, with their father walking at the head and two or four or five of the clowns and rogues following him with ropes around their necks, they never connected these sights in their minds with the *Downstairs* that their mother was always mentioning.

The woman was looking at him. 'Are you going down, Walther?'

The magistrate nodded.

'Oh, can I come?' cried the boy. 'Can I come, please?'

'No!' cried the woman.

The magistrate smiled. 'I've told you. Little boys aren't allowed there. Nor little girls neither,' he said, turning to his daughters, and chuckling.

'But I'm not a *little* boy,' said the child.

'Come on, we'll see,' said the magistrate. He leaned his elbow on the table. The boy eagerly jumped off his chair and put his elbow on the table and gripped his father's hand.

'Ready?' said the magistrate.

The boy nodded.

'Go!'

The boy strained, trying to force his father's hand down to the table. The father's arm didn't budge. The boy gritted his teeth. The magistrate looked out the window, started to whistle. He glanced at his daughters, and raised his eyebrows a couple of times. The little girls collapsed in giggles.

'*Two hands!*' cried the magistrate.

The boy slapped his other hand against the magistrate's fist and pulled as hard as he could. The magistrate wavered. His hand started to fall. He frowned as if in effort and surprise. The two little girls, as always, watched with wide eyes.

Then the magistrate swung his arm over swiftly and left the boy almost flat across the table.

'Not today,' he said, and he ruffled his son's hair, and stood up to go.

~

THE JAILER opened the cell door. The magistrate recoiled as the stench hit him. Then he went inside.

The fat man had grown thinner since the last time he had seen him. The other one was reduced to skin and bones.

The magistrate began.

'It's my duty to tell you that you'll be tried next week, on the first day after Kelmuss Week. You should think about what you're going to say. The best defence is to admit the truth.'

The fat one's lip curled disdainfully. 'Is it your duty to say that as well?'

The magistrate ignored him. 'If you admit everything,' he continued, 'you can be sure the judges will take it into account.'

'How?' cried Gaspar.

'Yes, how?' repeated Conrad mockingly. 'Will they shorten the noose? Or perhaps they'll make it longer. Or perhaps they'll ask the hangman to make a special knot. Tell us, please. My friend is *dying* to know.'

The magistrate glared at Conrad. The weeks in jail, half-starving, hadn't chastened him.

'We don't *need* your confession,' he said, 'don't think we do. I'm telling you this for your own good.'

'Take note, Gasparto,' said Conrad sharply, 'they don't need our confession. Didn't I tell you? We'd both be on the rack already if they did.'

The magistrate watched Conrad with distaste. He had completed his duty. He could leave now. But he didn't go. He remembered how the straw-haired man had made a fool of him the last time. The rogue had been so clever with his tongue, he had almost released him.

The magistrate glanced over his shoulder to check that the guards were still outside.

'You'll regret playing the Clever Eddy with me,' he said quietly.

'I'm sure I shall,' Conrad replied with mock apprehension.

'I talked to the innkeeper. Or perhaps I should say . . . he talked to me.'

'He always talks. Just ask him how he is and you'll be there for an hour listening to his complaints. Is he still alive, by the way? If that cough of his hasn't killed him already, one of his customers will.'

'He told us about the mule.'

Conrad didn't bat an eyelid.

'It was a fine mule, wasn't it? What did he give you for it, Conrad? Ten silver pieces? Twelve?'

'Fifteen.'

'Gaspar . . .'

'Come now, Conrad. He's only telling what he knows. Fifteen, wasn't it? Of course, five was for the saddle. Still, no need to be ashamed. You did well, to screw that much out of Farber. You ought to be proud of yourself.'

'Farber will say anything. Did you know he puts horse meat in his stew?'

'On the other hand, perhaps you could have done better with the saddle,' said the magistrate.

'Should never have given him the saddle,' muttered Gaspar resentfully.

'Quite right, lad. It was a fine piece. The merchant described it perfectly before the innkeeper handed it over.'

'If you really believe these lies,' said Conrad, 'it must be very disturbing for you, to think that the town's innkeepers deal in stolen goods. Isn't it your job to put a stop to that kind of thing? The council will start to wonder why it bothers paying you.'

'On the contrary,' replied the magistrate, 'the good Host Farber had no idea the goods were stolen. And why should he? When you came to him you told him the mule and saddle were your own. I'm sure you were very convincing.'

'Then it seems no honest traveller to this town is safe,' retorted Conrad. 'An innkeeper merely has to allege he's holding stolen goods, and you throw him into jail. Ride into town on your own mule and before you know it you're locked in a cell with every child in the town pissing on your head.'

'Oh, did they piss on your head, Conrad?'

'No,' said Conrad, pointing to Gaspar, 'on his.'

The magistrate clenched his jaw. He was a clever one, this Conrad. The sort you wouldn't forget in a hurry, even after he'd danced his last jig on the end of the rope.

'Didn't you say it was rings and chains that were taken?' said Conrad, and he gave the magistrate a puzzled glance, as if he were genuinely confused. 'And wasn't there some kind of purse? Or have I forgotten the charges?'

The magistrate shook his head in disdain. He turned to Gaspar, who was cowering on his mattress, gazing up at him anxiously. 'Admit everything,' he said. 'That's the best defence.'

'The best defence if you enjoy being hanged.'

The magistrate spun to face Conrad. 'You!' he said angrily. 'You and I will have some fun if you're not careful. The judges like to know everything about a man, and if he won't tell them, they'll ask me to help loosen his tongue. Sometimes I loosen it . . . *physically*.'

'Do you?' said Conrad.

'Have you ever seen, my friend, what a pair of pincers can do to a man? Or a piece of charcoal? Take a simple piece of charcoal when it's glowing red. Pain is a simple thing. It's very easy to provoke.'

Conrad glanced at Gaspar. He was watching with terror.

'No, I wouldn't worry about him,' said the magistrate. 'I think the judges will be much more interested in you.'

'I *am* more interesting.'

'Are you? Why?'

'You tell me.'

The magistrate shook his head contemptuously. 'You flatter yourself. You can talk, and you think that makes you some-body. I don't think you're interesting at all. A common ruffian and thief. Make no mistake. The mule would be enough to hang you, without anything else. Robbery at knifepoint? That's enough. Even if you'd only taken a hair from the mule's tail it would be enough.'

'Robbery at knifepoint?' Conrad laughed. 'I suppose the boy told you that as well. What an imagination he has! Where is he, by the way?'

'Safe from you.'

'He ought to be here with us. He must be lonely. He depends on us, you know. Where did you say he was?'

'Think about what I said,' the magistrate remarked, turning to the door.

'*You* have a boy, don't you?'

The magistrate stopped in his tracks.

'Yes. A boy. And . . . let me see . . . *two* little girls. You must fear for them, sometimes, upstairs, with all these criminals down here. Must give you sleepless nights. Just think, if one of us should escape, and find his way up there, what things he would do to them.'

23

GARNER ZEB laid Yoss down in the spice room. He hung a
lantern from the roof, and its light flickered over the sacks and
casks that were stacked against the walls. The workmen
brought a mattress of straw, and a pail of water, and they stood
on the threshold and peered in as Zeb knelt beside the boy and
bathed his cuts. Later Zeb sent the workmen away, and he
asked Tomas to call on his wife to say that he would not be
home that night.

The boy's injuries were severe. Bruises appeared under his
skin. His knee swelled. His neck became rigid, and blood
trickled out of one of his ears. Sometimes he appeared to be
awake, and sometimes unconscious, but this was not normal
sleep, and Zeb watched him with trepidation. Once, when the
boy opened his eyes, the foreman raised his head in his arms
and brought a cup of water to his lips, and tried to force the
fluid into his mouth, but the water ran out again. So Zeb took
up his position once more and watched.

Night came on. The lantern burned. The boy tossed
painfully on his mattress, or lay with eerie stillness. Zeb lost
track of time. He dozed, resting against sacks of cinnamon.
Then something woke him. He looked around. There was the
merchant's wife, standing in the doorway.

She was pale.

'May I . . . come in?' she whispered.

The foreman shrugged. He looked at the boy. The woman
hesitated a moment, then advanced gingerly. She stopped

beside the mattress.

'You've attended to him, Zeb.'

The foreman grunted.

The woman knelt. She tilted her head, to see the boy's face better. 'He's peaceful now.' She reached out a hand and touched Yoss' cheek. 'He sleeps.'

She reached out to the boy's cheek once more. Her fingers trembled. Suddenly she leaned forward and touched her lips to the boy's forehead. When she straightened up, there were tears in her eyes. She wiped them away, still gazing at the boy.

Zeb watched her. What was the point of coming down here, like this? In three years, she had never once come down into the courtyard but to hurry across it on her way out of the house. It wasn't her world, so what was she doing here now? If she had let alone, if she hadn't interfered and taken the boy to the upper floor, none of this would have happened. The boy couldn't have fallen down the stairs if he hadn't been at the top of them in the first place.

'Simon said it was my fault,' said the woman, as if in reply to the foreman's thoughts. The tears came faster, and as quickly as she wiped at them, others fell. Her shoulders shook. Suddenly she turned to look at the foreman. '*Was* it my fault?'

Zeb made no reply.

'He said that I had no right to speak to him. Not even to *speak* to him.'

The foreman didn't know what to say. In silence, the woman wept.

'I don't know too much about who has the rights to do one thing or another,' muttered Garner Zeb eventually.

'But it's true, isn't it?' she demanded, turning to him with reddened, anguished eyes. 'If I hadn't made you send him to me, this would never have happened. And you didn't want to send him, did you? I *made* you send him.'

'That's true, madam.'

'So it *is* my fault!' exclaimed the woman, and she put her clenched fist to her mouth, as she sobbed over the boy, and bit, as if to fix her sorrow in her flesh.

The foreman frowned. He could feel a tear starting in his own eye. How could one blame her? Where was the malice in what she had done?

'Madam . . .' he said hoarsely.

The woman didn't respond.

'I didn't tell him,' said Zeb. He hesitated. 'The master, I mean . . . I could have told him. I should have, but I didn't. Does that make it my fault?'

The woman took her hand away from her lips. She looked at him.

'I don't know why,' he said, as much to himself as to the woman who was listening. 'I've never done it before, kept a secret from the master like that. Never even crossed my mind to do it.'

The woman nodded. 'You're the most loyal of men, Zeb. Simon often says it. He values no one more.'

'No, madam.'

'Yes. Without you, he would be lost. Don't you see it? You're his greatest friend.'

Zeb stared at the woman in astonishment.

'Sometimes I've been jealous of you myself.'

'Jealous of me? Madam, look at yourself . . . And me . . .'

The woman smiled sadly. She turned back to Yoss. The foreman continued to gaze at her in disbelief.

'Come, Zeb,' she said suddenly, 'give me the key to the room.

You must be going home to your family. What will your wife be thinking?'

'The wife knows. I sent Tomas to tell her. I'll be staying here tonight. You go to bed, madam. Get some rest. I'll see to the boy.'

The woman nodded. 'I should have known.'

'Go, madam. Sleep. I'll be here.'

'Yes, Zeb.' She got to her feet. 'If there's anything you need in the night . . . if anything happens . . . send for me.'

'Good night, madam.'

'Good night, then, Zeb.'

The woman stopped in the doorway and murmured 'Good night' once more.

Zeb continued to stare at the empty doorway long after she had gone, baffled by the conversation, almost wondering whether it had really happened at all. Then there was a groan from behind him, and he turned back to the boy.

~

DURING THE NIGHT Yoss became feverish. Zeb dozed, and each time he fell asleep he was awoken by the boy, and he heard strange names, Herman and Moritz, heard the boy speak with his mother, heard him talk about a Cradle and a Middlesnag. The boy's body lay on the mattress but his spirit was far away. In the morning he passed water and it was as red as blood. Garner Zeb stared at it with horror. What did it mean? The lady called for the blue doctor.

The doctor's suspicions were immediately aroused. He gazed at the boy from the doorway. What kind of a room was this in which to keep an injured child? Before him stood the lady of the house and a man who was obviously one of her workers.

Where was the master?

'Who is this boy?' asked the blue doctor.

'One of my boys, sir,' said Garner Zeb. 'He works here.'

'How was he injured?'

'He fell,' said the foreman.

'Fell?' said the doctor. 'Down some stairs, I suppose.'

'Yes. He slipped,' said the merchant's wife.

'Ah, of course. He slipped . . .' The blue doctor gave the lady a knowing, complicitous glance. He had seen many 'slippages' of servants before. But it wasn't the servants who paid his fees, but the masters, and if the masters said it was a slippage, a slippage it was. Guilt made for generous clients, he had learned by experience.

The blue doctor approached the mattress and knelt beside it. He was a man with thick eyebrows, a large nose and a sharp chin. His head, smoothly encased in a close-fitting cap, had the look of a large bird of prey, and the long blue cloak that settled around him as he knelt was like the wings of such a bird as it settles on the kill.

The doctor felt the boy's pulse at the elbow. Then he put both his hands on the boy's face. He rolled back the eyelids with his thumbs and peered into the eyes. He poked a finger into a cut on the cheek. He leaned forward and smelled the boy's breath. He turned the head from side to side and peered into the ears. Yoss moaned at this. The doctor ran his hands quickly over arms and legs. Yoss shivered and jumped as his bruises were squeezed. The doctor pressed on both sides of the ribs, and leaned forward and listened to the heart. Finally, he pressed down on the stomach. A long, low groan came out of the boy's mouth.

'Blood?' he said, glancing over his shoulder. 'Blood in the water, you say?'

'Yes, sir,' whispered Garner Zeb.

'Have you got it? Show me.'

Garner Zeb went to get the pot. The blue doctor left the mattress and took the container from the foreman when Zeb returned. He held it up to the lantern and gazed into it. Zeb and the merchant's wife watched anxiously. He produced a long-handled spoon from somewhere inside his cloak and raised a spoonful of the water and tipped it back into the bucket, studying the flow of the liquid as it fell.

'No clots,' he said, in a tone that suggested this was a bad sign. He wiped the spoon carefully on his cloak and put it back in his pocket. Then he turned around and faced the merchant's wife with his arms crossed.

'No broken bones,' he said. 'Only bruises and concussion.'

'And the water?'

'Ah, the water. Yes, that's what'll kill him.'

The woman stared at him in horror. 'Kill him?'

'Probably. The heart's damaged and the blood goes to the bladder. The only way to save him is with a poultice. Honey, mustard, caraway . . .' the doctor looked around, searching for inspiration. His eye came to rest on a sack brimming with bright yellow powder. 'Saffron. Plenty of it. You want the boy to live, don't you?' he said in an insinuating tone. 'Slippages are always so inconvenient to explain to the magistrate.'

'Of course we want him to live!' cried the woman, who hadn't given a thought to magistrates or the inconveniences of explanations.

'Then spare no expense! Add a John's Wort infusion, to be drunk as often as possible, and not less than three time a day. Change the poultice twice a day. Have you got John's Wort? Don't worry, I'll send my servant with some. The poultice over the heart, by the way, like so.' The doctor returned to the mattress, tore open Yoss' shirt and slapped his hand flat on the centre of his chest.

Garner Zeb and the woman nodded. The foreman pulled out his stick and began slashing notches in it.

'And he'll live?' whispered the merchant's wife.

'Probably not,' said the blue doctor, and held out his hand.

The woman put a gold piece on the doctor's palm. He picked it up and turned it over, examining it.

'Good. I'll be back tomorrow. And I'll send my servant with the wort.'

~

THE FOREMAN and the merchant's wife tended the boy. When one was not present, the other was sure to be there. Zeb brought a chair into the room for the lady's use. They didn't dare to take the boy out of the spice room because of the merchant's command for him to be kept there. The workmen stopped at the threshold, to peer in and whisper an inquiry about the boy's progress, but were reluctant to enter. Perhaps, since the merchant's wife was now to be found there, they felt it had become part of the world of the upper floor, to which they didn't belong.

Sylvie, the maid, came with her mistress to see him. 'Hasn't he got a lovely face?' she said, gazing at Yoss while he slept.

'He has,' said the merchant's wife.

'Can I put the poultice on him when you change it this evening, madam?' she asked.

'No.'

'But, madam . . .'

'No. It's a very important job. The poultice has to be put on just so, exactly as the doctor showed us, and you didn't see him when he showed us, did you?'

'But I saw you put it on, madam, after he left, and *you* saw the doctor, so it's just as good, isn't it?'

'Don't be insolent. Go out now and don't come back until it's time to give him the John's Wort again.'

'But, madam . . .' said the girl.

'Go! Now!'

The maid left. The merchant's wife turned back to Yoss. She thought about what she had said to the maid. The application of the poultice was a simple matter. But she was jealous, she knew, of anyone else who touched the boy's tender skin. She sighed, and she gazed at his face, and when the boy moved and his face contorted in a moment of pain, her face contorted with it, and whatever it was that he felt, she felt as well.

The blue doctor came back the next day and poked around at the poultice and criticized its shape and size and added an ointment of Sow Thistle to the prescription – his servant would bring it around – and took another gold piece and left. He came back the day after that and peered into the bucket and examined the boy's water with his spoon.

'Mmmm,' he said. 'It's lighter. He might live.'

The woman's face brightened.

'Saffron, madam,' admonished the doctor, as he took his gold piece, 'plenty of saffron!'

Two days later, there was no blood in Yoss' water at all. The blue doctor found him sitting up on the mattress. And he was hungry!

The merchant's wife was waiting to hear what the doctor had to say before she fed him.

The doctor made a great show of examining Yoss, particularly spending a lot of time over his mouth and the smell of his breath. Finally he stepped back with his hands on his hips.

'He can eat.'

Yoss grinned.

'Chicken, and a small amount of honey. He should keep drinking the John's Wort infusion for another two days at least.'

Yoss made a face.

'Oh, yes, my boy' said the blue doctor, 'that'll teach you to go slipping downstairs . . .' The doctor waited, giving Yoss a questioning glance

The boy looked back at him blankly.

'That'll teach you to be more careful . . . not to have accidents . . . on *stairs* . . .'

The merchant's wife pulled out two gold pieces and thrust them into the doctor's hand.

'Thank you. Thank you, madam.' The doctor took one last look at his patient. 'Madam, you *will* tell people how I cured the boy? Of course, you don't need to tell them how he came to be injured,' he added hurriedly, 'but if you just tell them that I cured him . . . you understand . . . I'd be very grateful.'

'Yes, doctor.'

'The green doctor could never have done it. Saffron, you see,' he confided, lowering his voice, 'he'd never have recommended saffron. That was the thing that did it.'

'Yes, doctor,' said the woman, and she held out another gold coin to help the blue doctor on his way.

The blue doctor half-reached for the coin, but he stopped himself.

'You can also say that I never overcharge,' he informed her piously. 'All I ever take is the fee that's due. Even when I do save a boy from certain death.'

'Yes, doctor,'

'Yes, madam,' said the blue doctor, gazing at the gold coin until it disappeared back into the lady's pocket. He sighed.

'Well, I must go. Patients. Patients to see. Sickness doesn't wait . . .'

'Yes, doctor.'

'Good. Good. Well, goodbye, boy. Goodbye, foreman. Goodbye, madam,' and he bowed, and scraped a little, and sighed once more, before finally leaving the miraculous room of spices where the boy, whom the blue doctor had never had the slightest idea how to cure, saffron or no saffron, had somehow brought himself back from the dead.

24

THAT EVENING, YOSS heard noises from the street. At first there were shouts and whistles, and then the shrill music of pipes and the thump of drums. There were sudden bangs as well, and if they were loud enough to make Yoss jump in the spice room, outside they must be deafening.

'What's happening?' he said to Garner Zeb, when the foreman unlocked the door and came in with a plate of chicken.

The foreman put the food down. 'Kelmuss Week,' he explained. 'It starts tonight. Everyone's celebrating.'

'Let me see!' cried Yoss, jumping up excitedly.

'No, Yoss. You should . . . you stay here.'

'I'm sick of staying here. Beetle and Paulus have gone to see, haven't they? I bet they've gone!'

The foreman didn't respond to that.

'Don't lock me in again!' cried Yoss.

Garner Zeb hesitated at the door. Behind him, the boy pleaded.

'Don't lock me in. Please. I'm sick of being in here. Why can't I go out?'

The foreman turned back to him. 'You were ill.'

'I'm well now,' said the boy.

'No, you're still recovering, Yoss.'

'Let me out, please, I want to work again. I want to see the celebration.'

'I have to do what I'm told,' said the foreman.

'What you're told?' said Yoss. 'What does that mean?'

Zeb gazed at him wearily. He thought of his own son, as he often did when he looked at the boy whom the merchant had turned into a slave.

The boy frowned. 'Someone's *told* you to lock me in . . .' he whispered. 'Who? Who told you, Garner Zeb?'

'Who do you think?' muttered the foreman.

'The lady?'

Zeb shook his head. 'The master, Yoss. He told me to keep you here.'

'What if I want to leave?'

'You can't leave.'

'I can't leave . . .' Yoss frowned again. 'Why can't I leave?'

The foreman came back slowly from the door. He sat down opposite the boy, with his back against a sack.

'What do you remember, Yoss, about when you hurt yourself?'

Yoss thought. 'I remember . . . I looked up and saw you, Garner Zeb. And then you picked me up, didn't you? And you carried me. You must have brought me here. But I don't actually *remember* you bringing me here. Because the next thing I remember I was already here, on the floor.'

'What about before that?' said the foreman gently. 'Before you looked up and saw me.'

'Before that? I remember . . . I was upstairs with Master Hans, in the hall. And we were painting . . . I was painting some sky, I think.'

'And then?'

'Then I remember you picking me up.'

'So you don't remember what happened in between?'

'No,' said Yoss. 'I fell, didn't I? I must have slipped down the stairs.'

The foreman watched the boy, wondering what he should do.

'I'm not saying I'm going to leave straight away,' Yoss said after a moment, thinking that he was reassuring the foreman. 'I should tell you something, Garner Zeb.' The boy paused and glanced at the doorway, to see if anyone was listening. 'I helped to rob your master,' he whispered. 'You didn't know that, did you? It's true. Don't be angry, I wouldn't do it again. You wouldn't believe how it happened even if I told you. I didn't know I was doing it – robbing him, I mean. But I did it, I can't pretend I didn't. So it's right that I should work and make up for it. Don't you agree?'

'Perhaps,' murmured the foreman.

'Of course you do! I don't have to do it, though. It's only because I think I should. They took me to a magistrate, and he could have put me in jail. If he really thought I was guilty he would have, wouldn't he? Then your master said I should work for him, and I thought that's fair. But when I've made up for it, I *will* leave, Garner Zeb. I'm not going to be here for ever.'

'And when will you have made up for it?'

Yoss thought. 'I'm not sure,' he said. 'Soon, probably.'

Garner Zeb gazed at the boy for a moment. Then he slapped his thighs. 'Well, you're not leaving now, are you?' he said cheerfully, and he got to his feet.

'But you said I couldn't leave.'

'The master's away, Yoss, but he'll be back in a day or two. Kelmuss Week lasts for five days. You'll still see the celebrations.'

'But you said I *couldn't* leave.'

'I meant here. This room. Not until the master comes back.'

'No,' Yoss shook his head. He stared intently at the foreman. 'Don't lie to me, Garner Zeb. That's not what you meant.'

Zeb didn't have to reply. He didn't have to tell Yoss any more than he had already said, or even that much, in fact. As the merchant's foreman, it wasn't his place to reveal anything about the master's instructions. But it wasn't a foreman's place to watch his master throw a boy down the stairs, either, or to nurse the child back from the brink of death. The unease and dissatisfaction, that had troubled the heavy-browed man from the very moment he heard about the purchase of the boy, had increased with every passing day. The sight of the boy tumbling down the stairs had brought them to the boil. And now, not only was the foreman still overseeing this ugly business that the merchant had concocted, but, just as the boy said, he found himself telling lies on the master's behalf.

Suddenly the foreman understood: not only had the merchant made the boy a slave, but he had made him, Zeb, a means of the enslavement.

The boy's eyes were still on him. With a sigh, the foreman sat on the mattress beside him.

'You say you don't remember how you slipped, Yoss?' he said quietly.

Yoss shook his head.

'It doesn't really matter how,' said the foreman. 'You don't remember what the master said?'

'When?'

'Before you slipped.'

'Was he there?'

Garner Zeb nodded. 'He was there.' He gazed at the boy, wondering if he were simply playing the fool. But the look on his face was so earnest and innocent that the foreman couldn't believe he was dissimulating.

'He told you,' said Garner Zeb eventually. 'He told you why

you can't leave. Are you sure you don't remember? Think.'

'I can't remember.'

'Really?'

The boy shook his head.

'Yoss, you're his slave.'

Yoss stared for a moment, then he broke into a grin. 'His slave? How can I be his slave?'

'You're his slave.'

Zeb explained what the merchant had done, the bargain he had struck with the magistrate.

'He *bought* me?' repeated Yoss incredulously.

'Apparently.'

'But he just said I was going to work for him . . .'

'Is that what he said? Exactly?'

What difference did it make, the exact words the merchant had used? Yoss was still grappling with the idea. 'I've been bought?'

Garner Zeb shook his head. He felt sick at the thought of it

'How can you buy someone?' murmured Yoss. 'How can you *sell* someone?'

'Listen, Yoss. Outside this house you have no life. You're a dead man. A thief. If they catch you, you hang.'

'What about Conrad and Gaspar?' said Yoss.

'Who are they?'

'The two others. Did the magistrate sell them too?'

Garner Zeb smiled grimly. 'I doubt it.'

Yoss jumped up. 'No,' he said. 'You're wrong. How do you know all this?'

'I know it. The mistress knows it.'

Yoss was struck dumb again. The mistress knew it? All those afternoons, when she was feeding him cakes and honey, she was feeding someone whom she regarded as a slave? Why had she asked him about the village if he was never to return there?

He looked around the spice room. He tried to think. Suddenly everything seemed to have a different meaning. Everything that had seemed real now seemed false. He thought he had been working to make amends to the merchant, but he had actually been locked in against his will. What he thought he was doing by his own choice, he was doing according to someone else's design.

'What about Master Hans?' he asked suddenly.

'I don't know about Master Hans,' replied Garner Zeb.

Yoss looked around the room again. He glanced at Zeb suspiciously. The merchant's house was no better than Farber's inn. Full of lies and deception, both of them. Was there no one in the town you could trust? No word that meant what it said? Nothing that was as it appeared?

Yoss went to the corner of the room and sat on a chest. The foreman, still sitting on the mattress, was staring miserably at his feet.

'Well, if I'm a slave, I'll have to escape,' said Yoss at last.

Garner Zeb sighed. 'Yoss, I've told you, if they catch you, they'll hang you.' He got up and walked to the door.

'Will you help me?'

Zeb fumbled with the key.

'Garner Zeb, will you help me escape?'

The door closed. Yoss heard the key turn in the lock. He stared at the door. He didn't move. The foreman had left him. He felt as if he were alone, utterly alone, and there was no one who would help him.

He fought to hold back his tears. He thought of Moritz.

Moritz really had been alone, and if he had despaired, he wouldn't have survived.

And then, strangely, Yoss thought of someone else. Conrad. If he were alone, a man like Conrad would find a way to help himself.

But Conrad must be dead by now. They must have hanged him.

There was a loud bang from a Kelmuss firecracker. Good! Let them make noise! Suddenly Yoss felt strong and determined. Why should he expect Garner Zeb to help? Hadn't he learned by now that he could trust no one but himself? Alone, he *would* escape. He would rather take his chances, like Conrad, and hang, than be a slave.

~

GARNER ZEB heard the firecracker as well. He was standing on the other side of the spice room door, staring vacantly at the darkened courtyard. He was not at ease. He could close the door on the boy, but he couldn't close it on his thoughts.

He stood for a long time. The Kelmuss noise grew in the streets. And gradually, as he brooded, an idea occurred to him.

In the days that Yoss lay injured in the spice room, when they tended the boy by turns, something had happened between the merchant's foreman and his wife. It was the simplest of things. They began to speak to one another.

Before this, for three years, their paths had hardly crossed. The upper floor of domesticity, where the woman lived, and the lower floor of commerce, which was the foreman's realm, barely overlapped. And since their worlds barely overlapped, the opinion that each had formed of the other owed more to each one's preconceptions than to anything they actually observed.

The death of the first mistress from the lump in her neck, four years previously, had grieved the foreman deeply, more deeply, he sometimes thought, than it grieved the merchant himself. Even now he often thought of her. He could still see her with her head on the pillow, her cheeks gaunt and sunk, her mouth forced closed by the huge lump that had replaced her neck. Even in her last days, when she was as thin as a ghost and as pale as the linen on which she lay, she had called for him and wanted to know if all was well with his wife and children, just as she had when she was well. Up to the very end she spoke to him like a sister, not his employer's wife. But then she died, and within a year the new wife came along. Up the stairs she went, laughing with pleasure and glowing with beauty in her wedding gown, as the merchant carried her into the mansion he had bought with his new father-in-law's money. She was from one of the grand old merchant families of the town. Not like the first mistress. Too high and mighty to bother with the likes of me, Zeb had thought, as he watched her disappear up the stairs.

And in the years that followed, didn't everything about her prove that she was high and mighty, just as he suspected? Only came down the stairs to rush across the courtyard with her maid and stand impatiently as he unlocked the gate for her. Lucky to get a nod as he made an awkward little bow to her. Barely a word, never a conversation such as one might have with another human being, whatever their station. High and mighty, too high and mighty even to talk to him.

It never occurred to him that high and mighty might actually have been timid and uncertain. If just once he had thought of her not as the merchant's new wife from a family of wealth, but as a shy young woman, little more than a girl, he might have realized she didn't know what one should or shouldn't say to a workman, and because everyone assumed she knew, no one ever told her. He might have understood that if you don't know what to say, you may avoid the problem by saying nothing at all. He might have guessed that up there on the floor above him, with her maid and her servants, she was in a sense friendless and alone, and those who are friendless and alone will often speak more coldly than those who are surrounded by warmth and companionship.

But it wasn't only the foreman's fault. If Zeb fell victim to his own preconceptions, so the merchant's wife fell victim to hers. She had been brought up on the upper floor of a house just like the one in which she now lived, where she had been kept away from the workmen on the lower floor, and had been taught that they were rough and crude. On the morning after her wedding, when she gazed down from her window and saw the big foreman striding across the courtyard, heard him calling out to the workmen who lived in the stable, she shivered with trepidation. Even his head, with the large, overhanging brow, was threatening. Whenever she went downstairs to go out, he approached her with barely a word, as if to remind her that this was *his* domain. Struck her almost dumb by his gruffness. Gave her a brusque bow that showed how little he really thought of her. She could hardly wait for him to open the gate each time to get away from his disdainful gaze.

And so it went on for three years, each one misapprehending and misinterpreting the other, each misapprehension sowing the seeds of more misapprehensions in the future. One kind word from Zeb, as the woman rushed across the courtyard, might have unlocked the tenderness in her heart. And a kind word from her, as he opened the gate, might have unlocked his natural goodness. And then the boy lay injured in the spice room, dying, according to the blue doctor, and suddenly, in that room, their worlds finally overlapped. Distracted by their emotions, united by their fear for the child's life, they forgot their preconceptions. There wasn't space or time for them. There were things to be done, and they did them. There were words they felt compelled to utter, words of hope, or of fear, and they spoke them. They forgot that one was high and mighty and the other was rough and intimidating, and by the time they remembered again . . . they had discovered that they weren't. By the time the boy was well, they saw each other in a new light.

So Garner Zeb stood outside the door of the spice room, on the first night of Kelmuss Week, with the sound of Yoss' entreaties echoing in his mind, and he looked at the upper floor, where candles burned in one or two of the windows, and wondered what the mistress would say if he went upstairs to talk with her.

25

CONRAD AND GASPAR could hear the noise of the crowd in the streets. Torchlight flickered through the bars of their window. It was already late, but there was no end to the uproar. Outside, someone was clashing cymbals like a madman, on and on and on. Someone else began cursing. There was the sound of a scuffle.

'Kelmuss Week,' said Conrad.

Gaspar looked at him.

'You'll love it.'

They waited. They had no thought of sleep. Eventually a key turned in the door.

The jailer came in, carrying a lantern. Conrad motioned to Gaspar. Gaspar sat down on his mattress and began to take off his boots.

The jailer started to whisper. Conrad strained to hear him over the noise outside.

'At the end of the corridor, turn left. Take the first stairs you see. When you get to the top, go left again. You'll come to a door to the street. I've smashed the lock so it'll look like you've broken it. The guard has sneaked away to visit his mistress. He always does.' The jailer giggled. 'He'll have some explaining to do tomorrow.'

Conrad grinned.

Gaspar stood up, holding the boots in his hands. He gave them a wistful glance. Conrad snatched them out of his grasp and handed them to the jailer.

The small, sallow man took them eagerly.

'You'll get the rest of your reward,' said Conrad, 'don't worry.'

'Remember where we're meeting.'

'Tomorrow at dusk, under the New Bridge.'

'Under the Mill Bridge,' hissed the jailer.

'Of course, under the Mill Bridge. At dusk.'

The jailer looked suspiciously at the straw-haired man. His hand tightened around the boots.

'Come on,' whispered Conrad. 'Time's short. I'll be there, and you'll get what we agreed. Now, we just have to give you a bump so they'll believe we jumped you.'

The jailer nodded apprehensively. 'Who's going to do it?'

'Him,' said Conrad. 'I'm not a violent man.'

'Come on then, let's get it over with.' The jailer put down his lantern and turned to face Gaspar.

'Oh, there's just one more thing,' said Conrad

'What is—'

The jailer never finished the question. As he looked back over his shoulder, Conrad's fist smashed into his jaw.

The jailer stumbled. He bounced against the wall. Conrad was already on him, throwing him to the ground, his hands grabbing for his neck. The jailer tried to shout but the thumbs pressing over his windpipe choked his voice.

'Where's the boy?' demanded Conrad.

The jailer's eyes were bulging out of their sockets. His face was turning purple.

He struggled, but his arms were pinned by Conrad's knees. His legs kicked helplessly in the air.

'Where's the *boy*?' Conrad repeated. 'Tell me and I'll let you go. Shout and I'll strangle you.'

Conrad partially relaxed his grip. The jailer's chest heaved, sucking in air.

'What are you doing?' cried the jailer hoarsely.

Conrad tightened his grip again.

'All right, all right.'

'Where's the boy?' repeated Conrad.

'The merchant . . . has him.'

'The merchant?'

'The magistrate sold him to the merchant.'

'Sold him?' Conrad grinned, admiring the trickery of it. He glanced at Gaspar.

'I've told you. Now let me go!' wheezed the jailer, kicking his legs again.

Conrad shook his head. 'You wanted the rest of your reward. Why wait until tomorrow? You can have it now.'

Conrad's hands began to squeeze. The jailer's legs kicked and flailed. He bucked. He struggled a little longer. Then he was still.

Conrad got up. Gaspar was staring at him open-mouthed.

'I didn't know you were going to do that,' he whispered.

Conrad picked up the boots which the jailer had dropped. He handed them to Gaspar. 'See, you didn't lose them after all.'

~

OUT of the jail and into the town they plunged, into the Kelmuss crowds, where people were drinking and rollicking. Conrad shouldered into anyone who stood in his way and sent people flying. They came to a square. Acrobats were leaping on a platform. Elsewhere there was an enormous spit, and a whole ox was roasting. A crowd stood around it, clamouring for meat, their faces burnished by the fire.

'Let's eat,' said Gaspar, who had not tasted flesh in two months.

Conrad hurried on.

'Where are you going? Let's eat!'

Conrad turned on him fiercely. 'Would you like to be caught and taken back? Yes?'

'No.'

'Then follow me. You'll eat soon enough.'

They left the square. Conrad headed into the alleys of the town. Here, in the dark, twisting passageways, with their stench and muck, there were no crowds, only people who passed like shadows, heading for the festivities. Now the noise of the celebration came to them from afar, like a murmur, sometimes with loud exclamations. Still Conrad pressed on.

'Where are we going? Not back to Farber's inn!'

'Quiet, Gaspariño,' said Conrad, and suddenly his voice was soothing, as it had been in the early days, when Gaspar had first known him. 'Soon enough you'll see.'

Gaspar was light-headed and breathless. The long starving weeks in the cell had taken their toll on him. He followed Conrad blindly, as he had followed him so often in the past.

Eventually Conrad stopped. Now they were far from the centre of the town. The alley was deserted and the shutters of every house were closed.

'Wait,' whispered Conrad, and he stepped out of the alley cautiously.

Then Conrad's voice called to Gaspar from the darkness.

Gaspar stepped forward. He looked around. They were on the riverbank. Far away, up the river, there was an orange glow, which must come from a bonfire. The sound of a crowd came faintly from that direction. There was a bridge nearby.

Whether it was the New Bridge or the Mill Bridge, where they had promised to meet the dead jailer, or some other bridge, Gaspar didn't know.

'What are we doing here?' said Gaspar.

'We had to come,' said Conrad quietly.

'Why?'

'Do you know, Gaspar, sometimes there are things you don't want to do? You don't want to do them, and yet you must. And when you must, then you must, and you can't let yourself be weak. And so the best thing is to do them quickly, and not talk about them too much before.'

'Like what, Conrad?'

'Like the jailer, for instance.'

'Oh, the jailer.' Gaspar nodded. 'Well—'

Conrad hit him in the belly. Gaspar fell to his knees, gasping. The kick that caught him under the chin, and broke his neck, followed swiftly.

Conrad stood over the body. He looked around to see if anyone had seen him. Upriver, the water glowed in the light of the bonfire, as if it were burning. Here it was dark. Gaspar lay on his back. A memory came into Conrad's mind. It was a sunny day, the day he and Gaspar left Michele's mill. They were both on horseback. Gaspar was laughing at something, laughing, shaking his pot-shaped head until his hat almost fell off.

Suddenly Conrad kicked the body. He kicked it again, and then he was in a frenzy, kicking and kicking out the frustration that had built up while he was in the jail and the anger he felt at having had to kill Gaspar. Did he want to do it? Whose fault was it? If only he hadn't been so *stupid*. So *stupid*! So *stupid*! So *stupid*!

He stopped kicking, breathing heavily. He glanced around

again. He had heard a number of Gaspar's ribs crack. He felt somewhat sickened by himself.

Suddenly he grinned. Such quick fingers, he thought, staring down at Gaspar's hands, yet such a slow brain. One of the world's mysteries.

The force of Conrad's kicks had pushed Gaspar onto his side. His head was thrown back, the throat stretched. His legs were splayed. Conrad noticed his boots. He knelt and pulled them off. Then he put his arms under Gaspar's shoulders and dragged him to the river's edge. He lifted the body and cast it into the water. There was a splash. One of the feet was still caught on the bank, and Conrad kicked it away. The body bobbed, like a log, ensnared in the reeds.

Conrad went back to the boots and sat down beside them. He took off his shoes and pulled one of the boots on. It pinched a little, but not too much. The leather would stretch to accommodate him. He pulled the other boot on. He stood up and stamped on the ground, working his feet well into the boots. Then he picked up his own shoes and hurled them far away into the river.

Gaspar's body was starting to move. The current was working at it, pulling it out of the reeds. In the moonlight, Conrad could see it turning. Now it was moving away from the bank, bare feet first.

'You'd want me to have them, wouldn't you?' said Conrad aloud. 'You always loved them. You wouldn't want to waste them on the river, Gaspariño.'

Conrad stood on the bank, as if waiting for an answer. The body moved further away.

'Goodbye Gaspar,' he said, 'you really did have the fastest fingers I ever saw. I'll never forget them.'

Conrad laughed. Gaspar's body was disappearing, merging with the darkness of the water. The straw-haired man turned in his new boots and headed back into the alleys of the town.

~

AT DAYBREAK, two Kelmuss revellers walked home along the riverbank. They had drunk too much and spent a few hours sleeping in a gutter. Perhaps they were still somewhat drunk. Near the Mill Bridge, one of them caught sight of something snared in the reeds at the water's edge.

He stopped, and then stumbled over to see what it was.

It was an unusual hat, tall, black and pot-shaped. The man turned it in his hands, examining it. But the other man crept up behind him and snatched it and slapped it on his head. He laughed loudly. The first one tried to snatch it back, but the one with the hat ran off crookedly along the bank. His companion gave chase. Eventually he caught him, and grabbed the hat and put it on his head. Then the other one chased him. So they ran crazily beside the river, leaping and lunging at each other, each one trying to grab the hat and wear it, until one of them knocked it off the other's head with such force that it flew out of reach and bounced over the grass and rolled into the water.

And they both stood and watched as the river carried Gaspar's hat away.

26

ZEB STOOD AT THE TOP of the staircase. He had waited until morning, and then he waited until he was sure the mistress would be up, and then it had been very tempting to wait even longer, telling himself he'd just sort out one more delivery or oversee one more consignment, but he knew he mustn't. If he was going to go up the stairs, the time had come.

In three years, the foreman had not once been to the upper floor of his master's house. And now he stood there, gazing at a wood-panelled corridor with a row of doors along each side. There were tapestries on the walls, and chests between the doors. Each of the chests was elaborately carved and polished. Each of the tapestries showed a colourful scene in the country with young men and women.

Zeb stared. He knew his master was wealthy. With his own eyes, he saw the volume of the trade he did. And he heard people say that he accumulated gold at a faster rate than any other man in the town. But all of this was words. Wealth, gold, luxury. You made the sounds and out they came. You thought they referred to things with which you were familiar, like the things in your home. But Zeb suddenly realized that you didn't understand them until you saw what they actually meant. A dozen chests, and each one, probably, worth more by itself than all of the furniture in the foreman's own house. And the tapestries? How much each one of those might have cost, Zeb couldn't even begin to imagine. And the doors? Behind each one of those, who knew what objects were kept? It was too staggering. Yet he could still remember his master's first journey, when they had set off together with nothing but the small capital from the merchant's father-in-law, the baker. And it didn't seem that long ago. Fifteen years. Not that long.

Suddenly Zeb became aware that he was just standing in the corridor with his mouth open, like a peasant at his first glimpse of the town. He began to feel foolish. He looked at the doors, but had no idea which one he might open. He cleared his throat, and then he coughed, hoping someone would hear him.

No one came. The foreman began to walk past the doors. He walked up and down and soon he was back where he started without having seen anybody. There was a painter up here, called Master Hans, he knew, but he had never seen him. He wondered what he should do if the painter came out of one of the rooms. In Zeb's imagination, the painter was like some strange species of monster, and there was no telling what he might think or do and how one should appease him.

The foreman heard footsteps. He swung around. It was Sylvie, the maid. She was carrying a small tray with a cup and a jug on it. She stopped and peered at him in surprise.

'I'm looking . . .' Garner Zeb stopped. His voice, even to his own ears, sounded too loud for this place. 'I'm looking,' he began again, almost whispering, 'for the mistress.'

'Oh. Did she send for you?'

Garner Zeb shook his head.

'Oh,' said the maid again. 'Well, wait here.'

Zeb waited. Eventually the maid came back and led him into a room with a window on the street. There was a musical instrument in it that looked like a long, delicate desk with a row of white levers at one end. The woman was sitting at a small table, in an upholstered chair.

'Sit down, Garner Zeb,' she said, pointing towards another chair.

The foreman nodded. Suddenly, in this room, the lady seemed distant again, as she had always seemed in the past, high and mighty, unapproachable. But she smiled and said 'Sit, Zeb,' and he nodded once more and sat, perching himself cautiously on the edge of the chair that she had indicated.

'What is it, Zeb? It's not Yoss, is it? He's well?'

'Very well.'

'So long as we don't have to get the doctor back. If anyone can kill the boy, it's him,' she said, and she laughed.

The foreman nodded gravely. Doctors did kill people, everyone knew that, and it was a mystery to Zeb how they could sometimes cure and sometimes harm, and whether they ever knew what they were doing at all. When his own wife had been ill a couple of years earlier, with swollen wrists and toes and a bright red rash all over her, the doctor had changed his mind at least four times, and ended up curing her with the very treatment he had ridiculed in the beginning.

The mistress was still waiting. The foreman frowned, wondering how to begin.

'What is it?' prompted the lady again.

'It *is* about Yoss, madam. Not that he's not well,' Zeb added hurriedly, 'because he is. He's locked down there in the spice room just itching to get out.'

The woman smiled.

'No, you see, he's very impatient.'

'It's just another day or two, Zeb. Tell him he can come out when the master returns. Tell him . . . No, I'll tell him myself. I'll go down soon.'

'No, madam. The thing is, he doesn't want to wait. He wants

to leave.'

'Leave?'

'Escape,' whispered Garner Zeb, and he looked around, as if there might be someone else in the room who could have heard.

The woman smiled. 'Escape!'

'No, madam. He does.'

The woman frowned. 'How do you know?'

'He told me.'

'He hasn't told *me*.'

'He thinks you're like the master. He thinks you're part of it.'

'Part of what, Garner Zeb? What are you talking about?'

'Well, you see,' said the foreman, frowning, as if the memory of it was just as confusing to him as it would be to anyone else, 'I had to tell him. He asked. And after all, the master already told him, only he couldn't remember. Do you realize the boy can't remember anything from the moment he was painting until he opened his eyes at the bottom of the stairs? He's forgotten everything, including what the master said to him. But the master did say it, so I thought, since the master told him, he obviously doesn't mind if the boy knows. In fact, he probably *wants* the boy to know. The master isn't inclined to tell a person something if he doesn't want him to know it, is he? So if you look at it that way, then I *had* to tell him, because the master would have expected him to know and I bet he wouldn't count on the boy's forgetting!'

The woman gazed at Zeb in perplexity. How did those workmen ever get anything done down there, she wondered, if this was the way their foreman explained things?

'What I'm trying to say,' said Garner Zeb eventually, 'is that I told the boy he's a slave.'

'Oh,' said the woman.

~

THE MERCHANT'S WIFE stood at the window. In the street below, the Kelmuss crowds were already out again, even though the day had hardly begun. Last night, according to Sylvie, the town had paid for three oxen to be roasted in the Council House square, but that didn't satisfy them. Further up the street there was an inn with the sign of a duck, and a crowd of revellers was already outside it, drinking. Near them a hawker was selling sausages. 'Sausage! Best sausage!' he cried. Other cries came from further along the street. When she had been a girl, she could remember, and she had wanted her mother to buy her a sausage from a man like that, her mother told her that those sausages were filled with sawdust. She still half-believed it. Anyway, she had never tasted one.

A man stopped and bought one of the sausages. He broke it in half and gave a piece to a boy who was with him. The merchant's wife couldn't see the child's face. But she saw his small hand reaching up to take the food.

'What did you say to him?' said the woman eventually, still gazing at the street. 'Tell me again.'

Zeb threw up his hands. 'What could I say? I said the master had ordered me to keep him in the spice room and that's what I was going to do. But that didn't satisfy him. If people are going to treat him like a slave, then he's going to act like one, he says. He's going to escape.'

'And what did you say?'

'I didn't say anything, because he's right. If I was a slave, I'd want to escape as well. I don't know what I'd do . . . I'd *kill* before I gave up.'

The woman turned sharply. 'Do you think he'll kill?'

The foreman shook his head. 'No.'

The woman sat down. She sighed. 'Why do you tell me this, Garner Zeb? What do you want me to do?'

'I don't know.' The foreman stared at his hands. 'He wants me to help him. He wants me to help him escape. I've never betrayed the master, madam. I've never stolen, deceived him, or tried to deal in goods behind his back. But with this . . . there's something wrong.'

'So you expect me to betray him instead!' cried the woman. 'Is that why you're here, Garner Zeb? Well, he may be your master, but he's my husband. Does your wife betray *you*, Zeb? Is that what you're asking?'

The foreman looked up in surprise. 'No, madam,' he said hurriedly. 'Don't say that. It's just . . . I had a feeling . . . you don't think this is right either.'

'And?'

'And . . .' The foreman shook his head, lost for further words.

'Garner Zeb. My husband bought the boy. The money was paid. If he hadn't, the boy would hang. The others are standing trial next week. Did you know that? There's still time to add him to the list. So? He's been saved. You and I both know it, and now he knows it as well. Good! He ought to be grateful.'

The foreman stared at the lady in disbelief. He had misjudged her. Was this the same woman who had spoken so gently in the spice room? Perhaps he had imagined it. Perhaps, he thought in confusion, it was the rich odours of the spices that had addled his brain, made things appear as they were not.

'The boy probably *would* rather hang,' muttered Zeb. 'I would in his place.' He bit his lip, breathing heavily, to stop himself saying the other things he was thinking. He got up to go. He didn't belong here, in this room with its soft chairs and its musical instrument, or in the corridor with its chests and tapestries that were worth more than all the possessions he had ever had in his entire life. That was for the high and mighty, not for the likes of him. 'I'm sorry, madam,' he mumbled, as he reached for the door. 'It seems I was mistaken. I was mistaken. Don't worry, I won't betray your husband.'

'Oh, it would be easier if you did.'

Zeb stopped.

The woman shook her head in despair. 'How can you make a boy a slave, Zeb? Do you think I haven't thought about it? Do you think it doesn't make me ill? But it's done, and what to do now, can you tell me that? If the boy leaves, he's condemned, like the two rogues who deceived him. He'll hang. And if he stays, he's a slave.'

'He'll only hang if they catch him,' said the foreman.

'And *won't* they catch him? My husband will see to it that they will. No, he can't leave, it's too dangerous. But listen, Garner Zeb, I've been thinking. My husband could release him. He could live here freely. He needn't be a workman. He likes to paint with Master Hans. He's young, handsome, intelligent, like wax . . .' murmured the merchant's wife, hugging her arms around her bosom.

'Madam,' said the foreman, 'if he *must* stay here, then he's a slave, no matter what you call him. No matter what he becomes. Can't you see?'

The woman looked up. 'See what?'

'Couldn't the master return him to his village? He could send us to take him, Tomas and me. Why not? Now, in Kelmuss Week, who'd even notice? The whole town's full of peasants from the countryside. Put us in country clothes. We'd take him out of the town, back to his village, and no one would ever know. Madam,' Zeb continued urgently, 'why wait for the master? You could do it yourself. You could send . . .'

The foreman stopped. The merchant's wife was staring at him in horror.

'Take him to his village? Take him away?'

'Madam?' said Zeb uncomprehendingly.

The woman rose to her feet. She went to the window again. The foreman couldn't see her face.

'Go. Go, now, Zeb. The boy will be well. Don't speak of escape.'

~

ZEB retraced his steps along the corridor. He went down the stairs. Inside him, something was happening. A decision formed, shaped and hardened all in the space of those few moments. One for one reason, one for another, the master and the mistress had their plans. There was no help for Yoss up there, on the upper floor.

But if he, Zeb, were going to let the boy escape, he couldn't do it while the merchant was away. That would be too obvious, the finger of blame would point directly at him. The merchant would certainly dismiss him, if not worse. And he had a family to support, and must think of them as well. There were certain debts that he owed to the merchant, credit he had taken in times of emergency, when his wife had been ill, for example, and it took many bleedings from the doctor and many decoctions of expensive herbs to cure her. That was one of the debts he still had not paid, and when he thought about the amount that he earned and the amount that he required for his family, he was not at all sure that he would ever be able to repay it. If the merchant chose to call in his debts, he and his family would be on the street.

So a little patience, and a little planning, were required. The boy would have to understand.

Zeb crossed the courtyard to the spice room.

'You'll have your chance,' he told him.

'When?'

'Not yet. Not until the master returns. Until then you'll have to be patient.' Zeb gazed closely at Yoss, the eyes under his heavy brows searching him keenly. 'Will you be patient?'

Yoss nodded.

'Then I'll do it. That's my promise, Yoss. But it's as much as I can do. I tried to persuade the mistress to send me with you, but she won't. Yoss, it will be dangerous.'

'I don't care about that! All I want is a chance.'

'Think about it first,' cautioned the foreman. Before the boy made up his mind, he should at least know all the facts, even though Zeb doubted it would dissuade him. 'I spoke to the mistress. She doesn't want you to be a slave. She says you can stay of your own will. Perhaps you won't even be a workman, perhaps you'll be something else . . .'

But the boy wasn't listening. His mind was already far away.

'Yoss! Yoss, listen to me. It *will* be dangerous. They'll hang you if they catch you. It isn't a threat. It's true.'

'*If* they catch me!'

The foreman stopped himself from showing a smile at the boy's eagerness and confidence. Just like his own boy, he thought. Just like himself at that age.

'I can bring you clothes,' he said quietly.

'I've got clothes. See! What do you think I'm wearing?'

'And some money. Not much, but I can give you a little.'

'Don't give me your money, Garner Zeb.'

'What will you do?'

Yoss had no idea what he would do. Suddenly he thought of Conrad again. He thought of the dead man's cunning and bravado, his fast brain and beguiling tongue, his ability to seize an opportunity and benefit from it. Well, he would have to be like that. He would have to be clever, brave and quick. The town had swallowed him, perhaps, but in swallowing him, it had shown him what he must be like in order to break free. He would have to use all that the town had taught him, and be a Conrad to himself.

27

THAT MORNING, as the foreman climbed the stairs and was then rebuffed by his master's wife, Conrad made his way secretly to the old man who had bought the merchant's rings.

Wearing the clothes in which he had left the prison, without money or means, the straw-haired man was in danger, and no one knew it better than he. The bargain was straightforward. The old man, Onfluess, had no choice, and should have been shrewd enough to see it. So when he started to prevaricate, Conrad grew impatient. Time was short. The mask of amiability soon dropped from his face. Yet the old man continued to ponder.

'You want me to pay you for saying nothing? For doing nothing?' Onfluess shook his head for the tenth time, as if he couldn't quite believe it. He ran his fingers pensively through the strands of his beard. His expression was pained. 'It just doesn't feel right, Conrad. When you had something to sell, I always gave you a price. Can you say I ever didn't? But to give you a price for nothing? What kind of business is that? It isn't right.'

Conrad glanced at Margret, who was watching him stonily. There was nothing she would like more, he knew, than to see him turned away empty-handed. But she ought to have been able to see that it was just as important for her, as for the old man, that they reached agreement. Anything that implicated her father implicated her.

'Listen,' said Conrad, turning back to the old man, 'what I'm offering you isn't *nothing*. On the contrary, a man doesn't get an offer like this every day. It's your life, Onfluess. Your life and hers. Don't underestimate it. This is the most important bargain you'll ever make.'

'You're bluffing,' said the old man.

'Am I?'

Onfluess threw a cunning, complicitous glance at his daughter, before turning back to Conrad. 'Why would you go back to them?' he said slyly. 'You can't, Conrad. They'd hang you on the spot, like Simmy the Coin. This time they wouldn't even wait for the judges.' The old man cackled maliciously. 'Did you know Simmy the Coin, Conrad? Have I ever told you what they did to him?'

Conrad shook his head. 'You really don't understand, Onfluess? I'm not going back, because you're going to give me the money to buy a horse and get away.'

'But I've explained to you,' Onfluess replied, 'that it's *because* you're not going back that I don't need to give you even a farthing.'

The straw-haired man closed his eyes for a moment, breathing heavily. Onfluess, for some reason, refused to realize what position Conrad was in, and to ask himself what a man like Conrad wouldn't do in order to extricate himself from it.

Conrad opened his eyes. He spoke quietly. 'This is the last time I'll tell you, so listen well. If I don't get away, they'll catch me. And if they catch me, I'll tell them about you. Now, is that clear enough for you to understand? Make no mistake, I'll do anything to save myself.'

'Tell them about me? That won't save you!' exclaimed Onfluess derisively.

Conrad shrugged. 'Well, you see, I won't know unless I try.

So if you don't want me to find out, the way to protect *yourself*,' said Conrad, and he prodded a finger sharply into Onfluess' bony shoulder, 'is to protect me. The way to make sure they don't get *you* . . .' Conrad prodded again, '. . . is to make sure that I get away.'

'And what guarantee do I have that—'

'No guarantees!' roared Conrad, pounding the table with his fist. The old man jumped. Conrad stared at him fiercely. 'Just use your brain and work it out for yourself. That's your guarantee.'

'What about the other two?' demanded Margret.

'Don't worry about them,' he growled, barely glancing at her.

'So I pay you,' said Onfluess, lifting his cap and wiping the sweat off his scalp, 'and one of the others turns me in? Is that the bargain you're offering?'

'I told you not to worry about them. Dead men tell no tales.'

'Dead?' whispered Onfluess. 'Are they dead?' There was a glint in his eye, as if the thought of Conrad's violence excited him. 'Did you kill them yourself? Tell! How?'

'Shall I show you?' said Conrad, and he leaned closer to the old man, and reached out his hands towards his neck.

'No! No!' Onfluess threw a feeble arm up to protect himself.

'Then don't ask,' said Conrad, and he looked at Margret, who shook her head in disgust. Maybe he should kill the old man, thought Conrad, and then he would teach *her* a lesson, slowly, and at his leisure.

'How much?' Onfluess was saying. 'Five gold pieces?'

'Twenty,' said Conrad.

'*Twenty*? What are you, a prince? What kind of horse do you think you need?'

'Twenty of gold and twenty of silver as well.'

'No. Ten of gold and ten of silver.'

Conrad didn't reply.

'Twelve! Twelve of gold and . . . fifteen of silver. You're breaking my heart, Conrad. Eighteen of silver?'

Conrad watched the old man impassively. 'Don't bargain over this, Onfluess. There's no profit here for you or for me. I've told you what I need. I need a horse, I need to get away. I can't manage with less. Give it to me.'

The old man's eyes narrowed. He ran his fingers through his beard one last time. Then he glanced at his daughter and nodded.

Margret left the room.

Onfluess gazed at Conrad. He shook his head.

'You're thinner, my boy. Never seen you so thin. You were always a big lad. And the beard you've grown . . . well, maybe it suits you.'

'Maybe.'

The old man nodded. Then he started to chuckle. 'Nothing would surprise me about you, Conrad. Killed 'em both, eh?'

'More or less.'

'More or less? What's more or less? Here you are asking for my money and you can't even tell me for sure. A man's either dead or he ain't.'

'One's dead. The other soon will be.'

'And he never saw me, did he?'

Conrad shook his head.

'Well, kill him if you want. I don't care.'

Conrad stared with hatred at the old man, who sat safely in his house and took the gains that other men obtained through daring, feeding on them like a leech.

The old man grinned. 'You . . .' he said, wagging a bony finger at him, 'you're the coldest villain I ever met, Conrad Bellyguts. The blood in your veins is ice.'

'How do you think I learned to be like that?'

The old man ignored the question. 'Yes, from the very first time I met you, when you came here to sell those candlesticks – do you remember, those candlesticks, heavy as rocks and pure silver? You bargained for them as steady as you like, and I knew you were cold. It was the way you bargained. How old were you then? A young thief like that, you should have been trembling in your boots. Shitting in your pants. Should have taken the first thing I offered. But you didn't. I gave you a good price that day, just out of pleasure at seeing you swagger.' Onfluess laughed. 'Thought you'd be dead before I ever saw you again. How is it you're still alive after all these years? You should be dead, Conrad. You should be dead five times over.'

'But I'm not.'

'Because others are,' observed the old man.

'That's what you say.'

'And what do *you* say?'

Conrad didn't reply. Margret returned, holding a purse. Conrad snatched it out of her hand and tore it open.

'Well?' said the old man.

Conrad counted the coins out one by one.

'No need to be so suspicious, Conrad. Have a little trust.'

Conrad snorted.

'Take them and go,' said Margret. 'Don't come back for more because there'll be nothing for you.'

'Most gracious, madam,' said Conrad, his spirits beginning to rise again as he gathered up the coins and felt their weight in his hands. 'After all the trouble I've taken to protect your father from the noose! He oughtn't buy other people's rings if he don't want to be disturbed now and then.'

'He'll buy no more rings from you, Conrad Silvertongue. Don't ever come back.'

Conrad returned the coins to the purse. 'Never?' he said.

'Never,' said Margret.

'Not even if I've got the queen's own rubies to dispose of? Rubies as big as pigeons' eggs, they say, and diamonds to match.'

'Never, Conrad. I said never.'

Conrad glanced at Onfluess. The old man rolled his eyes. For rubies as big as pigeons' eggs, he'd make an exception.

~

CONRAD set to work. His first stop was a barber, where he had his beard trimmed – not removed, as one would expect from a man who had entered jail clean-shaven, but clipped and tidied. Then he slipped into the market, and he bought old trousers and a tunic from a dealer in used clothes, and he purchased a country cloak off the very back of a peasant who had come to the town to sell rustic flutes and rattles to the Kelmuss crowds. The man was wearing a low, slouching hat such as peasants wear, and Conrad bought this as well. It would shield his face from prying eyes, and together with the cloak it made him look like a country man who had arrived for the festival. He changed his clothes in an alley behind the market. A woman came past as he did it, and stared at him, but he scowled at her and she hurried away. He left his clothes where they fell, for some starving urchin or beggar to scavenge.

He also guessed, and he was right, that the soldiers in the town had been told to look for a fat man with a thinner, pot-headed companion, but he no longer had the companion and the weeks that he had spent in jail ensured that he was far from fat. Thus the lean, bearded man who emerged from the alley in his cloak and slouching hat bore little resemblance to the escapee that the soldiers were seeking.

Perhaps, to complete the transformation, he should have disposed of Gaspar's boots. What country man would possess such finely worked footwear? But people don't look at shoes. If someone did, Conrad could always think of an explanation. He could say, for instance, that he had won them at cards. And it would be a shame to get rid of them. They had already saved his life once. They might do it again. Besides, they weren't only finely worked, but strong and sturdy. Even if they didn't save his life they would serve him well enough on his feet.

So he kept them. Now he was ready to find out the rest of the information that he needed. And the best way of finding out what you need isn't necessarily by stealth, Conrad knew, but by doing precisely what your opponent least expects . . . even if it means walking straight up to him in broad daylight.

~

EVERY AVAILABLE SOLDIER was out in the town. Extra sentries had been posted at the gates, on the bridges, in the squares. One of the sentries stood at the end of the New Bridge. Now and then he shouted out to the people crossing the bridge and demanded to know their names. He got all kinds of stories. Half the town was drunk. A country man sidled up to him, clutching a big tankard freshly filled with beer.

'What are you doing here?' demanded the peasant belligerently.

'Go away, country boy,' barked the sentry.

'You weren't here yesterday when I came through.'

'Well, I'm here today.'

The peasant took a mouthful of the beer. He held out the tankard to the sentry. The sentry looked around, took the tankard and drank greedily. The beer overflowed around his mouth and ran down his chin.

'Careful! Give it back.'

The sentry handed the tankard over.

'You *weren't* here yesterday,' said the country man. He looked into the tankard and took a mouthful of beer.

'Well, yesterday two terrible murdering thieves hadn't escaped.'

'And have they escaped now?'

'It'll frighten you, the story,' said the sentry with relish. 'Killed the jailer and three of the guards, smashed the door down and ran off.'

'Killed the jailer *and* three of the guards?'

The sentry nodded. 'We're on the lookout,' he said confidentially. He glanced at a man coming towards the bridge, leading a donkey. 'What's your name?' he shouted, as if to demonstrate to the country man how a sentry in the town looked out.

'William, a glassblower,' replied the man

The soldier scrutinized him suspiciously. 'Why aren't you blowing glass, William?'

William stopped, holding on to the donkey's harness. 'I'm going to get a chest for my sister. She bought it from Beatrice, the wife of Thomas the whitewasher. That's why I've got this donkey. I borrowed it from Gerrard the invalid.'

'Why has Gerrard got a donkey if he's an invalid?' demanded the sentry.

'He inherited it from his uncle, Fronch the Loom. He died under a beam that fell from the roof. It broke his leg. Henry the

Bone tried to set it but the gangrene came and he was rotted to the hip before he died. Richard at the graveyard dug his grave and broke a shovel doing it. It was only last month. Perhaps you heard.'

The sentry shook his head. William waited obligingly for another question, patting the donkey's nose to keep the animal quiet.

'Go on, William,' said the sentry eventually, as if he begrudged him the fact that he wasn't one of the terrible murdering thieves. 'Not fat enough nor tall enough,' he explained to the peasant when William and his donkey had passed by. 'One of them's a terrible fat glutton, and the other's as tall as a beanstalk with a head that looks like . . . I can't remember, a pea or something.'

The country man nodded. He handed the tankard to the sentry again. The sentry drank. He almost finished the beer. People passed by on the bridge and he ignored them. Finally he handed the tankard back to the peasant and wiped his mouth with his hand.

'So they were in the jail?' said the peasant.

'Who?'

'The thieves. The ones you're looking for.'

'They were. Terrible, murdering thieves, they are. Killed the jailer, four guards, and slaughtered the jail dog with a single kick to the head. That's how powerful the pea-headed one is. He's the one to watch. The fat one's too heavy and slow to worry you.'

'Really?'

The sentry nodded.

'Thieves, you say? Who did they rob?'

'The merchant Siebert . . . Hey, you! What's your name?'

'Elizabeth, a launderer.'

'Go on, Elizabeth.'

'I thought you were looking for two men,' said the peasant.

'Yes,' murmured the sentry slyly, 'but they could be in disguise. Don't you think her head is a bit of a pea?'

They both gazed at Elizabeth the launderer. She was wearing a brown kerchief tied tightly around her head. Perhaps her head was a little smaller than normal.

'The merchant Siebert?' said the peasant. 'Let me see . . . Didn't I once deliver some grain to a merchant Siebert? Or was it Sabert?'

'I don't know a Sabert.'

'This one wasn't far from the Mill Bridge. You know the little alley that leads up the hill . . .'

'No, no. That's not him. This one's in Grain Street. Got a great big house, just as you'd expect. Near the House of the Duck.'

'The House of the Duck?'

'Listen, country man. You go to the town square, where the Council House is. You go into Love Lane . . .' he winked, poking an elbow into the peasant's ribs, 'and at the end of that, past the sign of the Lodge, you'll find Grain Street. No, you have to turn at Mussel Walk first. Hold your nose for the stink. Half way down Grain Street you'll find the House of the Duck. Tell them Vogel sent you. They'll give you good beer.'

'Are you Vogel?'

'No, I'm his cousin. The sister-in-law of his brother's stepson owns the Duck.'

The peasant nodded. He looked down into his tankard, tipped it up and drained the last mouthful of beer.

'Do you think you'll find them?' he said. 'The thieves?'

The sentry snorted. 'Not likely! They'll be well gone by now. Who'd stay in the town after killing the jailer and half a dozen guards?'

'I suppose you're right. The House of the Duck, you said? In Grain Street?'

'That's it. Not far from the merchant Siebert's house.'

'They have good beer?'

The sentry grinned. 'They have good beer and they have bad beer, just as you expect. Tell them Vogel sent you.'

The sentry peered into the peasant's tankard. He took it out of his hands and set it upside down on top of the peasant's slouching hat.

'Go on,' he said, laughing. 'You've run dry.'

The peasant reached up and took the tankard off his head. The sentry was looking at someone coming across the bridge.

'Hey, you!' he shouted. 'What's your name?'

'Gaspar, a woodworker,' answered the man.

Gaspar! There was a coincidence, thought the country man, as he slipped away.

28

———

THE MERCHANT'S VISIT to Rosteck was a triumph. He could not have dreamed of a greater success.

He had ridden hard, arriving before any of the messengers from his rivals. Rosteck was old, wily and inscrutable, but behind his unfathomable expression he liked the merchant immediately. He was a man who stayed abreast of developments at the Exchanges in other towns and already knew of his visitor as a young, shrewd and ambitious man who had built his business from ten gold pieces of capital borrowed from his father-in-law. Just as the merchant had guessed, Rosteck was impressed that he had ridden personally with the news of Grossfuss' demise. He invited him into his palatial house. Over the next two days, the merchant watched the messengers from his rivals arrive in Rosteck's courtyard to deliver their letters. As Rosteck unfolded and perused each one, sitting in an opulent armchair before the fireplace in his counting room, the merchant was on hand, sitting in a chair drawn up beside him, to help with all the small but important details of which Rosteck, for all his efforts, might not be aware. There was Merchant Pressler's letter, for example. Now, before Rosteck accepted Pressler's proposal he might want to know that Pressler was yet to pay for a consignment of ceramics that he had received from a merchant called Reisbauer two years earlier. Of course, Pressler was a friend of his, the merchant confided, and must have his reasons, and there was a court case in progress, something about a few broken pots, but court cases took years, and in the meantime Pressler had sold the remainder of the goods and reinvested the money while poor Reisbauer struggled to receive his due. Nor was it the first court case Pressler was involved in, and people – not Pressler's friends, of course, but other people – were even beginning to whisper that he was, well, making a habit of it . . .

Or Master Muntz, for example, whose proposal arrived a little later. Well, the merchant murmured, the rumour around the Exchange – not that he wanted to blacken anyone's name, not least the name of a fellow merchant just when he needed every ounce of help he could get – but the rumour around the Exchange was that Muntz was going under, badly damaged by a large speculation in hops for which he had borrowed heavily, and that if he didn't find a fresh supply of capital he was finished. Did Muntz suggest an injection of capital in his letter? An advance, perhaps to fund the new partnership? The merchant leaned over and peeked at the letter. Well, *that* was a coincidence . . .

One by one, the merchant smeared doubt across every proposal that came to Rosteck. When he wasn't able to discredit an offer, he promised to better it. Rosteck warmed to him more and more. To come to him so brashly, to denounce every one of his rivals so brazenly, even those who were friends, was an act the old merchant understood and admired. It reminded him of what he himself might have done in his younger days. By the end, Rosteck had come to an arrangement with him – providing Grossfuss was really dead, of course, since official confirmation was yet to arrive. That came on the following day. The messenger from the Grossfuss family finally rode into the courtyard with a black-edged letter. Obviously, wrote Grossfuss' son towards the end of it, he would expect to continue the mutually profitable relationship that his father had established with the estimable Merchant Rosteck. The estimable Merchant Rosteck laughed out loud. That Grossfuss' son was a fool and a spendthrift was well known to anyone who had dealt with the Grossfuss family, and to suppose that any intelligent merchant would want to continue business with him showed just what a fool he was. The estimable Merchant Rosteck, still cackling, showed the letter to the estimable Merchant Siebert, his new partner.

When the merchant left the next morning, he was carrying not only an agreement for delivery of seven cases of furs and ten cartloads of pine lumber within the month, but a letter from Rosteck to Grossfuss' son commiserating over the death of his father, which, unfortunately, must bring relations between their two houses to an end. What a cruel twist that it should be *he* to bring the message! Rosteck himself had thought of it, and sealed the letter before the merchant's eyes with a malicious chuckle.

The merchant's spirits were high. As he passed out of the town gate and set off on the road that would lead him home, he congratulated himself on his judgement, his audacity, his persuasiveness. How the Exchange would buzz with excitement and envy when the merchants learned of his manoeuvre. As they sat on their behinds, waiting for the drinking and banqueting of Kelmuss Week to commence, he had outflanked them all! He wished it were Zeb, and not Gregor, who was riding with him, so he could talk and laugh and boast about it, as in the old days when they would ride home together from their journeys and laugh out loud at the shrewd bargains he had struck with wool traders and peasants. Those bargains were mere crumbs compared with the golden pie he had just baked in Rosteck's house. They were worth only a few coins, and the arrangement he had struck with the old merchant would deliver riches for years to come. One day, young merchants would come to him, as he had gone to Rosteck.

The merchant turned in his saddle to glance at Gregor, who was riding on a mule behind him. No, he could never talk with Gregor, not as he could talk with Zeb. Gregor was unpredictable and often surly, and the merchant would never have trusted him with his secrets. He was just a servant. He wasn't the one who had been with him in the early, hard days, not so much servant as companion, guard, confidant, accomplice and brother-in-arms. That was Zeb. Well, it would simply have to wait, that was all, until he got home and could sit down with Zeb in the counting room, with a tankard of ale for each of them, to tell him the story and exult in the scale of his success and the irony of the letter until they were breathless and teary with the deliciousness of it.

Zeb, he thought. To sit down with Zeb again in the counting room?

After such a triumph, the merchant's only concern should have been where he was going to store all the new merchandise that Rosteck was sending him, a tricky question, it was true, but the kind that a merchant relishes. Yet as he rode away a sense of uneasiness settled over him. While he was with Rosteck, he had considered nothing but the matter in hand, beating his rivals and gaining the attachment of the old merchant. Hardly another thought had crossed his mind. But now, as he rode home, everything began to come back. The boy had been upstairs, his wife had arranged it, and Zeb, who had known all about it, said nothing. That shook the merchant more than everything else combined.

The merchant had no idea what to do about it. For once, he

was at a loss. He could punish the foreman, but what would punishment achieve? The kind of trust he had felt in Zeb – the kind of love, which is not too strong a word – was not something that could be purchased by favour or preserved by threat. It was rare. The merchant, whose very lifeblood was shrewdness and calculation, knew just how rare it was.

Now, when he thought about Zeb, he was in pain. He sat listlessly in the saddle. What wouldn't he give to change things so that it had never happened! But it *had* happened, the foreman had betrayed him, and the merchant felt a kind of emptiness and grief, as if he had lost something, or someone, inexpressibly dear to him.

There was nothing to do but watch the road, or gaze at the bare, harvested fields through which they were passing, and dwell on it. The merchant's spirits plunged. He sank deep into confusion and gloom. They stopped at an inn for the night and he lay awake, pondering, as Gregor snored on the floor beside his bed. It was the boy, thought the merchant, that was the problem. None of this would have happened without the boy. He dug into his memory, trying to recall each time he had spoken to the foreman about him. Zeb had put the boy in the stable, done what he was asked to do. He never objected. He didn't argue. He put the boy to work. The boy worked well. When he had asked about him, Zeb was satisfied. He never said much more. Maybe, now that he thought about it, the foreman's replies were more curt than usual. But what of it? The foreman wasn't much of a talker at the best of times. Was this disapproval? From Zeb?

No, not from Zeb. But how else to explain it? Perhaps his wife had been talking to the foreman. The merchant remembered the last conversation with his wife before he left for

Rosteck. It still made him angry. Children, the lack of children, that was always at the bottom of things. And then to accuse him of not being able to treat anything except as an object to buy or to sell! Is that how he treated her? Did she lack for anything? When she asked for a painter, hadn't he found her the best and most expensive money could buy, that fat bug Master Hans who had extorted an extra fee out of him for a little sketch of his wife that he would probably toss off in an afternoon? The merchant turned on his bed, trying to drive her words out of his mind. But they wouldn't go. Perhaps, in his heart, he feared that they were true.

It was the boy, he thought again. None of this would have happened without the boy.

In his bones, the merchant began to feel a chill. Doubt oozed out of his marrow and made his skin prickle with apprehension. Had he overreached himself? There had been times, of course, in the past, when he wondered whether a venture that he had undertaken was too big and too risky, or when half his fortune had been at stake, dependent on the safe arrival of a single ship or the quality of one season's harvest. But those were risks that any man must take who starts with a large ambition for wealth and a tiny capital of twenty gold pieces, the life savings of his father-in-law. This risk, with the boy, was unnecessary. Pride, thought the merchant, trembling with doubt, what if it was only pride? What had he done? To make the boy a slave, an actual slave . . . Pride goes before a fall.

Doubts! The merchant turned and turned on his bed. He couldn't get the doubts out of his head. The night dragged on, dark, close. Gregor snored. When a merchant starts to doubt, he's finished. This was what the merchant believed. Only those with audacity and confidence could succeed. It was clear. He had gone too far with the boy. He had told the magistrate to play God in his jail and he had played God in his house. And if he needed proof, look what it had done to his wife. She had turned against him. Look what it had done to Zeb. He had betrayed him. It was becoming a curse and he had brought it on himself. Soon his business might start to fail. He had heard of things like that, even seen it, merchants who suffered one unaccountable loss after another until there was nothing left, speculation after speculation that should have succeeded but turned to dust. With Rosteck he had sealed a partnership that would bring him greater riches than he had ever attained before. But perhaps it was an illusion. Perhaps this success was not a beginning, but the end. Perhaps he would never reap its fruits. The doubts! When a merchant started to doubt, he was finished.

But what could he do? Having made the boy his slave, he couldn't release him. To hand him back to the magistrate would mean the boy's death. His wife would never forgive him. And he . . . no, he couldn't do it either. Now that he had taken the boy, he was condemned to keep him. It was grim. It was a punishment in itself. He was a slave to the slave!

And if it really was a curse? What if other things started to go wrong? How would he get rid of the boy then?

The merchant hardly slept. In the morning, he was pale and worn. His eyes were haunted. His mind wasn't clear. As he reached the town, he was tired and troubled. He guided his horse distractedly through the streets, crowded with visitors for Kelmuss Week. He didn't even notice the soldiers posted in the squares, and when they challenged him, he left it to Gregor to say who they were. There was always trouble in Kelmuss Week, he said to himself, glancing disdainfully at the crowd on foot around him, replete with beggars and drunks, and he didn't give the soldiers a second thought.

At last he turned into Grain Street and rode towards his house, clattering past the sausage-sellers who cried their wares for the Kelmuss crowds and the revellers drinking outside the House of the Duck.

But to a certain straw-haired man, watching from a dormer window on the third floor of the inn, the pair wending their way up the crowded street might just as easily have been coming towards him on a quiet and desolate marsh, so quickly did he recognise them, the merchant on his horse and his white-shirted servant, beside him, on a mule.

29

'WAS IT A HARD JOURNEY?' asked the merchant's wife.

'No, I didn't sleep last night, that's all.' The merchant tried to smile. 'Inns!'

The woman examined her husband anxiously. He didn't look himself. Was he unwell? Perhaps the journey wasn't a success.

'Simon . . .'

He didn't meet her eyes.

'Simon, is there—'

The door opened. Josephus came in with food and drink. The woman waited until he had gone.

'It was a success with Rosteck?' she said.

'Yes,' said the merchant, looking at the food. He sighed. 'A great success. I'll have all his business. I'll have to look for more storerooms.'

'Garner Zeb will be busy.'

The merchant nodded. He picked up a joint of veal and began to chew on it vacantly.

'So you're happy then?'

'What?' said the merchant, looking up for a moment.

'You're happy with Rosteck?'

'Oh, him? Yes, I'm happy.'

The merchant ate. His wife watched him, baffled.

He put the bone down on the table. He hadn't eaten much. He drank some wine.

'Well, I'll go and wash. Then I must go to the Exchange,' he said.

'Can't it wait until tomorrow?'

'No. Better see them today. Best to give the news myself. People will be envious. Besides, even young Grossfuss has friends. I should see how they react.'

But the merchant didn't leave the table. He fingered the veal bone.

Eventually he spoke in a low voice. 'Is the boy well?' he asked.

'Yes,' said his wife. 'He almost died.'

The merchant looked up quickly. 'Almost died? How?'

'His heart was damaged by the fall. The blood went to the bladder.'

'And?'

'He's cured of that.'

The merchant nodded. He looked down at the bone again, picked at a strand of flesh that was attached to it. How strange it would have been if the boy *had* died, setting him free of his slavery forever. Perhaps that would lift the curse . . . No, perhaps it would make it worse, and the boy would haunt him from the grave.

'I called the blue doctor. We nursed him.'

'We?'

'Garner Zeb and I. You had him locked in the spice room, remember?'

'And you didn't move him out?'

'Do you remember what you said to Zeb?'

'Do you remember what you said to *me*, Eleanor?'

'Simon . . .'

'I am cursed, Eleanor. Cursed!' the merchant cried out suddenly, and his head rolled in torment.

The woman stared. 'What do you mean? What's happened?'

'Nothing. No, nothing.'

'What do you mean, then? What curse? Who's cursed you?'

'I have cursed myself.'

The woman took a deep breath. 'How have you cursed yourself, Simon?'

'With the boy,' said the merchant despairingly. 'What should I do? Tell me, what should I do, Eleanor?'

The woman shook her head. She got up and came to her husband and he reached for her convulsively and buried his face against her belly.

'I'll tell you what to do, I'll tell you,' she murmured, stroking his hair.

~

ZEB unlocked the door of the spice room. Pungent, heavy odours came rushing out. The merchant peered inside. A lantern hung from the ceiling. Underneath it was the boy, sitting on a mattress.

He looked pale. There was a cut on his cheek that was healing.

The merchant entered the room. His wife followed him, and Garner Zeb came in last.

At first the merchant didn't speak. The boy watched him with an unsettling intensity. Was it hatred? Anger? How much did he merely imagine?

He crouched beside the mattress. 'Are you well, Yoss?' he asked eventually.

'Yes,' said the boy.

'I heard you had an injury. I didn't intend any harm. You understand that, don't you?'

'I don't remember how it happened,' said Yoss simply.

'But didn't anyone tell you?'

'They said I slipped down the stairs.'

The merchant glanced over his shoulder. His wife nodded.

'Have you been in here all this time?' the merchant said to the boy.

Yoss nodded.

'As you said,' added Garner Zeb from behind him.

The merchant looked around the room. It was large enough, but mostly filled with sacks and barrels, and there was too little space if you looked at it as a place to live. 'Do you want to come out now?'

'If you wish,' said Yoss.

'If I wish,' muttered the merchant. 'Tell me, Yoss, what do *you* want? Do you want to work with the other men? Zeb says you enjoyed it. He used to tell me, you know. Don't think I ever forgot about you. Of course, you'll have to recover your strength. Zeb won't work you too hard, will you, Zeb? Eh?'

'No,' said the foreman.

Yoss shrugged.

The merchant frowned. 'Well, it can be something else' he said, hoping to find a spark of interest in the boy. 'What about the painter? Do you want to work with him? Can Master Hans use an assistant, Eleanor?'

The woman smiled. 'It'll take him forever to finish that ceiling.'

'It'll take him exactly as long as he chooses,' muttered Yoss, 'assistant or no assistant.'

The merchant's wife looked at Yoss in surprise. 'I thought . . . I thought you liked working with him.'

Yoss stood up. He did nothing else. He merely stood and waited.

The merchant stood up as well. He was tired and his patience was wearing thin, and he still had to go the Exchange. He threw a glance at his wife. He had followed her suggestion, offered the boy whatever he wanted, yet the boy had nothing to say for himself. 'Let him out of here,' he muttered to Garner Zeb. Then he turned to the boy, and he tried to speak gently. 'We'll talk again. Just think about what I said, Yoss.'

'He'll think about it, won't you, Yoss? He'll think, Simon,' said the woman hastily, as she followed her husband out.

Garner Zeb watched them from the doorway. The merchant and his wife stopped in the courtyard. The man shook his head, the woman placed her hand soothingly on his arm. Then he turned to leave by the gate, and she walked slowly, thoughtfully towards the stairs.

'Well,' said Yoss behind him, 'he's back.'

'And you should be more grateful!' replied the foreman, turning to him angrily. 'Listen to what the master said.'

'He's not *my* master,' retorted Yoss. 'I don't want anything from him.'

'Why, you! I should put you back to work right now, that's what I should do. That'd make you think again.'

'You must let me go, Garner Zeb.'

'After that? After you spoke to the master like that?'

Yoss didn't reply. That was no reason for Zeb to break his promise, and the foreman knew it just as well as he.

Zeb sighed. It was one thing to talk about freeing the boy when the master was away, another to do it when the master returned. Another betrayal, and greater than the last! Yet he had promised. And there was not a promise the foreman had made in his life that he had not kept, or at least tried to keep.

'Are you sure, Yoss?' he said after a moment. 'Think about what he said.'

'Nothing will make me stay.'

'What will you do? If they catch you, Yoss, they'll—'

'I know. You've told me.'

Zeb gazed at the boy, and nodded.

'Let me go now. Why wait?'

'Not now,' said Garner Zeb.

'Why not?'

'He's gone to the Exchange. It would look suspicious if you disappear when he's out. He has to be in the house.'

The boy looked at the foreman doubtfully. The man himself didn't know whether he believed his own reason, or whether it was one last moment of procrastination, to protect the boy from the danger that awaited him outside, to protect himself from the final betrayal.

'Then do it when he comes back,' said Yoss. 'Do it then.'

The foreman hesitated.

'Do it then, Garner Zeb. Today. When he comes back.'

Zeb nodded. 'When he comes back. I'll leave the gate unlocked. Then if you want to go, go. But you don't have to, Yoss. Think about it carefully. Remember the danger. Once I lock the gate again, there's no way back.'

Yoss grinned. He took out a small sack from under his mattress. He raised his shirt, and began to fasten the sack around his body with a piece of cord.

'What's that?' asked the foreman.

'Nutmegs.'

'Where did you get them?'

'Where do you think?'

'You can't take the master's nutmegs!' cried the foreman. 'You *are* a thief.'

'I'm not a thief,' retorted Yoss. 'They're for my village. I'm taking them back. It's just a few. He can give me a few nutmegs after throwing me down the stairs.'

'Who told you he threw you down the stairs?' demanded Zeb in surprise.

Yoss laughed. 'You and the mistress should watch what you say when you think people are asleep.'

'Yoss!'

Yoss finished tying the sack. He lowered his shirt and looked seriously at the foreman. 'All right, Garner Zeb. I'm ready.'

30

CONRAD SAW THE GATE of the merchant's house swing open. At his window in the Duck, overlooking the street, he lowered the brim of his hat and watched the merchant walk away.

He had been sitting at this window for hours. When he had arrived at the House of the Duck on the previous day, Vogel's brother's stepson's sister-in-law pointed out the house of Siebert as she gave him his beer. Conrad spent the afternoon mingling with the Kelmuss crowds, examining the building from every angle. It was a large, imposing house. There were no windows on the ground floor, and only a single gate. All the windows on the upper floor were barred. At one point a woman appeared at a window and Conrad slipped into an alley. Later, from the opening of another alley, he saw the gate open, and he caught a glimpse of a courtyard and storerooms beyond. A wagon left and then a tall, heavy-browed man came out, peered up and down the street, and closed the gate again. Shortly afterwards Conrad sauntered past, hiding his face under the wide, slouching brim of his hat. He pushed on the gate discreetly as he went by. It was locked. The heavy-browed man probably kept it locked all the time.

There didn't seem to be any easy entry. Besides, Conrad wasn't about to go breaking in anywhere yet. First, he needed to be sure he had found the house where the boy was being kept. To be caught and taken back to the magistrate for breaking into the *wrong* house would be a folly of truly Gasparian magnitude. No, he needed to see the merchant to be sure. Until he saw the merchant, he wasn't going to do anything.

So he took a room at the Duck and began his vigil. When the hostess discovered that he wanted a room with a window overlooking the street, she doubled the price and demanded the cash in advance. He found himself in a filthy little alcove on the third floor. Food was sent up, a greasy stew that almost made him hunger for the turnip and potato broth of the jail. He ate it at the window, still watching the street. He watched late into the night, as the Kelmuss crowds milled and the street vendors sold their sausages, doughnuts, sweets and beer. Once, he would have suffered agonies at the sight of the food on display below him, but now it didn't distract him. He had another obsession, and nothing could divert him. He slept for hardly an hour. At dawn he was already watching again, while the drunks still lay in the gutters. And as the hours passed, he continued to watch, fingering one of his knives, or gnawing on his knuckles, waiting for the merchant to appear.

And the waiting had its effect. Nothing to think about but what he would do . . . what he would do . . . what he would do when the moment arrived.

Then he saw the merchant and his servant, coming down the street on their animals, just like the first time he ever laid eyes on them in the marsh. They went inside. So it was the right house. But the gate was locked. Conrad watched. Sat at the window and watched. That was the house and the boy must be inside and the gate was locked. And then the merchant came out again, on foot this time, and Conrad watched as he walked away on the street below.

Wagons came and went through the gate. Each time, the tall, heavy-browed man would step out of the courtyard and peer around the street before pulling the gate shut behind them.

Conrad knew the type: officious doorkeepers. You could usually bribe them for a couple of pieces of silver. Sometimes you couldn't. It was impossible to tell just by looking at them. This one looked harsh and severe, but sometimes those were the most corrupt of the lot. He went to his own home at night, Conrad knew, having seen him leave late in the evening before, and he had a key, Conrad knew, because he had come back and let himself in early in the morning.

Conrad tapped his knife, tapped it and tapped it, against the sill of the window. It was as if something had been released in his mind. Now it moved, tramp, tramp, tramp, and he couldn't stop it. There were the barred windows. There was the locked gate. For him, the gate was the only way in, and he knew it. He wasn't made for climbing up to balconies or leaping across rooftops, just as his fingers weren't made for the deft movement of cheating at cards. That was for people like Gaspar. Conrad's advantages were his brain, his bulk and the surprising strength in his wrists. To know one's own weaknesses is as important as knowing one's own strengths. Knowing this was itself one of the strengths that Conrad had.

To get through the gate he would need a key. To get the key he would need to get to the man. Was he bribable or not? If you don't know, assume not. That meant Conrad would have to attack him.

But the idea of attacking the heavy-browed man was troubling. Not that he couldn't prevail. With sufficient care and planning Conrad believed he could beat anyone. Follow him one day, choose a spot for an ambush and surprise him on the next. If he spotted you the first time, wait three days to allay his suspicions. But the days added up. Two, three, four, perhaps five. The thought made him uneasy. It was time to leave the town. To stay for a day or two was a provocation, an amusement, like turning around and thumbing your nose at someone who was chasing you. It was also something that no one expected, so it was clever. But after that the cleverness wore off. Each extra day was another day in which you could be discovered, especially when you were just sitting in one place. People talk. 'I've got an odd bird in the front room on the third floor,' Vogel's cousin's brother's sister-in-law, or whatever she was, might say to a customer, 'he came for Kelmuss Week but he never goes out,' and the customer, who might just happen to be an ambitious soldier in the magistrate's guard, might just climb the stairs to have a look.

And another murder? It was too much. Every killing entailed risk, created uncertainties, provided information to your old enemies, generated new enemies to pursue you. Getting rid of Gaspar and the boy was a matter of tidying up. No one cared for either of them. Were Gaspar's body even to be found, no one would know where he came from or whose son or brother he was. As for the boy, well, the merchant had bought the boy like a mule. In the eyes of the law, he had no rights to him. The law might even have something to say about the little bargain that the merchant and the magistrate had cooked up. To whom was the merchant going to complain? Hush it all up, that's what they'd do. But the heavy-browed man, well, he had a home that he went to. There'd be a family, relations. Someone would care. Killing him might create even more things to tidy up. And to create new things to be tidied up, merely in order to tidy up other things that had happened before, didn't seem very clever.

The afternoon wore on. The air in the room was warm and close. There was a bowl with the leftovers of cold stew on the floor. It was from breakfast or even from the night before, Conrad couldn't remember. The serving girl had been up and taken something away. There! Another person who had seen him and might talk . . .

Somewhere in Conrad's mind, there was a thought that he should leave the boy, forget him, use Onfluess' money and get out of the town as soon as he could. As if someone were speaking to him from the other side of a noisy room, the straw-haired man knew this thought was calling to him, he knew he should be trying to listen, but he couldn't quite focus his attention on it. The boy was there, close, somewhere on the other side of the gate across the street. *That* was the thought that obsessed him, it drowned out everything else. By eliminating the boy, Conrad would eliminate the risk that the boy posed. If he left him, the danger would always remain. The boy would always be out there, somewhere, like an axe poised over his head.

But in Conrad's position, the immediate danger of discovery, if he continued to stay in his room at the Duck, far outweighed any future risk that the boy might pose. If it had been a game of cards, the straw-haired man wouldn't have hesitated to give the signal to lay down the cards and go. In those hours of watching from that room at the inn, something had happened to Conrad's reasoning.

For the first time in his life, perhaps, at a point that was so critical, the straw-haired man was not thinking clearly. The ruthlessness of his logic, the cold calculation that had been both his weaponry and his protection for so many years, had deserted him. Something else was making him stay, and he himself didn't realize it. It was the thing that had been released in his mind. Its origin went far back, to his own boyhood, to the days when he had been as innocent and hopeful as Yoss.

Ever since that time it had rested quietly, tiny, silent, undetected, like a seed. But over the two months that he had spent in the cell with Gaspar, it had begun to grow, and now, at last, it was free, and it moved, tramp, tramp, tramp, and he couldn't stop it. Hatred and the desire for revenge were swollen and raging within him. Even as Conrad told himself that he wanted the boy only to silence him, these were the emotions that actually impelled him.

Conrad gnawed his knuckles. The boy was somewhere in there, just across the street. He could almost feel his windpipe under his thumbs.

He sat and watched. From some distant corner of his brain, he knew the voice of reason was calling to him. He sensed risk all around. Sometimes he imagined that he could hear soldiers coming for him on the stairs, and he clenched the hafts of his knives.

Yet he stayed, gazing at the house and its barred windows and its ever-shut gate. He was close. Anything might happen. The doorkeeper might leave the gate open by mistake. Or the boy might just walk out, for instance, and into the street.

31

THE SCENE AT THE EXCHANGE was perfect. Not even a company of actors could have staged it more dramatically.

The merchant arrived. The others turned to look at him, wondering where he had been when the Kelmuss festivities commenced. They all suspected he had been up to something. He headed straight for young Grossfuss, and by the time he reached him, there was such a hush in the Exchange that you could have heard a coin clink, even if it were only a tiny copper coin and its clink was of the quietest.

He pulled out Rosteck's letter, presented it silently to young Grossfuss, and retired to his usual desk to watch the result.

Young Grossfuss, without stopping to ask himself why this letter was being delivered by a rival merchant, and as if to prove how foolish he was, tore it open at once. Before he had finished it, five other merchants had read it over his shoulder or upside-down. In less than a minute the news began to spread. The merchant could literally *see* it moving, turning head after head towards him. The first of his rivals sauntered over to him, and then he was surrounded by an excited, babbling crowd shouting offers and proposals.

It should have been a moment of triumph. But the merchant's thoughts were bleak. Having more success, he realized as his rivals bobbed around him, merely made more agonizing the prospect of losing all.

The Exchange closed early in honour of Kelmuss Week. Pressler and Krantz attached themselves to the merchant. On left and right they bubbled over with ideas for ventures. The merchant pretended to listen to them. He was weary. He wanted to get away. When they reached the pig market he shook them off.

At once his shoulders sagged, his eyes clouded and his gait became dejected. He continued alone through the crowds of people that were coming out for another night of Kelmuss celebration. How to lift the curse? If the boy didn't want to stay, then he must go. But how? It must be done safely. If the boy were hanged, the curse would be written in blood, and would never be lifted.

The merchant turned into Grain Street. He was still thinking, still struggling with the problem. He stopped in front of his gate and searched for his key. He must have left it behind. He clanged on the bell for Zeb to let him in.

Once inside, the merchant saw the boy sitting on a barrel beside the stable door. He walked past him and went into his counting room. A moment later he came out again. The foreman was still standing by the gate. The merchant called for him, then disappeared into the counting room once more.

Garner Zeb looked at Yoss. The boy was watching him intently.

The foreman hesitated for a moment. Then he nodded. He unlocked the gate, threw a last glance at Yoss, and went to join his master.

Yoss jumped to his feet. But before he could get across the courtyard, Beetle appeared, rolling an empty barrel. The workman stopped, sat down on the barrel and raised one of his feet to peer at the bottom of his shoe. He began to pick at something with his fingernail.

Yoss waited for Beetle to start moving again. He could feel

his heart pounding. He glanced at the gate. His eyes went wide. The gate had opened! It had swung back by itself. Anyone who looked at it would see that it was open.

Beetle got up off the barrel. Shoulders hunched, eyes on the ground, he was rolling it again.

~

CONRAD had seen the merchant return. The heavy-browed man opened the gate and let him in. Conrad stayed at his window, gnawing his knuckles. His gaze didn't waver. He had no patience now for elaborate plans. He was beyond that. What would happen if he just went up to the gate and rang the bell? The doorkeeper might let him in. He wouldn't know who Conrad was. He could make up some story, pretend to be a merchant . . . No, his clothes weren't right for that. Pretend to be selling something, perhaps? The doorkeeper would go to fetch the merchant. He might have a minute or two. Maybe the boy would be standing right in front of him. It was possible. Why not? But what were the chances? Too much risk, too much risk at every turn.

Conrad shuddered, hunched, gnawing on the skin around his knuckles until there was blood between his teeth.

He sat forward with a start.

His eyes narrowed. The gate was open. But no one was waiting to go in. No one came out. What was happening? Could the doorkeeper have forgotten to lock it? Perhaps the merchant was about to come out again. Conrad watched. No one appeared. Something was going on. His instinct told him.

He jumped up, took his daggers and stuffed a length of cord in his pocket. He pushed his hat down low on his head, threw on his cloak, and slipped out of the room and down the stairs.

~

'So, you want to let him go?' Garner Zeb was saying, sitting opposite his master in the counting room. There was a tankard of beer for each of them.

'Yes, Zeb,' said the merchant.

'That's good,' said the foreman, and he took a sip of his beer.

'But where, Zeb? How?'

Zeb smiled. 'Send him to his village. No one will find him there. I could take him myself.'

The merchant smiled. Simple! He rested back in his chair. Suddenly he felt an enormous wave of relief. He raised his tankard. Here was his foreman again, Zeb, just as he should have been, his friend, confidant and brother-in-arms. He nodded. 'Of course.'

'All we need to—' Zeb stopped. He jumped to his feet.

'Zeb?'

But Zeb had already run for the door.

~

Yoss was at the gate. He went through the opening. He was out.

Which way to go? People were everywhere. Through the milling crowd one figure was striding purposefully across the street. Someone spun and stumbled in his wake. Yoss glanced. Something about the figure caught his eye. What was it? Hat, cloak, boots . . . Those *boots*!

Yoss gasped. He looked up. Conrad! Or was it a ghost? A thin, bearded ghost of Conrad, leering greedily from under the brim of a hat. Hands reached out to grab him.

Yoss yelled. He turned and ran for the merchant's courtyard. He got through the gate, saw Zeb come out of the counting room towards him. But now Zeb's eyes went wide and Yoss felt a hand fall heavily on his shoulder and a moment later an arm swung around his chest.

Conrad pinned him tight. Yoss felt a blade against his throat.

'Stay still!' shouted Conrad. '*Still!* Or I'll kill the boy.'

Conrad began to drag him backwards towards the gate. Yoss saw Zeb, Tomas and the Beetle all watching, frozen. Then Conrad stopped. His arm pressed even tighter. And Yoss knew exactly what Conrad was looking at.

The merchant was standing in front of his counting room.

Conrad's breathing was heavy.

The merchant took a step towards them.

'You . . .' muttered Conrad. He took a step forwards, pushing Yoss in front of him. And this moment, Yoss would later think, was the point at which he understood that Conrad – Conrad of all people, the coldest and most calculating man he had ever met – was not in control of what he was doing. Whether he really did it perceive it at this moment, or realized it only in later years, he would never know. But if Conrad hadn't stopped and taken a step forwards, if he had kept moving backwards instead, he would have reached the gate, and once he got through the gate he might have got away, either with or without Yoss, and lived.

But he did stop, and he did take a step towards the merchant, and Yoss could feel, in the clenching of his arm, the heaviness of his breathing, the muttered words that came out of his mouth, a surge of terrible, blinding hatred.

'You. . .' growled Conrad again. 'Want your property, do you? Trading human beings now, are you? Call *me* a thief! What can you steal that's more precious than a man's liberty, Merchant Siebert. Tell me that!'

'I'll release him. I promise. Let him go.'

'Release him, will you? Answer my question!'

The merchant frowned. What question? His expression was puzzled and helpless. Yoss would never forget it. The look on the merchant's face in the last seconds of his life burned itself into his memory.

'I'll show you, then,' said Conrad.

Everything happened quickly.

Yoss felt the arm around him relax for an instant, heard something whoosh beside his ear, saw a flash in the air, and a jet of bright red blood spurted out of the merchant's throat. But already there was a second knife at Yoss' neck, and the screams of women were coming from the windows above the courtyard and Garner Zeb and the workmen were rushing to their fallen master and Conrad was dragging him towards the gate and then something plummeted through the corner of Yoss' vision. There was a thud. The arm that held him dropped away. Conrad was on the ground and blood was pouring from his head under a tangle of metal and somehow there were candles rolling around and the dagger that Conrad had held was jackknifing and bouncing across the ground until it came to rest on its side, glinting brightly against the cobblestones.

The dagger bounced, bounced out of the shade and into the sunlight, out of Conrad's hand and into Yoss' memory, where it would lie shining, glinting, forever.

Yoss looked up.

The painter was leaning out of the window above him. It was he who had thrown the candelabrum that had felled the murderer. And already Tomas had rushed across and was standing with his foot on Conrad's neck.

'Yoss, remember what I said,' called Master Hans.

Yoss shook his head. He was still dazed.

'Go, Yoss,' called the painter. 'Go now.'

Yoss gazed at him a moment longer. Then he understood. He ran, without looking back, through the open gate.

~

IN GRAIN STREET, a boy raced through the crowd, bumping into bystanders and stumbling past them. People turned to watch. Some of them cursed him for his haste. He swerved and skidded. But even before he was gone, something else had taken the crowd's attention. People glanced at one another apprehensively. One by one, they fell silent. Conversations stopped. Even the street criers paused. There was a hush.

Now there was only one sound in the air, eerie, piercing, a woman's wailing that rose from within the courtyard of one of the great houses nearby.

32

Yoss ran. He pushed past the people in the street and he didn't know what he had left behind him, what was happening in the yard. The merchant must be dead. Conrad's knife had embedded itself in his throat and the blood had spurted bright. And Conrad, under the weight of the candelabrum, with Tomas' foot on his neck? Dead or merely injured? And the merchant's wife? It was her screams that he had heard. Where was she now? Crouching over her husband, keening, weeping? He ran and the images flashed through his mind, some seen, some imagined, like so many pictures that Master Hans might have painted, and he was numb with them. His feet took him deep into the alleys of the town, heedless through refuse and muck, past the ragged children who played there and the drunken revellers who staggered there, and eventually he found himself at the river.

Here he stopped. Evening was coming on. He remembered the first time he had seen the river, in the moonlight, when the boatman had taken him across the water in the boat that was like a fairy pod. Perhaps he wasn't far from the place where the boatman had left him that night, because he could see a bridge close by, with houses jutting out over the water. It seemed a long time ago, too long to be imagined. Now, as night began to fall, lights were appearing in the houses. There were boats on the water, each with its own lantern. The boats were filled with people and Yoss could hear their cheerful shouts. But this time the boats seemed to be like long, predatory insects crawling across the water. He heard a woman's playful shriek, and he shivered. It reminded him of the sound he had heard as he ran out of the merchant's yard.

He shrank back against a wall. He was in danger now, if the things that Garner Zeb had said were true. Out here he was a criminal. And now that the merchant was dead? Somehow, Yoss felt, they would blame him for that as well. Wouldn't the merchant's wife, when she rose from her husband's body, demand to have him found? Perhaps he *was* to blame, at least in part. The merchant wouldn't have died if not for him. But it was the merchant himself who brought him into his house and locked him in.

Yoss shook his head, staring out at the river uncomprehendingly. He didn't know how it had come to this, that two men lay dead in that courtyard, that the cobblestones were stained with their blood. What had he done to make it happen? And yet he must have done something, because it had happened over him. How could everything suddenly become so complicated and irreversible? He remembered, when he was a little boy, he had a toy wagon, and when one of the wheels fell off his father had stopped his crying by saying 'What can be fixed isn't broken', and had fixed it for him. When he was smaller he used to repeat this to himself whenever he had done something bad. What can be fixed isn't broken. He said it to himself now. But why did he remember it? And why repeat it? None of this could be fixed, not the death of the merchant nor the death of Conrad, nor the woman's grief.

Yoss started walking again. It was dark in the alleys. Through an open door he could see a woman skinning a hare by the light of a candle. Her hands were bloody to the elbows, and the skin hung from the pink, slippery body of the hare like a winter coat that the animal was shedding. He watched. It reminded him of the village, and of his mother, whom he had often seen skin a hare in just the same way.

Suddenly another thought struck him. Gaspar! If Conrad was after him, then they hadn't been hanged, and Gaspar couldn't be far away. He turned and looked back down the alley. It was empty. Gaspar was somewhere out there in the town, waiting, and when Conrad didn't come back, and when Gaspar found out what had happened, as he must, there would be one other person who wanted to find him.

Suddenly it struck Yoss that it was strange, to see Conrad wearing Gaspar's boots. Gaspar loved those boots almost as much as life itself.

'*Boy!*'

Yoss jumped. It was the woman who had been skinning the hare. She had come out into the alley with a jug of water, and was rinsing the hare's blood off her hands.

'What are you standing there for, *boy?*' she demanded, squinting into the shadows.

Yoss didn't reply. He hurried away.

The woman shouted something after him. Her voice was shrill and angry.

How to get out of the town? It was late and he didn't know how to reach the town gate. He could ask someone, but they might ask why he didn't know, and what would he say then? Perhaps he could follow the river, he thought, as he walked through the alleys. That would take him out of the town. But where did it go? It might take him further away from the road that led back to the mountains.

Suddenly he just wanted to stop. He sat down right where he was, in the alley, and leaned his back against a wall. Everything around him seemed harsh and hostile. The merchant's wife was after him. Gaspar was after him. If the magistrate found him, he would hang him. If a woman merely saw him in an alley, it seemed, she shooed him away. He gazed at the wall opposite. Light came out of the chinks in a shutter nearby and the wall gleamed with a moist, slimy film. The very bricks of the town seemed to ooze disdain for him. Perhaps he would just stay here like this, just sit, in the dark, without thinking or moving . . .

A man walked into him. Yoss jumped up. The man came after him and tried to kick him. Then he turned away, cursing. Another man walked past. Suddenly Yoss wanted to get away from the darkness. He wanted to get away from his thoughts. He could hear noise coming from the direction the two men had taken. He went towards it.

He came into a square. There was a crowd, and in the middle of the crowd was a raised platform, with torches burning at each corner. A man flipped into the air above the platform, turned a double somersault, and landed on his feet. Another man jumped on his shoulders, sprang into the air and fell with a twist and turn. The crowd roared. Yoss went closer, gazing stupidly at the tumblers. Cries of street vendors were in the air. He smelt meat. He felt dizzy. A boy tugged on his arm, holding out a hat. Yoss looked down. What did he want? He shrugged him off and turned away. On the other side of the square was a man eating fire, and beside him a man swallowing a sword. They looked so alike that they might have been brothers. They were twins. They were the same person twice. There were trestle tables, and people were drinking, and there were kegs of beer on the ground between the tables and men who stood filling tankards. They wore long aprons, like slaughterers. There was a bear standing on its hind feet with a chain through his nose, and a man was goading it with a stick. A crowd around it shrieked and roared. Yoss saw a building with columns and a porch. It seemed familiar. Yoss stared at it. He had slept there once, he remembered.

There were beggars in the square. Now Yoss began to notice them. Four were sitting together at the edge of the crowd that was watching the tumblers. He went to look at the four but he didn't recognize them. Elsewhere he saw a woman with a baby. He remembered – it seemed so long ago – a woman flicking a fly off the head of an orange-haired infant. What did they call her? Eyes with Babe. He went across to her but she showed no sign of recognition. Maybe she had forgotten him. He started to walk around the square. Beggars looked up at him but their faces were blank. He peered at each one. They held out their hands. He heard some of them curse as he moved on. Then he came across two of them sitting together, not far from the bear that was being goaded.

He hesitated. They looked at him blankly.

'Legs,' he said.

Legs and Seven Fingers gazed at him for a moment longer, but their expressions didn't change.

'Legs, it's me, Yoss. Don't you remember?'

Legs looked away and held out his hand towards someone who was passing by.

'You must remember,' said Yoss. 'I was Deaf 'n' Dumb.'

'Go away,' hissed Legs out of the side of his mouth.

'But Legs . . .'

'Go away!' said Legs, turning to face him. 'Decided to come back, have you? Have a bit more fun with the beggars? See if they'll sit still for another beating? Very entertaining.'

Yoss shook his head. 'I'm sorry . . . It wasn't my fault.'

'Wasn't your fault? Well, let's see.' Legs paused and scratched his head, as if he were trying to remember a very complicated series of events. 'I've been begging at the Zendel Gate for years. Never once had a beating. A tap on the head now and then, perhaps, but never a proper beating. And then, the very first time I go with you, I get beaten black and blue. What do you think, Fingers? No connection? No, I agree. None at all.'

Yoss didn't reply.

'Been having a good time with your merchant friend, have you?'

'He wasn't my friend,' muttered Yoss.

'Ah, well, doesn't matter, as long as they feed you.'

'He was after me.'

'Yes, and that's another thing,' remarked Legs. 'Correct me if I'm wrong, Fingers, but I seem to recall asking our young friend here if there was anyone who was looking for him. And I seem to remember him telling us there wasn't. Or did I dream it all?'

'I've escaped now,' said Yoss.

'Good for you,' said Legs.

'Today. Just now. It's taken me all this time.'

'To persevere is to prosper.'

'And he's dead,' said Yoss. Suddenly all the fear and the guilt and the horror of what had happened welled up and burst out of him. 'He's dead! Are you happy? He'll never kick you again. He's dead and so is Conrad and his wife's a widow and if you want someone to blame then blame *me* and kick *me* if you want because I don't care!'

And he ran off, stumbling into the crowd and being cuffed and shoved as he pushed a way through, and everything was blurry through the tears in his eyes.

Someone called his name. He kept going. He heard it again but he didn't stop.

He felt a hand on his shoulder.

He jumped. His heart stopped.

But it wasn't Gaspar. It was Legs, peering at him closely.

'What's wrong? Why don't you stop when a person calls you?'

Yoss shook his head. He couldn't speak.

The beggar looked around anxiously to see who was watching, and gave an agonized grimace, as if he were in excruciating pain. 'It's no good if people see how fast I can really go,' he whispered to Yoss. 'I shouldn't have to remind you.'

~

'YOU DON'T have to tell us, you know,' said Legs quietly.

'I know,' said Yoss. He chewed the crust Legs had given him, and took a sip of the beer dregs that the beggars had scrounged at the end of the night. It was late now. The beggars had gone back to their porch.

'We never ask questions, do we, Fingers?' said Legs. 'That's one of the rules.'

'I know that,' said Yoss.

'In fact, it's better if we don't know,' said Legs. 'When you don't know about someone, you don't think good or ill of him without reason. You form your opinions from what you see yourself. People change. All we need for you, young Yoss, is to get you a caper.'

'I don't want a caper. I'm not staying.'

'Not staying? That's what a lot of people say at first, eh, Fingers?'

Seven Fingers nodded earnestly.

'No, really, I'm not staying. That's why I want to tell you.'

Yoss looked out at the square. Most of the crowd had dispersed. The platform on which the tumblers had somersaulted stood abandoned. A few figures shuffled in a drunken dance to the sound of a slack bagpipe. Others lay slumped against walls or in the gutters. Some people were sprawled across the trestle tables. The men in long aprons were going from one to the next, throwing each of them on the ground.

He wanted to leave. When the town swallowed a man up, it changed him, and turned him into something he should never become.

'I *am* going to leave,' he said, as if to confirm it one last time.

Legs nodded. 'Well, if that's the case, and you want to tell us . . .'

Most of the other beggars under the porch were going to sleep. They were stretching out under their rags, like long black bundles, just as Yoss had seen them on the night he ran away from Farber's inn. Maybe he would start there. It was such a long story, and it got so complicated, that it was difficult to know where to begin.

'Just start at the beginning,' said Legs.

Seven Fingers nodded.

The beginning? 'Well, I come from a village.'

'*Which village?*'

They all looked around in surprise.

'Rosie, go away,' said Legs, 'this is a private conversation.'

Rosie quacked.

'Go on, go away.'

Rosie glared at Legs for a moment. Then she went off to the other end of the porch, and quacked a few times, until people started shouting at her to be quiet.

When the noise had died down, Legs turned back to Yoss.
'Now, you come from a village?'

'In the mountains.'

'Ah . . .' said Legs, and he nodded, as if he knew the story so
well he could have told it himself.

33

THE TWO SOLDIERS AT THE GATE folded their arms with satisfaction. They were in for some entertainment! A wagon bringing hay into the town had broken down. It jolted over a rut, lurched back, lost a wheel, dipped to the side and ended up stuck at an angle, one corner almost touching the ground, blocking the gate.

People stopped to watch. The driver ran off to retrieve his wheel, which had rolled into an alley. He shouted, as he brought it back, for the onlookers to come and help him push the wagon out of the way. The onlookers were laughing. A couple of people had already walked off with armfuls of hay that had spilled on the ground. The driver started scrambling around, collecting the rest of it. The soldiers grinned from their post beside a wall. They shouted at the driver to get the wagon moving, to make him scramble faster. In the midst of the commotion, only the horse that had been pulling the wagon seemed calm, standing unperturbed in its harness.

Another vehicle pulled up inside the gate on its way out of the town. It was the coach of a landowner who was going back to his estate after having come to the town for Kelmuss Week. The landowner put his head out of the window to see what was happening. He shouted at the soldiers to get the wagon out of the way. The soldiers looked back at him and shrugged helplessly. One by one, a few bystanders went reluctantly to push the wagon. The driver was now standing by the horse, pulling on its harness. The horse took a step forward and stopped. With much coaxing, it took another step and stopped again. The soldiers watched with interest. Occasionally they glanced back at the landowner to see whether he was enjoying the proceedings.

While all this was happening, it was still possible to get around the wagon on foot. A trickle of people made their way in and out of the gate. The arrivals were mostly country people from nearby villages, carrying sacks of produce for sale. Many of those leaving had come to the town for the Kelmuss festivities in the Council House square on the previous night. The soldiers, when not watching the slow progress of the wagon or stealing a glance at the landowner, shouted to ask who they were and where they were going, as they had been instructed to do. And thus, as the driver continued to tug on his horse's harness, and a few people pushed half-heartedly at the back of the wagon, the soldiers saw three beggars making their way towards the gate, and one of the soldiers called out.

The beggar at the front turned and let his hood drop from his head.

'Legs!' cried the soldier, grinning. 'I didn't recognize you. Where are you going?'

'Wait a minute,' said the second soldier, 'there's something's different about him.' The soldier walked towards the beggars, rubbing his chin. 'What is it?'

'What?' said his companion, following him across.

'There's something . . . I know there is . . .'

'I know,' cried the first soldier. 'He's got both legs! Legs, you've got two legs.'

'Yes, it's a miracle,' replied Legs without elaboration.

'How did it happen?'

'I prayed a lot. And now I've had enough of this town. I'm going to seek my fortune.'

'Quite right, too, now that you've got all your legs.'

'Your fortune!' exclaimed the other soldier contemptuously. 'Beggars going to seek their fortune! Whatever next?'

'Who's with you, Legs?' said the first soldier.

'Seven Fingers. You know him.'

Seven Fingers nodded at the soldier.

'And this one?'

'Don't you recognize him?' said Legs. 'You must have seen him a hundred times. It's Dumb Jarrow, of course. Look, I'll show you. Say hello to the soldier, Dumb Jarrow.'

'Hello,' mouthed the third beggar without making a sound.

'See, dumb as a baby on the day it's born.'

The soldier nodded. 'Of course, I remember him. Off you go. If you find your fortune, bring some of it back for me.'

'Only if we find *your* fortune!' called Legs over his shoulder, leading the other two away.

The soldiers watched them go.

'Prayed a lot,' said the first one, shaking his head with amazement, as they walked back to their post. 'Good for him.'

'What did he mean, only if he finds *your* fortune?' said the other one. He frowned. 'And what was that about babies? Babies aren't dumb when they're born, are they?'

The first soldier thought. 'That's a good question . . .'

'Beggars!' muttered the second one. He turned to look for them again, but the three beggars had gone through the gate and were out of sight.

'Look over there,' said the first soldier, nudging his companion in the ribs. 'He'll have a stroke, I swear. I'll bet you a pint of Stampfer's best beer.' And they both grinned at the landowner, who was still waiting for the wagon to move, almost choking with impatience.

~

THEY TOOK the road which Yoss had followed with Conrad and Gaspar when they first brought him to the town, through the plains and into the marsh. At night they slept in the open, under their rags. They ate food that Legs had bought before they left the town. From somewhere in his clothes he had produced a few copper coins, and even Seven Fingers produced a couple, and they purchased bread and cheese and onions to carry with them. This journey was a very good idea, Legs pronounced, he hadn't eaten better in years. And the air! He had forgotten how fresh the air could be. And this was the only clue he gave that he had ever been outside the town, because still he didn't tell Yoss anything about his earlier life, nor did Seven Fingers, maintaining the beggars' rule of secrecy.

Once they were out on the plains, and past the wagons that were heading for the town, they saw few people. Every time Yoss heard horsemen behind him, he jumped off the road into the ditch, thinking that it might be Gaspar, or men sent by the merchant's wife, or soldiers from the magistrate. He didn't know that Gaspar was dead, floating somewhere in the river, and that the merchant's wife, fearing the curse that had caused her husband's death, would have done nothing to bring him back, and that the last thing the magistrate wanted was to be forced to explain how he had handed this boy over to a merchant. So he was safer than he knew, as safe as the day he left the village. But unaware of this, he feared that at any moment the town might reach out, as with a giant hand, and haul him back.

They came to the place in the marsh where Conrad and Gaspar had robbed the merchant. Yoss remembered it, or thought he remembered it, from the hillock where he had gone to retrieve the merchant's mule.

'So this is where it all started?' said Legs.

Yoss nodded. He walked to the edge of the ditch. 'This is where some of it started. That's where I hid, down there, until Conrad called me. When I came out they were holding both of them with knives.'

'And you really didn't know they were robbing them?' said Legs, and he glanced at Seven Fingers with disbelief.

'No,' said Yoss, and he could hardly believe it himself. 'I'd know now.'

'I bet you would,' said Legs. He stood in the middle of the road, hands on his hips, and looked around from one side to the other. The marsh stretched away to the horizon in each direction, and it was empty, silent, except for the harsh calls of waterbirds. 'Come on,' he said eventually.

They followed the road. It took them out of the marsh and into the forest, and two days later, after they had left the road and followed the stream that ran through the trees, they found themselves at the edge of the lake.

High in the air, like two horns of white cloud, floated the peaks of the Cradle.

~

'THAT'S where I live,' said Yoss.

Seven Fingers stared with his mouth open. Legs nodded, but his gaze was distant, clouded, and Yoss couldn't tell what he was thinking.

'Will you come with me?' said Yoss.

Legs looked at him abruptly. 'Is that what you plan to bring back?' he demanded. 'Two beggars? The village will really thank you!'

'But I thought you said people *need* beggars. They need to be able to give, to help others who are less fortunate than themselves.'

Legs glanced at Yoss. He raised an eyebrow knowingly.

'Come with me anyway, Legs. And you too, Seven Fingers.'

'You wouldn't want to go up there, would you, Fingers?' said Legs.

'Wouldn't you, Fingers?' said Yoss.

Seven Fingers blinked in confusion.

'See,' Legs said to Yoss, 'he wouldn't be happy.'

'How does he know?'

'He knows, Yoss. Trust me, he knows what's best for himself. Right, Fingers?'

Seven Fingers looked at Legs. He nodded, then he started fiddling with the bandage on his hand.

Yoss frowned. He didn't think he understood what Legs was saying.

'It's all right, Yoss,' said Legs quietly. He glanced towards the mountains. 'You should get going.'

Yoss nodded. He began to say something, but Legs shook his head, and Yoss could see he wasn't going to change his mind. Yoss lifted his shirt and began to pull at a cord beneath it.

'What's this?' said Legs.

'Nutmegs,' replied Yoss.

Legs and Seven Fingers watched as he unfastened the sack.

'I didn't tell you about them,' Yoss admitted apologetically. 'That's what I was going to take back to the village.' He held out the sack.

Neither of the beggars made a move to take it.

'Go on,' said Yoss. 'I haven't anything else to give you.'

'Do you think we want payment?' demanded Legs.

'No. But you haven't got much. And you spent your money on food.'

'Don't you see we always get by?'

'Take them,' said Yoss. 'I never really thought it was a good idea anyway. I just couldn't think of anything else.'

'And what will you take back instead?'

Yoss shrugged. 'I don't know.' He grinned. Suddenly he felt wildly happy. There wasn't any reason for it. 'I really don't know!'

Legs grinned as well. He reached out and took the sack. Seven Fingers watched uncomprehendingly.

'You can sell them,' said Yoss. 'They must be worth something.'

'Maybe I will,' said Legs.

'You could be a merchant.'

'I could be, Yoss. Who knows. Next time, you'll work for me!'

Suddenly they were both silent. The grins drained away from their faces.

'Goodbye, Legs.'

'Goodbye, Yoss. Good luck.'

~

Yoss went around the lake. He was alone again, as at the start. A day later he was in the hills once more, and eventually he reached the Middlesnag. He was back in the pure, dry air and the soaring silence of the slopes. All he had to do was walk around the mountain and down through the trees to be home.

But he didn't go down at once. He turned off the track, and he climbed higher, up the slope of the Middlesnag and around its crags, until he could see the entire village spread out beneath him in the valley. And he sat there, and he gazed down at it, for a long time.

He didn't know what he was bringing back. No nutmegs, and nothing else he could show nor any new skill that he could demonstrate, for all the time he had spent away. People would laugh. And yet at the same time he felt that he was bringing back more, much more than he could ever have imagined. And it was true, he was. It was so much that even he himself did not understand it all until many years had passed, and he had married, and had children of his own, who had then had children of their own, and it seemed like another life, Legs bounding after him on his crutch through the crowded square, and Master Hans suspended like a giant spider under his ceiling, and the merchant's wife offering him cakes made with honey, and Garner Zeb frowning pensively in the spice room, and Conrad and the merchant lying dead in the courtyard and the dagger bouncing, bouncing and glinting in the sunlight, forever glinting, forever shining, were distant memories of people long gone, like so many pictures that the painter might have painted, like a dream that he had once dreamed, and he was an old man, Yoss, the Speaker of the village.